Mind

Merry Christmas 2014

Ryan -

Happy Readings -

[signature]

Mind Travelers

To Oliver and Simon.

Contents

Mind Travelers - Chapter 1

Time Travel – The Naked Truth

I remember the first time it happened to me. How could I forget? How could anyone forget their first time jump? The way it happened wasn't anything like I remember from the old movies, you know, where someone would jump and stick to a big white circular wall with a black spiral painted on it which would morph into a funnel and suck them down a time warp spitting them back out in the past or future. There is no 'Time Machine' to step into either. No metal can with wires and buttons where you punch a bunch of numbers into a keypad or hit a switch or pull a lever and wait for the buzzing to reach a loud crescendo till "poof" you're gone. There are no visible mechanics involved and the process is much more subtle than you would imagine. The entire physical action of a time jump is very subtle, nearly imperceptible with the exception of two things, the visual experience and the adrenaline rush. The visual experience is accompanied by a super-heightened awareness, and the adrenaline is a by-product of the visual sensation on top of the conscious realization of the experience in progress.

It really is like nothing you've ever been through before. It's an out of body experience with an expanded awareness that gives you a 360 degree conscious and mental imprint of your surroundings. This includes an instant understanding of the thoughts and emotions of every person or animal within a radius of perhaps two or three hundred feet. You instantly know all the details of every conversation that is taking place around you at that exact moment. One way to describe it is like you have walked into a room with a very familiar movie on TV that has been placed on pause. You know the movie intimately, you've seen it dozens of times and can recite the lines as if you've acted the stage play. You see it from all angles as if you wrote and directed it and are now within it. You are the main character. I know this doesn't sound like anything that would give you much of an adrenaline rush, but now the fun begins. You are about to take this familiar movie out of pause mode and into real-time and with it the main character, you, and all the supporting actors come to life.

The first time for me was absolutely surreal. In what seemed to be an entire minute, only a fraction of a second elapsed. It was a frozen moment in time where the physical world stood still but my mental processes continued to work, and at an incredibly accelerated pace. Oddly I had an exceptionally detailed awareness of my surroundings. It seemed like I had been captured in a still photograph for several seconds and then the scene changed ever so slightly. At the time I thought I detected just a little movement but I quickly dismissed it from my mind because I was somewhat disoriented and uncertain of what was really happening. 'Is this a dream?' I thought to myself. I recognized this place and the people, but why were we frozen? Then the scene clicked again and there was another small visual change. Things had shifted position just slightly. This time I knew it wasn't my imagination. Then it clicked again, and again. The time between each click was getting shorter and the scene was beginning to come to life. It was like one of those animation books that you flip the pages to see the movement. Only this was happening to me and my entire surroundings.

Click, click, click and the scene changed frame by frame, each one getting shorter. Click, click, click, click; faster and faster until the time between each flicker had reduced enough to make everything appear nearly normal. Well it looked almost normal now but imagine how I felt when I realize that I was not in a dream. I was watching a much younger version of myself relive an experience that I vividly remembered having as a teenager.

While this slow flicker effect was happening, I also realize that I was totally naked. Naked at least for the first thirty or forty freeze frames. For some reason inanimate objects take longer to re-constitute after a time jump than the human anatomy. I later learned that being naked for a short time doesn't cause problems as long as you are not seen by other people. If someone does see you emerge from a time-jump they are usually so shocked to see a human being materializing before their eyes that they fail to notice that the human materializing was naked for the first half second.

But how does it happen? How does someone actually break the space-time continuum? Well that's a good question and not an easy one to explain. For now, let's just say it's similar to solving a mathematical equation. I don't know anyone who can accurately explain how we do it, but we all know that we can feed a simple math question into our brain then allow it to take over and solve the question. The main difference in this case is that it's not a mathematical question, but instead a destination. A destination in time and space; coordinates that I feed into my brain and my mind does the rest.

I Have Seen

There's a definite art to remaining hidden during a time jump. You really don't want someone to see you land, trust me it's just too awkward. Each jump consists of departure coordinates which are your current location and time, and destination coordinates for where and when you want to go to. First, the departure point is important because it's also where and when you will return to later on and continue in your present life. When you return to the present, no time will have transpired but your mood may be drastically different than when you left, especially if the adrenaline has any say in the matter. For the people present upon your return, it may appear like you just took a shot of speed or ran a hundred yard dash and for no apparent reason.

At first I preferred to depart in the evening and to be out doors in a secluded area like a park, or between two buildings. I had a series of close calls before I realized that all I needed to do was use a washroom. It was an acceptable excuse to have a few moments of privacy. I could leave for days if I wanted to, then come back to my present time, regain my composure, flush, wash up and walk out like nothing happened. Back to my seat at the table in the restaurant with Devin my wife; back to my desk at work; back to the meeting; back to life as it is happening now, in the present. I would just join back in on the conversation as if I was only gone for a few minutes even when sometimes I had been away for weeks. Thank goodness for the heightened awareness, I sure wouldn't be able to remember the conversation I was returning to, certainly not after several days.

    And now there's the destination place and time to consider. This could be in the future or in the past. It can also be a great distance from where you currently are. Short jumps are easy because you have more accurate control over the coordinates and time of day that you want to land at. All you need is to have a real destination and time planted firmly in your mind and that's where (and when) you will end up. The more detailed the time and destination is in your mind, the more accurate the landing. By 'detailed' I mean if you can remember the time of day that you ate dinner on your 10th birthday for example and think about the bedroom of the house you lived in at the time, you will emerge in the bedroom on your tenth birthday while your younger self is having their birthday dinner with the family in the dining room, kitchen, back yard or wherever it originally took place.

The trouble with greater distances and time gaps is that they are more difficult to stick the landing. Buildings get renovated, demolished, rebuilt. Land masses shift a little every year, earthquakes, volcanoes and landslides alter the landscape. Over many centuries, mountains shoot up, weather grinds them down, and glaciers cover them in ice hundreds of feet thick.

Jumping accurately into the past is not as difficult as hitting the mark way ahead in the future. The past has already happened so there is a naturally greater level of accuracy in jumps to the past simply because of the physical connection we have with history. The future, on the other hand, has not yet happened. This causes a number of issues because the future that will happen is constantly being influenced by the future that could happen. An endless list of possibilities exists for the future that could be, an infinite number of 'IF – THEN' statements that determine the forward course of mankind.

Think about it this way, whether it's a conscious decision or not, your actions today can and will affect the way the future plays out. If you eat tainted food today, you could be sick tomorrow. So you get sick from tainted food and miss an interview that would have resulted in landing a role in a company that would have required you to move to say Chicago, where you would have met your future wife (an American), settled down, had kids, who would have had kids of their own, one of whom lets say would have discovered the cure for cancer sixty years after that job interview. But instead of making it to that interview, you lie in bed for two days with mild food poisoning, interview for a different position in a different company a week later, land the job, stay in Toronto, meet and marry a nice Canadian girl, decide not to have children, become wildly successful in your career and enjoy traveling the world with your wife. The cure for cancer may still be discovered sixty years later, but in this particular alternate timeline it may be discovered by someone in say China. Every action of every person on the planet has a direct impact on the future outcome of the planet.

Action is not the only thing that affects the future, it is also impossible not to impact the future by returning to the past. By simply existing simultaneously with your previous self, you create a circumstance that requires matter to be displaced from its natural course of space and time and to exist in a state of duplication. There are a variety of effects caused by this duplication which will be discussed in a later chapter.

As I mentioned earlier, longer jumps through time and space are much more difficult to accurately hit the mark and require substantially more thought and planning in order to avoid some very serious pitfalls. Going 3000 years in either direction has countless dangers for obvious logistical reasons as previously described. How do you know if the place you are landing was build yet, or has been torn down since, or if having moved a couple meters over time has an impact on your ability to stick the landing out of site? What if you land in the middle of a snake pit, or inside a glacier or volcano? These considerations are usually not major issues but they could be. The saving grace is that the first two seconds of the landing seem like a minute in time. This allows you to think about what immediate action, if any, you may need to take.

But even more important than sticking the landing, is how your actions in the past will impact the present and future. What if you are seen? What do you say to someone who sees you emerge? It depends when this is happening and who is asking. If it is happening in an era when time travel is accepted, practiced and widely adopted, it doesn't make much difference; if it's in the past during a time when the capability is believed impossible, that's a whole other story.

Either way, short jump or long jump, it just takes a little common sense not to jump into the middle of an audience like say at the front of your high school math class or worse, how about landing on the pitcher's mound in the middle of a baseball game?

Batter Up!

It was the bottom of the 9th. Bases were loaded. Brent Schuhmacher was at bat with a full count, 3 balls, 2 strikes. The stands were packed. It was 7:14 p.m. on Wednesday, October 12th, 1977 and I found myself emerging from a time jump right on the back of the pitcher's mound!

Brent Schuhmacher had moved to Wisconsin from Germany two years before and was the league's heaviest and most dangerous hitter. He was in the running for MVP again for the second year in a row. The game was about to finish with a bang! Brent was about to hit the grand slam home run that would catapult his future into the big leagues. It would lay the groundwork for his baseball career and ultimately land him smack dab in the middle of the 1985 World Series. Brent was until this moment in time, destined to lead the Kansas City Royals to a 4 game to 3 win against the St Louis Cardinals eight years from now. But all of that changed in the blink of an eye.

This is how I remember it from behind the plate that night...
I was sixteen years old at the time. As catcher for the team, it was my responsibility to suggest what pitch I thought should be thrown next. The pitcher, Steve Bolins had been my friend since grade school. We hung out during the summer breaks at our favorite beaches. We fished together and camped. We played on the same volleyball team six years in a row. He was the setter, I was the power hitter. Steve made me look great on the court. I did my best to make Steve look great on the field. I had an excellent record for making the right call, although Steve didn't always go with my suggestion. When he did, however, seventy five percent of the time he got a strike.

Now here we were in our senior year of high school. Brent Schuhmacher was at bat and this was it. Full count and bases loaded. The pressure was on. I gave Steve two fingers down then one to my left which meant a fastball with a slight left to right break. Steve nodded, checked the men on base, settled, wound up and let the ball fly. That's when it happened. My eyes stayed on the ball traveling sixty eight miles an hour towards me, (pretty fast for a high school pitcher), but my eyes caught a flicker just behind Steve on the mound. A slight sense of déjà vu came over me. It was strong at first then quickly faded into a tingle that spread over my scalp. I had never experienced déjà vu before. My eyes were focused on the ball as the flicker appeared and disappeared several times behind Steve. I couldn't bring myself to take my eye off the ball. There was too much at stake.

The flickering of that image lasted less than a second, but in the moment, given the circumstances and my heightened level of awareness caused by the adrenaline of the game, that half second seemed like a long time. The ball had now covered more than half the distance from Steve to the plate and I could see Brent's swing had begun. My motor skills had taken over and as my glove hand opened and my arm moved slightly down and to my left, I took my eyes off the ball to verify what my mind was processing from the periphery. The flicker I saw was like a translucent sepia tone image and appeared to be a man, flashing in and out of view over and over. Like a silent movie playing on a projector that is struggling to get up to speed. The image of this man looked like a life sized still poster of my self.

I saw the flickering image gradually turning into a three dimensional real person as the ball traveled even closer toward me. The ball was almost at the plate now and Brent was mid swing. The tingling from my scalp had moved across my entire body. I had a strong feeling about what I was seeing. I clearly saw only the final three flashes of the image just behind Steve then Brent's bat wiped across my field of view from top to bottom. With a loud SNAP, the ball landed solidly in my glove and the flickering image was gone. In that short moment of quietness between the snap of the glove and the roaring cheer from the crowd, it became crystal clear in my mind that I had just witnessed a very brief appearance of a future instance of myself.

I remember seeing a small but distinct puff of dust just a few inches above the mound on Steve's right, and thinking this was the final proof I needed to confirm what I had just seen. Steve's stance after releasing the ball was the same every pitch. Feet shoulder width apart, knees slightly bent and there was always, always a small puff of dust on Steve's left caused by his right foot coming out of the place where he plants it to anchor his throw. This time however, there was the usual puff on the left, but absolutely, undoubtedly an additional one on the right. I looked around to see if anyone else possibly witnessed what I had, but based on reaction, or lack there of, I guessed that I was the only one. It was only four or five seconds before the team had surrounded me and I was being pushed out towards Steve who was coming in towards this mad huddle.

I turned and shot Brent a quick glance through the chaos of gloves and hats and team mates faces yelling. I could see that he was still staring at the mound and was white as a ghost. He rubbed his eyes as he turned and began walking slowly back to the dug out, head down and shaking side to side. I almost expected him to put the ball out of the park and now for some reason felt a tinge of regret and even a little bit guilty that Brent hadn't won the game. He was an opponent so why did I feel guilty?

It happened so fast. By the time I actually processed the situation it was long over. The crowd was cheering as the team celebrated all around me. This was not the time to focus on a strange half-second visual that appeared before my eyes in the most crucial moment of the game; or to grow feelings for the opposition. We had just claimed the 1977 regional championship for our high school. Out of twenty seven teams, we were number one. But throughout all the cheering and celebration I couldn't help thinking of the appearance of my future self and wondering why did it happen? Why there and then? Was it really me? Of course it was. I felt it before I even looked, and when I did look there was no doubt in my mind although it took several seconds after the image vanished for it to fully sink into my brain. I focused on the image for less than one tenth of a second but it was enough to burn it into my retinas and register in my head. I started to wonder when I was going to learn how to time travel. I knew what I had seen but I also knew I couldn't talk to anyone about this. People would think I had hallucinated. Everyone would think I was crazy. Everyone, that is except for Brent Schuhmacher.

24

Swing and a Miss

Did I mention I remember the first time it happened? How could I forget? How could anyone forget their first time jump, especially when they land smack dab in the middle of a baseball game.

This is how I remember the event from a different point of view. From the point of view of a thirty five year-old who has just mastered the art of time travel. Well I shouldn't go so far as to say I had 'mastered the art' but perhaps I could say 'accomplished his first unassisted time jump'. The problem of course is that I hadn't fully considered the landing coordinates and time so as to conceal my re-entry from onlookers. The coordinates would have been fine if I emerged a half hour further into the future. Who am I trying to kid? I stumbled on it quite by accident and had no idea what the hell was happening. Here's how it went that first time.

I was upstairs in our loft meditating quietly on the love seat with Oliver and Simon our two dogs. The three of us meditated there nearly every morning and afternoon since we moved into this house about six months previous. The ideal way to practice Transcendental Meditation is to simply focus on repeating your mantra over and over and when you become aware that your mind has wandered off your mantra, you come back to repeating it. Sounds simple doesn't it? You'd be surprised how many people claim they can't do it.

Having practiced TM for over twenty years, at this point my body pretty much slips into a transcendent state of consciousness in very little time. This state of consciousness is similar to a dream state or REM but with a complete awareness of your surroundings. When meditating, I usually reach this REM-like state within the first two minutes, and will experience this four or five times during a typical twenty minute meditation. The average adult experiences four or five REM cycles over the course of a night so for me, meditating is kind of like getting a full night's sleep in twenty minutes. You could say meditation is a sort of time travel of its own.

During my meditations around this time, I found that my mind had been wandering to a place where it was recalling extensive amounts of information on quantum physics. Stuff that I had studied back in high school and digested from several books I had read over the last fifteen years. My meditative REM brain activity around that time had also included another common theme in addition to the physics, sports, and in particular a game called 'capture the flag'. I never played capture the flag growing up so I don't know where this was coming from, but all the same it seemed to be coming into my brain more and more frequently during my meditations. In fact this capture the flag game which I had never played in my life, and didn't even know the rules, seemed to be taking over more and more of my mental process during meditative REM.

When I was meditating, my mind would wander off on various thoughts as it generally tends to do. As usual I would become aware of my mental meanderings and return my focus to my mantra. Today was a very special day however. I was in that semi-conscious REM state and was experiencing an extremely detailed and entertaining visual activity. I was standing in what looked like a play-ground surrounded in a fog. In front of me were several people playing this capture the flag game, running, dodging and jumping sometimes even diving into these odd looking slits hovering above the ground. There were three of these slits and when anyone would dive or jump through one of them, they would disappear. Often, soon after someone disappeared, another player would appear nearby out of one of the other slits. I recognized some of the players who had jumped through the slits earlier and then reappeared a few moments later. What a strange dream I thought. I knew this rather curious activity was related to the capture the flag game somehow but I couldn't understand what the disappearing part had to do with it. I didn't know what the rules were or what the objective was. It did look like they were having a lot of fun.

I watched with curiosity, trying to understand the

objective of the game and as I watched I began to feel a growing urge to join in. There was no fear at all on any of the players' faces; in fact they seemed to quite enjoy the game. They seemed to be chasing one another in and out of these portal-like slits, trying to catch the person in front of them. I wanted to mentally experience this interesting disappearing act and to understand more. I wondered where I would end up if I did jump in. As far as I knew all of this stuff I was witnessing was just brain activity going on in my imagination during REM. I was now feeling an overwhelming sense that I had to try it for myself. What could possibly go wrong? After all, this was only a dream.

I mentally began to run towards the odd vibrating slit closest to me and dove into the black opening head first. As I did I was suddenly reminded of a man sliding into home plate. I recalled a memory from years and years ago just then, and at the very instance of my impact with this hovering shimmering black hole, I was thinking of the most important baseball game of my high school career. A game we lost in my senior year to our rivals which ended in a grand slam home run. In my mind I was visualizing the final pitch from the viewpoint of the pitcher's mound. What happened next surprised and shocked not only me, but several hundred onlookers.

I visualized myself standing behind Steve Bolins on the pitcher's mound. His wind-up was complete and he was just beginning to accelerate the baseball through the pitch. The ball in his hand was literally a half inch away from my nose. Over top of the ball I could see my younger self squatted down behind the home plate some sixty five feet away. This whole scene around me was completely still and lasted what seemed like ten or twelve seconds. I thought, 'how real does this look and feel?' It's like being there in a virtual 3D version of the actual event. Hell, screw the virtual part it's like being right there in real life but in a freeze frame image.

Everything faded to black quickly then a short time later appeared again, only this time, Steve's hand and the ball was maybe six inches away from my face. The same scene was clearly in focus and surrounded me, just a little changed from the first glimpse. I did not hear the din of a crowd but I could hear voices in my head that seemed to give me a pretty good sense of the mood as I remembered it back some nineteen years ago. I could sense exactly what my younger self was thinking. He was really focused on the fact that Steve had taken his advice and was throwing a fast-ball with a left to right break. I could also sense what was going on emotionally within a number of other people. Brent, for instance, was intent on hitting a home run to win the game and felt confident he knew what pitch was now coming his way. The coaches for both teams were emotionally charged at this pinnacle moment. I could feel all kinds of emotion in the air, then everything faded quickly to black again.

As the scene immediately reemerged, again very little had changed. The ball was ten or twelve inches further along in the pitch, people in the stands had moved ever so slightly. I could see very clearly every person that was in my field of view. I recognized many of my old class mates, the cheer-leaders and even some parents. Brent's stance had begun to shift a little and I could see the baseball bat he was holding was now at a slightly different angle. As the succession of freeze-frame images progressed they started to accelerate in frequency with shorter and shorter times between fade outs.

I remember thinking how I had never experienced anything like this before. I knew the human mind was capable of recalling events and memories in exceptional detail, especially if hypnotized, but the detail I was experiencing here and now of a memory so long ago, and from a different physical perspective than what I had originally witnessed…well this was blowing my mind. And why could I hear so many conversations? My head was like a radio that was picking up a hundred channels all at the same time. What had I jumped through to get here? How were the people playing capture the flag related to this? Was this experience my imagination on steroids or had I finally meditated to a state of Cosmic Consciousness? I wasn't looking forward to seeing Brent strike out again and lose the game. I remembered that I had called for a fast ball down and left and I could see from the ball's trajectory now that Steve had thrown my pitch; the pitch that ended our season in a huge win right in our home turf.

I was aware that I had come here during meditation and that my mind had most certainly lost focus of my mantra. I didn't really want to leave this scene but out of habit I began repeating my mantra again now figuring it would bring me out of this super vivid dream state. I quickly realized that it wasn't making a difference. Click, click the images came and went changing just a little each time. I felt I was no longer in control of my conscious state. I began to feel anxious that this mind-blowing 3D animated flip-book experience I was in may continue to play itself out whether I liked it or not. Maybe I had fallen asleep and was actually dreaming. The ball had been released from Steve's hand now and was on its way to the plate. Click......click......the scene flashed. I could sense my younger self was having strong déjà vu. I hadn't given myself over to the experience yet and kept repeating my mantra. For some reason I wasn't coming up out of this dream so I decided I would just ride it out. What else could I do but let it happen?

Then suddenly I remembered the event that took place when I was sixteen years old; what my younger self had experienced from behind the catcher's mask. Yes, this was *that* moment, the moment that haunted me for months after that game. How could I have forgotten the ghost behind the mound, the image of myself appearing right before my eyes the day we won the regional championship? Like a dream, it had faded over time, retreated and filed in the archives for future reference if needed. And now it came back to me in a rush of excitement. Could this possibly be happening for real I thought? Am I actually time traveling?

Click.....click.....click... the scene continued to progress faster and faster. The sound of the crowd was starting to rise ever so slowly from an extremely low pitch. It sounded as though I were scrubbing through a sound wave file at slow speed and gradually getting faster. The voices were audible but I could not make out any of the words. My head was still filled with hundreds of thoughts and internal conversations.

The ball was half way to the plate now and I could start to sense that people were becoming aware of my presence behind Steve on the mound. Wayne Mc Donald saw me first from right behind home plate. Then Wayne's daughter Judy who was sitting next to him and Ted Williams sitting up two rows and a few seats to Judy's left noticed me as well. The number of people that saw me grew exponentially with every click until I couldn't make out how many people were witnesses to my presence. As the ball progressed along its path, the number of people becoming aware of my presence began to diminish. I suppose because all eyes were now either on the ball or the man at bat. I knew that there were at least fifty to sixty.

Click...click...click then as the ball reached the plate and the bat swung to meet it, the clicking stopped and the air was cut in half by the snap of a hard ball slapping the pocket of my past self's leather glove. The sound of the crowd was now at a normal pitch, and as the cheers came up Steve left the mound and began to run towards home plate. I was left standing on the back slope of the pitcher's mound with at least a hundred people watching me.

I don't know how long I was standing there but I could tell a lot of people were aware of my presence. I could feel their attention on me and this feeling was accelerating quickly. I felt a hand on my back. It was a warm, soft and gentle touch that I felt move up from my upper middle back to my neck and up the base of my skull. There was a tremendous flash of light and I instantly found myself back in the loft sitting comfortably where I had begun meditating fifteen minutes earlier.

My body had just jumped as though I had shocked myself out of that state of consciousness in-between awake and sleep. I wasn't accustomed to emerging from a meditation in such an abrupt fashion and my heart was beating a little faster than usual. Ten minutes had gone by so I closed my eyes again and continued to meditate and reflect on what I had just experienced. I could feel Oliver by my side but Simon was gone. Odd I thought as it's usually Oliver who bails from the love-seat to bask in a patch of sunlight on the carpet. I'm always aware when either of them jumps off the love seat, but I did just come up from a very deep state.

At first I figured I had dreamt the whole scene, you know just an old memory that I turned around in my mind to imagine what if. What if Brent had struck out that day? He never would have survived the loss and gone on to be the great ball player that he became. It couldn't have actually happened because I remember the outcome. Brent hit the ball and it was an amazing home run, a Grand Slam in fact.

As I thought deeper about the overall experience, the detail of the crowd and all my surroundings, how I sensed people becoming aware of my presence, how as a sixteen year old I wondered if anyone else had seen this crazy event that I witnessed from behind the plate, I was convinced that what I had just experienced was in fact time travel. I believed that I knew how I got there, and I was sure that the black-hole slit was the portal. The memory of the high school baseball game must have caused the time and place to be set as the landing coordinates. But how did I get out of there? Whose hand had I felt on my back and neck? Why was I removed, taken out of the scene, and why didn't they reveal themselves to me? I had so many questions for this person. This was such a wild rush of an experience I knew I was going to have to attempt it again soon. I knew for sure I wouldn't be able to wait long.

The Atom Exchange and Déjà vu

While there are countless atoms in existence throughout the universe, man has long tried to understand the stuff that atoms are made of. We are made of atoms so how do they relate to our existence? How does our existence relate to all atoms within the universe?

They say every seven years the human body replaces each and every one of its cells and hence each and every one of its atoms as well. This obviously doesn't happen on the last day of the seventh year, like changing your car, but gradually, day by day, every day of your life. And when your life comes to its end, the atoms that make up your body at that time are then absorbed one way or another by mother earth to be eventually combined and aligned into many other things. During cremation, for example, atoms are converted into ashes and gas, heat energy, smoke vapor. Many of the atoms rise up and become part of the atmosphere. They get pulled back down with precipitation and become part of the earth again as water in a lake or in the earth being absorbed by plants for example.

There's no escape for an atom. It just moves along from one material to another pretty much for all eternity. Oh some atoms of course don't move around much. These atoms just hang around a long, long time say for instance as part of a mountain or desert. Atoms that make up living things like plants and people on the other hand move quite frequently. Think about a water molecule for a minute, made up of two hydrogen atoms and one oxygen atom. Coming from a lake or river through a water processing plant, out of your kitchen tap, into an ice cube tray, it gets frozen and later placed into a cocktail. The water molecule now part of a solid mass which then melts back into a liquid state, sticks to the side of your glass, evaporates into it's three components (two Hydrogen atoms and one Oxygen atom) and floats away into the air. Maybe the oxygen atom is inhaled by you and sent from your lungs through your blood stream to your muscles to enable you to do the work it takes to lift your glass and take your next sip. Then the oxygen atom may combined with other atoms in your body to form say uric acid (C5H4N4O3) and get expelled, flushed down the drain and processed at a sewage processing plant before being sent back out to the lake to once again cycle through another adventure in transformation. The oxygen atom which was once part of the original water molecule is now once again part of a different water molecule. It's combined into the same substance that it once made up only this time it has teamed up with two hydrogen atoms that were not part of the original molecule.

As substances transform from solid to liquid to gas, the atoms themselves don't actually change. They just join to make up molecules that vibrate at different frequencies usually based on the external temperature in the immediate environment. Atoms just move around like people visiting friends and relatives, starting out in a family (water) then going off on their own for a while (air), joining with others to form one substance (uric acid) and then another and so on. So how do humans and atoms relate in the universe?

Déjà vu is not what you think it is. When you visit the recent past, by recent I mean less than seven years ago, your physical body from the present still contains some of the atoms that were contained in your past instance. That is to say that your body has not yet entirely replaced every atom within it. This causes an overlap (or duplication) of atoms existing at the same time within the same object; you. This duplication of existence is what creates a strange feeling of familiarity.

At the atomic level, the matter that has been through the experience once before is confused as to where it belongs. This confusion is due to a memory effect that occurs in the older atoms that are brought back in time to exist alongside their earlier selves within the same object. The atoms have a strong urge to go to where their duplicate counterparts are and as a result, vibrate at a much higher energy level than they usual do. There is a resonance between the two bodies that causes the younger atoms to feel the memory effect from the older atoms. What one senses then is the physical memory of an experience that they have already had. Your normal memory tells you that you haven't been here before. Your mind says this experience is new but on the atomic level there is a part of your physical body that knows and screams 'I have been here before'.

It turns out that the intensity of déjà vu is directly proportional to the quantity of overlapping atoms present in the two instances of your body at that given moment in time. Over the course of seven years, as more and more of your atomic make-up dissipates and moves on, the effect becomes less and less.

So a time jump of more than seven years produces little to no déjà vu because there are very few, if any, overlapping atoms within your body. Your body has already replaced the entire lot of them. A five year jump will give a mild feeling of déjà vu because there are still a few million duplicates. A two year jump will create a very strong déjà vu because there is an overlap of several billion atoms, and a two week jump causes such a strong sensation it will nearly cause a person to faint. This effect only occurs for the instance of the person who is having the experience for the first time. So when you jump into the past, your past instance will have the déjà vu. When you jump ahead in time you get the feeling of déjà vu when you emerge. The future instance of you will not.

There's one more very important thing you should know about duplicating atoms. Atoms are energy vibrating at very specific frequencies. They in turn combine to make up matter which again is just a form of combined energies vibrating at their own combined frequency. Because energy cannot be created or destroyed but only transformed from one form to another, when an atom's existence is duplicated it is as if we are creating energy from scratch. This is something only Mother Nature herself or God was intended to do, and when we duplicate atoms through time jumps in the material world, it goes against all natural laws of physics. As stated earlier, it is impossible not to impact the future by returning to the past. By simply existing simultaneously with the atoms that made up your previous or future self, you have created a circumstance that requires matter to be displaced from its natural course of space and time. And it's not nice to piss off Mother Nature or God for that matter.

No single atom was meant to exist more than once ever, so when duplication does happen a shock wave is created that leaves a distinct and lasting mark in the vicinity of the occurrence. When a person time jumps they are essentially duplicating trillions of atoms. Even though the atoms that make up their body at the destination time may be dispersed amongst the lakes and rivers or plants and air, the duplication still occurs and so the mark is created. Though the mark, rip or portal is imperceptible by most people it is created none the less. Like a tear in the fabric of the universe it appears like a dark slit about two feet wide and three feet high, hovering just above the ground like a doorway into a black cavern that looks exactly the same from all sides. It carries a colored aura around it that presents like mini northern lights shimmering blue, lime green and red in an up and down direction. Contained within this aura like a DNA fingerprint, is all the information about who caused this un-natural occurrence, exactly when and exactly where they came from and went to. The rip or portal if you will is recognizable only to a trained eye. That is anyone who is a trained time traveler and of course dogs.

- Excerpt from The Time Traveler's Handbook

Messing with Timelines
Part 1 – Take a Mulligan

Have you ever wished you could go back in time and change something? You know hind-sight being 20-20 and all, wouldn't you like to go back and have a do-over; A mulligan? Take knowledge from the future and change something; something small like a university exam that you wanted a better grade on, the outcome of which would have had a great impact on your career as an adult. Or even something bigger like taking yesterday's lottery numbers back a few days and buying the winning ticket? What about a childhood memory that haunts you? Perhaps you would like to change the course of events that caused a friend or relative to die at a young age say thirty years ago? Well as noble or fiendish the idea may be, as small or harmless the do-over might seem, messing with timelines is an extremely sensitive matter. Every Mulligan you take increases the risk of seriously altering the present and the future.

A slight change in an event that has already occurred may have significant impact on the status of the present and the greater the time gap, the more significant the impact. Imagine if you inadvertently caused a direct ancestor of yours to miss out on the opportunity to enter into the relationship that eventually produced your lineage? Let's say your great, great grandparents met on a ship sailing from France to America in 1890. And you just happened to jump back to the day before the voyage and inadvertently detained the old boy. So in this altered time line, he never made it aboard, never met your great, great grandmother, and as a result, your whole existence never came to be. The only way to correct this is to go back and make sure he gets on the ship. Problem is you need to act fast, because the moment the ship sets sail, the present day *you* will be gone. The entire timeline of your future family tree will instantly cease to exist the moment there is no longer a chance of your ancestors meeting when they were destined to. So as a rule of thumb, it is best not to get too close to anyone in the past, or interact with people at all...on any level. It's a small world and you never know who you might run into.

Something had changed that day of my first time jump. Jumping through that portal, going back to the game and being seen if only for a fraction of a second had caused something in the world to change. When I went downstairs I felt disoriented at first. I walked past the laundry room where I place food and water for Simon and Oliver in their four dishes every day, and I noticed there was for some odd reason, only two dishes there. I felt hungry and went to the fridge to eat some left-over pork tenderloin that I had barbecued the night before. When I opened the fridge I felt like I was in the wrong house. My head began to hurt.

There were no pork leftovers. There was nothing resembling what I had remembered being in this fridge less than two hours ago. There was a half eaten roast chicken, plenty of cold cuts, and take-out containers from a Chinese restaurant that I had never heard of let alone remember ordering or consuming. There were six bottles of beer and two bottles of wine, one wine bottle was opened. That was enough to alarm me. It was Wednesday, and we never consumed alcohol during the week. We never even kept alcohol in the kitchen fridge during the week. I had a beer fridge in the garage and Devin had her wine fridge downstairs. What the heck was going on here? There was sushi; my god, sushi, my favorite tuna rolls salmon rolls and plenty of them. This was really weird. I hadn't eaten sushi in the few months since we moved here so what the hell was it doing in our fridge? Oliver was by my side as usual when I had the fridge door open. He and Simon always followed me to the fridge. Simon where the hell is he?

I closed the fridge door and walked to the top of the stairs that lead down to the lower level.

"Sweetie, do you have Simon with you?" I called downstairs to Devin who was working in her office.

"What? Did you say Salmon? What are you talking about?" Devin replied with an agitation in her voice.

"Never mind, I'm being silly." I yelled back down to her.

"Salmon rolls are in the fridge." She yelled back. "Help yourself I don't want any more."

I thought about the baseball game I had dreamt about in my meditation. There was something missing in my mind about the outcome of that game. For a second I thought Brent had hit the ball on that last pitch and won the game, but something told me that was not the right ending. I turned around and leaned against the laundry room door. I stood there looking at the single set of dog dishes in amazement, stunned at Devin's words that had come up from the office. Devin didn't eat sushi. Where was Simon and why was there only one set of dog dishes? My head was pounding now so I went to the medicine cabinet in my powder room and took out the Advil. As I opened the bottle I grabbed my iPad and called up my photos. I knew I had lots of shots of the two dogs on it, but now there were none to be found. I knew for certain that I had altered the current timeline when I showed up on the field. For some reason we were now a couple who ate sushi, roast beef, take-out and consumed alcohol on weeknights! That was the good news. The bad news, we were now a one-dog family. My little guy Simon was missing in action. According to the timeline we were now living in, he had never been part of our family at all.

My headache began to subside. I looked at the iPad and blinked a few times. I couldn't remember why I had the iPad out or why I was feverishly looking at photos of Oliver. Something felt odd about the ending of the game I had just meditated on but I knew deep down that Brent had struck out. The game had ended in my meditation ten minutes ago just like I had seen it happen in real life nineteen years ago. Why did I have Advil in my hand? I didn't have a headache.

I was hungry so I went to the fridge to get some left-over sushi that I had picked up on the way home from work yesterday. Tuesday night was always 'Sushi-Night' at our house.

Late Night Training
Part 1 - Martin and Sheila

Sheila awoke startled and in a sweat, the kind of sweat caused from running a quarter mile or a few one hundred meter dashes. Her condition concerned her not because the feeling of exhilaration was foreign, but because she knew she could never reach this level of exhilaration in a dream. No this was a sweat accompanied by heavy breathing that was a result of a far greater physical investment than could possibly be achieved while lying still in bed, dreaming about running for the flag. It was the same game that she had dreamt about playing every night for the last eight or ten nights. This recurring dream was very familiar to Sheila now, with the exception of the outcome. The winners of the game and the people on the opposing team seemed to change each night. Martin and Harold were the two consistent characters in her dream, each night Martin playing along as her teammate and Harold coaching them both.

Sheila's current physical state wasn't unfamiliar to her, but it concerned her because awaking from a dream in her bed, feeling the same intensity and fatigue that she was accustomed to feeling after playing a basketball game just didn't make sense. Then a quick wave of realization rolled over her as she recalled the dream that she had just awoke from. The sequence of events that Sheila recalled made her current physical state seem to make sense if, in fact, those events took place in reality. But she knew it was just a dream and as such made no sense to cause her to be in this state. Something inside of her said it was real. The welcomed flash of light each time she jumped through one of the portals, the instant teleportation to exotic and beautiful destinations that seemed so vivid and real. The air and temperature was different on the other side of the flash. And her limbs, she was aware of her arms and legs. She was entirely lucid in the dream. The running, the dodging, Martin, her father Harold, the flag, the burning muscle fatigue, the fast breathing, perspiration, adrenaline, exhilaration, the feeling was far too real to dismiss. It seemed as though she had been playing Capture the Flag on a team with her boyfriend in her dreams with her Father acting as their coach. They played each night against other teams of two, the participants of which in this moment seemed familiar but were not entirely recognizable. Then the feeling passed, and the memory began to fade as dreams normally do once one awakens.

She looked over at Martin sleeping next to her. She couldn't help but notice that he too was sweating as if he were in a heightened state of physical exertion. It was at this precise moment in time that Sheila came to the realization, or at least the suspicion that she shared the same recurring dream with Martin. But that didn't make sense. How could they be having the same experience in their dream state? It was indisputable that Martin was in the same physical state that she was. No doubt about it, Martin, a fine athlete, was sweating and breathing at a rate consistent with the level of activity Sheila had just been dreaming about. She woke in a sweat from a dream that Martin was present in, and here Martin was before her eyes breathing hard and glistening.

There was no way Martin could be in this condition just because of a dream. No, Sheila knew that someone with Martin's athletic prowess couldn't reach his current state without substantial physical exertion. The fact that Martin was still asleep made the moment surreal. It just made no sense on one level that they could be sharing the same dream. But deep down, there was a vibe that resonated within Sheila that screamed there was something much grander at play than she could imagine.

Sheila's boyfriend Martin Saunders came out of high school as most Wisconsin graduates who earn a hockey scholarship do, with wide eyes, great enthusiasm and the dream of one day making it into the NHL. He was on top of the world now in University reveling in the knowledge that one day soon he would be playing professional hockey somewhere in the country. It was almost a given that he would escalate up to the pros. After all, eight out of every ten players on the Badger's varsity team moved up to the FARM league and half of them made it to the big time. He knew that his odds were

47

greatly increased because Sheila's father Harold was head coach of the varsity team. Over the next couple years Martin's path to becoming an NHL'er seemed almost pre-destined. And now about to play his first season on the Washington Major junior league team, Martin looked back at the journey with a great respect for Harold, his coach, his mentor, his future father in-law.

Harold respected, envied and lived vicariously through Martin. He had coached Martin through university and was instrumental in moving him along to the Major junior league. No one knew just how instrumental Harold had been in fast-tracking Martin up to the semi-pros. The two were very comfortable working together. Harold was exceptionally good at coaching Martin. It could be said that Harold could coach Martin in his sleep. The two worked so well together that Sheila felt there was something odd about their relationship. He pushed Martin harder than anyone else on the team and Martin always embraced it without question. Sheila chalked this up to Harold overcompensating for fear of the possibility that the coach could be accused of favoring the prodigal soon to be son-in-law. But other onlookers who were slightly more removed from the family dynamic could sense a different connection between the two. There was an unbalanced sort of intense competitive expectation of Martin's performance level within Harold. He exhibited an entitlement or ownership of Martin's performance almost like he was leveraging inside knowledge to motivate him to exert more effort than anyone else. Despite the outward appearance of over-expectation, Martin worked as hard as Harold demanded every time.

Sheila was remembering more detail of her dream now, running together with Martin, and her father was there too. The same dream she had last night and for the past week at least she thought, only this time it was much more real and much more intense. Running and diving through a series of holes in the air that enable physical jumps from one location to another. Running in short spurts with a sense of urgency to make it in time, but in time for what? She sensed there was a quick window of opportunity and somehow she needed to decide which way to dodge and which hole to jump into each time. She knew she had to select the portal she thought her opponent had gone through, and knew she was doing it well. She just didn't know HOW she was doing it. The other piece of the puzzle that made no sense was the possibility that she was experiencing the same dream that her father and boyfriend were also in. Dreams were not reality to Sheila, or to anyone else that she knew. How could Sheila's experience within a dream possibly be shared with someone else at the same time? And how could a dream cause her to work up such a sweat?

Martin awoke startled and in a sweat. Sheila stared at him with a questioning look, but Martin was oblivious to her gaze. It took Martin several seconds to gain awareness of his surroundings, and acknowledge his girlfriend's presence. Even then, Martin's breath was rushed and his pulse was high. The perspiration on is forehead was obvious, and anyone would think that Martin had just come off the ice after a tough third period shift. Martin focused on Sheila and realized that she was awake, propped up on one elbow, the full moon shining into the room from over her shoulder. She was looking down at him and looking very hot. Their eyes met with an instant mutual emotional desire. Martin didn't notice the shine of perspiration on Sheila's face, and as she opened her mouth to ask him about his dream, he rose up and kissed her. A warm rush came over both of their bodies as Sheila fell into his strong embrace. There was no discussion about dreams.

Mind Travelers - Chapter 2

Messing with timelines
Part 2 – Travel Companions

Dinner with Lisa and James is always a treat. The girls talk about the important things in life such as celebrities, jewelry, fashion, food, wine and decor while the boys talk about sports. The girls love their wine and nibbles, the boys, beer and pepperoni. The one topic that always brings the four of us together into a single conversation is travel. We love to travel together and have extensively done so for several years, predominantly through Europe. In recent discussions we agreed to some destinations including Hawaii and a few South American cities.

I raised my glass to James and proclaimed.

"Another eight weeks and we'll be sipping Malbec by the pool. Hey James, we should bring our clubs and play a round or two."

"Not me, I'll just rent clubs if we actually manage to get out to a course. My guess is we'll be too busy carrying the ladies shopping bags around town." James quietly reported as if speaking low, three feet away from our spouses would keep the words concealed. "I'm looking forward to Buenos Aires but I hear there's been a lot of crime there lately."

"I suppose if you get in with the wrong people it could happen. Have any tourists been involved?" Lisa chimed in.

"Yeah there were some Americans and a Canadian kidnapped; I think three or four just in the last couple of months." James added matter-of-factly.

"If you act like a tourist anywhere you'll be a target. What do you know about the kidnappings? Were they rich foreigners or just dumb-ass tourists?" Devin queried.

"Hang on I'll 'Google' it." I said as I switched on my iPad.

James continued by adding, "I don't know all the

particulars but I heard that it seemed all pretty random. They weren't of significant wealth; they were part of a group looking for investors, maybe on a business conference."

"And what happened, did the kidnappers get away with it? What was the ransom? ", Lisa asked as she sipped her wine.

"That's the funny part. There was no ransom and no demands at all." I said while looking at the article on my iPad.

Lisa continued, "So why kidnap someone if you're not going to ask for anything?"

This didn't sound right to me either. There had to be more to the kidnappings than what was in the online article that I was now reading.

I read the highlights of the article out loud to the group, "There were three similar kidnapping incidents one weekend four months ago. All three victims in the same hotel knew each other and were there for a technology conference. They claim they never saw their captors, never heard voices, no ransom demands or threats and no harm came to any of them. They were simply taken to a holding cell and detained for an undisclosed period of time. Then they were eventually released without harm. Two guys, Anthony Peroni aged 21 from Vancouver, Ralph Miller 22 from Miami, and a woman, Rita Boyer, 21 from New York."

"So how long were they held? Was the holding cell at least decorated nicely?" Devin added with her usual humorous sarcasm.

I continued communicating the contents of the article, "These are three separate kidnappings. Sadly there is no mention of how the holding cells were decorated, but apparently the food wasn't all that bad. According to this article all of the three victims say they were fed very well.

One actually said that they served him his favorite spicy dragon rolls."

"Sushi in Buenos Aires served by your kidnapper, I wonder how they knew he liked sushi." James questioned, "And Dragon rolls to be specific."

"I wonder why they were so nice to the victims." I continued. "It also says here that the victims have no recall of how they were transported to and from the room they were held in. They were all taken the same way. Each on the way back to their hotel room someone came up from behind with a rag soaked in ether. They woke up in a holding cell with good food but non-descript decor. Rita was held for two days, Anthony for two and Ralph for one. Not one of the three can remember leaving the cell. They all assume they were put under again with ether in their sleep, and then moved out of the room. They all came to in their respective hotel rooms just around check out time on the last day of the conference."

"Are you guys worried? Devin asked, "I mean what if Lisa and I are kidnapped and fed a diet of chardonnay and chocolate cake? Then forced to make out with some gorgeous hunks?"

"Or eat steak and drink Malbec…" Lisa added, "mmmm yummie."

"Excuse me I need to use the little girl's room." I said as I rose up from my seat.

"Time to break the seal mate?" James asked.

"You got that right."

"Clink clink". I could hear the sound of Devin's ring tapping against a near empty wine glass.

I rose from the table and topped up Lisa and Devin's chardonnay. With iPad in hand, I went down the hall and into my powder room. The clock on my iPad read 8:37 and 43sec. I set my mind to Buenos Aires ten weeks into the future so I could have a short preview of the last day of our vacation. I figured that if nothing had happened to any of us by then, we could go ahead and proceed with the holiday completely worry free.

I landed in the washroom of our hotel unit. As I emerged the déjà vu hit me good and solid. I was standing in the hotel room's bath tub with my head and body tingling so hard I was barely able to maintain my footing. I managed to kneel down on one knee and hold my balance until the vibration within my body subsided and my eye sight came back. I sensed a few dialogues going on around me, none that were alarming just your basic vacation type emotions. There was happiness and contentment and I could feel Devin, Lisa James and my self all reflecting a bit of last-day-of-vacation blues.

Lucky for me there was a shower curtain that kept me concealed from the person who was just now walking into the bathroom. It must be James I thought; it was definitely a man, his shoes clicked as he entered the room and walked to the toilet where he began peeing standing up with his back to me. With the déjà vu almost completely worn off, I slowly and very quietly rose up. I now could see through the window above the bathtub that faced outside to the pool. I saw Devin sitting in the shade reading, Lisa next to her soaking up the sun, and I could see myself walking around the far side of the pool. It's always so strange to see another instance of yourself in the future, or the past. It's even stranger when you know you are being visited by another instance of yourself, like when the déjà vu hits you and you just know that your future self is somewhere nearby.

This must be James I thought having a pee in the washroom here on our vacation in BA. I thought for second that I could really scare the hell out of him right now. Just jump out and scare the livin' daylights out of him. But James and Lisa didn't know about my ability to time travel. Neither did Devin for that matter, at least not yet anyway.

Stay quiet I thought to myself, another few seconds and James will leave; I can take a look around and get out of here. The man was finished at the toilet, flushed it and walked to the sink. I suddenly got a strange feeling. I could see through the small opening in the curtain the reflection in the mirror on the vanity revealed a man that he was fully dressed. It looked like he was wearing a suit. As he walked, his shoes made the sound that dress shoes make when walking on a tiled floor; a soft sort of click as the hard leather hits the tile. Why was James wearing a suit while the three of us were poolside? I heard a clink sound as the man set a small bottle down on the sink less than two foot away from me. It reminded of the chardonnay I had just poured for Devin as she sarcastically beckoned with the clink of her wedding ring against the glass like Susan Sarandon in the movie Igby Goes Down. That's when I heard my own voice outside the window poolside, and the entire situation got much clearer and much, much more real.

"James, I gotta break the seal, how's your beer?" I heard myself say.

"I'm ready mate, thanks." James answered back instantly.

I could hear the sliding glass door open as my future self entered the hotel room. There was a pungent odor in the air. Ether I suspect, but why, and what was he going to do?

The man stepped to the side and took a position behind the washroom door. As my future self walked in the man stepped out and caught my arm from behind, quickly placed the ether soaked cloth over my mouth and nose and braced my body from falling down. In less than three seconds future me was out like a light. The man gently lowered me to the bathroom floor with his back to the tub. I took a chance and peeked out through the small gap between the shower curtain and the wall at his reflection in the mirror. I could only see his back in the mirror and couldn't get a clear view of his face. He was blond, tall and looked stocky but fit. He took out a cell phone and hit a speed dial number. The other end connected and I heard the man's voice.

The man in suit said quietly, "Zee package is ready."

Almost instantly, as he closed the call on his cell phone another man in a suit entered the room. He was also tall and blond and spoke quietly to his accomplice in a low tone and in German. Peeking out through the small gap I could see the backs of the two men in the mirror and myself sitting on the floor with my back against the wall, eyes closed as if I were sleeping. I remained still and watched with no clear view of their faces, and then something struck me. A familiarity about the way the second man carried himself. The second man had a large dark cloth bag that he quickly pulled over my limp body. My heart was pumping through my chest. I had to stay quiet even though I felt the need to gasp for air. I moved back from the crack in the curtain with a view of the mirror for fear that I would give my presence away. When I looked back only a second or two later the two later the men and me were gone. Had they dragged future me out of the washroom? I didn't see where they went. It happened so fast, and I didn't hear footsteps or the sound of the hotel room door. It didn't matter at this point because I wasn't going to follow them, I didn't need to. I didn't need to see the man's face either. I knew there was something familiar about him, the way he carried himself, his stance and the voice. The voice was one that I recognized and remembered from nineteen year ago. I knew without a doubt that it was Brent.

I immediately left the bath tub and went back to my powder room, at present time so I could get more information from my iPad. The clock read 8:37 48sec. Five seconds had been consumed in transitioning to and from the South American hotel bathroom where I had just discovered I would be kidnapped approximately ten weeks from now. I scanned the online article again on the iPad, this time for dates and the name of the hotel that the three victims stayed at so I could find them and attempt to answer two questions that were now burning in my brain. Why did Brent kidnap those three people, and more importantly why did he want to kidnap me in ten weeks?

I had to work fast. After all, according to my wife and guests I was merely relieving myself in the powder room right now. Every moment I spent in here was a moment away from the conversation in the dining room. At this point I had been away almost one minute. It was now 8:38 and 37sec. More than 3 minutes away would seem suspect so I quickly found the info and checked the time once again. It was 8:39 05sec. Shit, a minute twenty gone already. As I set my mind on the next destination, this time four months into the past, I was well aware that I wouldn't be able to come back and check my reference materials again. When I returned I would have to rejoin my wife and guests without a doubt. For now though, my goal was to get close to the second kidnapping and see what I could find out as an observer. I concentrated on the coordinates that would land me just ten minutes before and close to where the second kidnapping happened, November 5th 2010, 6:20 p.m. the Home Hotel.

Emerging in the third stall of the washroom in the Home Hotel, I now felt a slight panic set in. I had left my powder room in such a hurry that the anxiety over the elapsed time had amplified in my mind during transition causing me to forget the names of the people that were kidnapped. Who was it that I was coming here to look for?

Within my sphere of awareness I picked up on four conversations currently in progress. Two were mundane; a guy trying his best pick up lines on a young lady; another conversation were two women talking about their spouses. The third conversation was very interesting, a group of people discussing ideas having to do with advancements in the luxury travel industry; and the fourth seemed more like a monologue, someone talking to them self about going home, or thinking about being away from family, homesick. I thought because the first kidnapping had already happened, there would be some conversations about it, but no one at all was talking about the first kidnapping.

I left the stall and was relieved that there was no one present in the washroom at this time. I walked out of the washroom and down the hall into the bar where I found myself a seat facing the group of young professionals talking about technology. The names came back to me and I was now listening specifically for conversations that included the names Rita, Ralph or Anthony.

"Vhut ill it be?" The bartender asked.

"Beer." I answered.

It dawned on me that the bartender was not a local. He appeared to be German with a pretty thick accent but I didn't think much about this other than sensing he was the homesick one I had heard during my entry. I was still trying to remember who I came here to look for. Laughter erupted from the group of six young professionals occupying two tables half way across the bar, four women and two men. The hyper-awareness had faded so I could no longer hear the conversations in my head and had to listen as carefully as I could for any of the three victim's names. There were two other occupied tables in the bar, two of the other conversations I had detected, but could no longer hear. None of the conversations fit with what I was looking for, except maybe the technology conversation.

Judging by the sun light outside, I guessed it was getting close to sundown. The group was discussing new technology being developed for the hospitality and luxury travel industry. I figured out that these people were a team of under funded, highly skilled techies developing some new cutting edge experiential applications for an elite hospitality market. They were inventors of some really interesting luxury hotel room features looking to engineer a unique customer experience, completely tailored and customized to the individual consumer. I caught something about environmental controls that auto-adjusted based on the movement of the consumer; aroma, lighting, sound and even visual media following the consumer from room to room.

Half way through my beer, one of the women excused herself from the group saying she was going to get ready for dinner. This could be Rita I thought, but didn't hear anyone refer to her by name. One of the men got up and left with her, claiming he was going to do the same. The group bid them farewell and the two headed for the lobby. I felt the urge to follow the couple but resisted. Instead I decided to find out what I could about the remaining four while I had the chance. Besides I figured if this woman was Rita I wouldn't be able to find out enough about her on the walk from the bar to her room, and she was with company now regardless.

I kept my eyes on the TV screen above the bar but was listening in to the conversation to pick up what I could from it.
I caught a snippet about "…voice-activated wallpaper-television." It was being described as a "…floor-to-ceiling hi-definition screen and the image moves with you from living room to bathroom to bedroom. Speakers are laid in the ceiling and walls strategically around the suite so the sound can follow you as well."

I was still listening for Rita's name, or Ralph or Anthony. The bartender looked at me and saw that my glass was still 1/3 full. He turned and exited the room through the door behind the far side of the bar.

The conversation in the corner continued. "Through voice activation a customer can order any television show, sporting event or movie, listen to any music accompanied by visuals of the artist's recording in studio or live on stage."

I heard Rita's name but couldn't tell if she was still at the table or if she was in fact the woman who left the bar.

The bartender came back after being gone no more than 30 seconds. I noticed he was looking a little pale. He pointed to my empty beer from the far end of the bar. I nodded yes and he proceeded to draw a pint from the tap. As he brought it down to my perch I heard Rita being addressed in person assuring me that Rita was still at the table. He placed the beer on a new coaster, picked up my empty glass and my moment of relief over discovering Rita's presence quickly turned into a rush of anxiety. As he turned and walked away I caught the distinct odor of ether. The same odor I caught in the bathroom when my future self was abducted before my eyes only a few moments ago, in fact it was going to happen 19 weeks from now. As he walked away I noticed the stocky build, the blond hair and the suit jacket all fit with the image of the man in the bathroom that I had seen kidnapping my future self. Then I remembered that it was Rita the second kidnapping I had intended to come here to scout. Accidentally I targeted the first kidnapping by mistake. It was Anthony who was the first one kidnapped. I remembered now the article said that it happened at 6:30 today…less than a minute ago. Rita's time of abduction was to be much later, 11:30 this evening.

In my heightened state of anxiety, my mind began to race through all the reasons I could think of as to why these young folks were being targeted. They were young energetic and bright professionals working on new technology that really didn't have a wide market anywhere. Or at least I hadn't heard of any of this yet… Hadn't heard of it yet…YET! That was it. Someone from the future has come back to take ownership of an emerging trend. Capitalizing on future technology by manipulating its inception to control the development of what they know becomes a successful and lucrative enterprise in the future. It made sense, the abduction in my hotel room. The man appeared immediately, the two left without using the door. How far in the future had the idea come from? Who was behind this?

The beer was making my mind wonder off in a number of tangents. I was beginning to think about the financial potential a monopoly of this magnitude could have, especially if you consider controlling something this big for a very long time? Imagine receiving $10 for every television that was installed in any hotel anywhere in the world for say a hundred years? What if the number was $20 per TV in every hotel room for only 20 years? I wonder what that would amount to. Or what if you received $100 per room each year for every Hilton Hotel, or Marriot or Holiday INN around the world? Still, I couldn't fathom the revenues even one hotel chain would generate for a contract that covered a multitude of products and services.

Now at least I thought I knew what the angle for the kidnappings was, these strange kidnappings with no demands or at least no obvious demands. Of course, the only demand was that the victim be absent from a very specific event at a very specific time, the main outcome of the event being the future relationship that would develop between a group of entrepreneurs and investors. Brent or someone he worked for wanted to plant some of their own people in a partnership that would eventually flourish and grow into a multi-billion dollar business. The demand was contained within the action. It was simply a way to distract the three potential principals of the future company long enough to divert and influence the investor's direction. A kidnapping would facilitate the immediate short term requirement that the kidnapper had, plus it would have an emotional and mentally distracting effect that would last for days or even weeks; long enough to keep all three out of circulation without actually harming them physically.

I put $20 down on the bar and was getting up to leave (through the washroom of course) when out of the corner of my eye I glimpsed a recognizable figure. The same one I now knew was going to put a bag over my head and abduct me on the last day of my upcoming vacation. Brent had just entered the bar from the far entrance and was quietly greeting the bartender, his accomplice. I quickly diverted my eyes downward and tried to turn before he saw me, but I was too slow.

"Wictor?"
Shit, he saw me.
"Wictor!"

I should have turned back, raised my head and tried to explain what I was doing there but instead I kept moving towards the washroom as if I wasn't who he thought I was. My heart was pounding as I was trying to figure out all the ways this could play out. I could come back from the washroom and claim I didn't hear him, or I heard him but needed an emergency visit to the toilet. Or I could pretend it wasn't me and simply vanish. I knew it was the worst thing to do because there was a very large chance that Brent wouldn't buy it. After all he had impeccable eye sight considering he was meant to be a pro baseball player in an alternate timeline, one that I had caused to go off the rails. How the hell did he recognize me? It's been at least fifteen years since we last saw each other last, near the end of University.

As I walked, I put my hand up to my left ear to give the impression that I was on a cell phone. This may help me form an excuse if I needed to come back and confront this situation. I needed to get back to my dinner party and now after two additional beers I really did need to break the seal. I walked into the washroom, it was empty. I headed for the third stall and made a snap decision to relieve myself before going back home mainly because I knew I couldn't take more than a minute to resurface to the dining room once I got there. I also assumed Brent would have dismissed the sighting as his mistake or maybe would remain occupied with the bartender talking about what most kidnappers talk about for the next forty seconds or so. I was wrong. Half way through my well needed relief I heard footsteps approaching and the bathroom door open. The footsteps came inside the room. The same footsteps I heard from inside the bathtub before the abduction of future me. The footsteps came into the room but didn't stop at the urinals or the row of sinks. The footsteps kept coming closer and suddenly stopped at the first stall. I heard the door swing open and bang against the inner wall of the toilet stall. Then the footsteps came closer still and stopped outside the second stall. Again I heard the door swing open and smack hard against the wall this time right next to me. Then two more steps slow and sure before they stopped just outside of the third stall, my stall, the stall I was standing in still urinating. I was close to completing the task, feeling relief in my bladder when I heard the distinct click of a pistol being cocked. I didn't wait for what was about to happen next. Penis in hand, urine fully flowing, I caught a quick but distinct smell of ether as I left just in time to save my life.

I re-emerged in our powder room back home. Thanks to the slow-motion effect during re-entry, I managed to "get a grip" on the situation so to speak and not cause too much mess. I aligned my stance to the toilet as fast as I could and finished my business. I cleaned up and checked the time on the iPad again. It was 8:40 and 15sec now, a total of 2 minutes and 30 seconds had elapsed in present time. I felt a bit flushed with anxiety over the thought of having a gun cocked less than two feet behind my head, and the beers I had consumed didn't help that anxiety much either.

Meanwhile back in Buenos Aires, the man standing outside the third toilet stall who had just cocked the pistol heard the sound of a solid stream hitting the water in the toilet bowl come to a sudden stop. He kicked hard at the stall door causing it to buckle inwards and slam against the inner wall to reveal that the stall was empty. The man with the gun was not surprised.

I got back out to the dining room within three minutes and as I did, I became acutely aware of the fact that Brent now knew I was a time traveler. Worse than that, when he saw me in the bar it was four months ago. I had advertently given Brent an advantage. He would likely figure out the reason for my visit was his kidnapping caper, and I now understood why in another ten weeks he would take action by kidnapping me in the Home Hotel room.

"Hey baby." Devin greeted me as I re-entered the kitchen.

"Hey. What are we discussing now?" I asked.

"Lisa and I were talking about the drapes. I told her how difficult the decision was to pick these." Devin explained with a bored tone.

"I know right? You were torn between these and the..."

"Don't mock me." Devin pouted, "I _was_ torn. Lucky I have you to bounce all my decorating ideas off."

I rolled my eyes in the air towards James' direction. James returned the eye roll.

"Sweetheart," I started, "I keep saying you should become a professional interior designer. You could make gazillions and you would have all sorts of clients and assistants to bounce your ideas off of. You wouldn't need my lame opinion. Win-win you see."

"Your opinion isn't lame." Devin rebutted as she rolled her eyes sarcastically at Lisa. "Besides, I couldn't deal with trying to impart my taste and style onto people who don't get it."

"Hey what if you could template the designs and let people pick their own combination. You know on car websites like mini-cooper where you can 'build your own', pick tires and rims, leather interior and paint color etc... Then you won't need to convince them of anything, just give them the pre-formatted choices and execute on the ones they choose."

"O.K. but how will they get the choices to pick from?" asked Devin in a quiet tone.

"Any number of ways, online, mobile or tablet, I could build you a virtual studio app that has a catalogue of furniture, fabric swatches for the furniture, drapes, paint colors, accessories the whole nine yards." I ranted on, "Even throw in a bunch of 'Designer Picks', combinations that you know work tastefully together. And the virtual tour can be a 3D fly-through or a 360 degree panoramic image."

"And I suppose the customer just punches a few selections and the price is quoted." Devin began to sound negative.

"Of course" I said, "and in what ever currency they want to pay in."

"I like it. Can you build it next week?"

"Of course, Ughhh." I said as I rolled my eyes at James again.

"It would be better if the REAL material and paint could change, then I'd never get tired of our living space, just change it to suit my mood."

"So three times a day basically?" I added.

"Hardy har." said Devin.

There was a sudden loud 'clunk' noise that came from the powder room down the hall.

"What was that?" Devin yelled, "I heard something down the hall."

Oliver barked once and ran down to the powder room door then began barking hysterically.

"I'll take a look." I said heroically.

I went down the hall to towards the powder room. Oliver was barking his head off. The door was slightly open but the light was off. As I approached I thought I saw something move inside. I opened the door and turned on the light but saw nothing. I caught a faint smell of something that was familiar but couldn't put my finger on it. I could see the portal I had left from my two time jumps was still there. It would remain for a day or so. I wondered if Brent or the bartender had come and gone. Maybe he followed through my portal to locate me. I picked Oliver up in my arms and walked back out to the dining room.

"Good boy, Ollie. That's enough," I said consolingly "nothing there sweetheart. James, can I get you another beer?"

"I'm ready mate." was James' quick reply.

"Ladies, more chardonnay," I offered, "Hey you switched to red wine?"

"I swear Victor you've got the shortest memory of anyone I've ever met. We've been drinking red all night. He makes up for it with his looks though." Devin muttered sarcastically in Lisa's direction.

I had topped them both up with Chardonnay just before I went to the powder room. I guess this little real-time continuity switch to red wine was a bi-product that was somehow caused by Brent's sighting three months ago. I wondered what else in the present had changed because of that little mistake.

As the night went on I found myself thinking more and more about the situation. It was difficult to remain jovial and I was pre-occupied thinking about the events. It was getting late, our guests left and we retired for the night. Lying in bed I could not stop thinking. I was not entirely comfortable with the responsibility that came with this incredible ability to travel across time. It seemed like I had more of an obligation to right the wrongs of the world than to use it as a gift for my own enjoyment. But I guess that there are two sides to every story.

I knew Brent would be on the hunt for me. The only way I could remedy this problem was to somehow get Brent back on his natural path to baseball stardom as was meant to be. To accomplish this I needed to intercept his employer and pre-empt his corruption. Actually I should try to find the moment that the idea was conceived by his employer and pre-empt the conception of the idea itself. Then his would-be employer would not think to involve him. I assumed that the idea was to be conceived far in the future because of the fact that the technology was just emerging now, and the kidnappings were an indication of the timing for the beginning of the technology company partnership.

Initially I had changed the outcome of Brent's baseball career when I jumped back 17 years to the pitcher's mound at my high school game and caused him to strike out instead of hitting a grand slam. The trip I took back to the past had given Brent a four month head start on me, so I couldn't make the assumption that the next sighting I would have of Brent would be in ten weeks. Brent could choose to come after me at anytime.
Was my future kidnapping a direct result of Brent's seeing me months ago, or was he already planning to kidnap me for another reason? After all I had gone forward first and back second from my powder room so there was no reason to believe that my future kidnapping had anything to do with my visit to BA in the past. My head was spinning with the myriad of thoughts and possible scenarios. My last thought before I fell asleep was that I needed to figure out how to fix this.

Jump across Time
There's an App for That

It's a fact that we only use 10-15% of our mental capacity. Einstein probably came close to harnessing 20%. In case you didn't know, he focused mainly on understanding the universe and how everything worked together within it. He was a "theoretical physicist" with an incredible capacity to visualize complex situations, generate mathematical equations that related specifically to the mechanics of the situations, and devise experimental methods to prove the outcome of those situations. His hypotheses were devised from pure imagination and although he was a strong mathematician, he relied heavily on his wife to review and verify or revise much of his mathematical formulae.

With the ability to use one's imagination anyone can visualize themself in an environment that is purely made up. Most people however lack enough imagination to effectively accomplish such a task or perhaps find it silly or juvenile. This is mainly because we allow ourselves to be mentally molded at a young age as we conform to society through our upbringing and into adult life. Society teaches us to act like everyone else and to expect everyone to act like us. Most of us are schooled to develop logic rather than creativity so we stifle our imagination which in turn reduces our true ability to develop the creative mind. It is the creative mind however that enables "out-of-the-box" thinking. Einstein once said "I will never let my schooling interfere with my education". And he didn't.

Everyone has the ability to time travel at their immediate disposal. Actually every human brain invokes this ability whenever we enter into the REM dream state. Unfortunately most of us have been conditioned to believe that dreams are "a succession of images, ideas, emotions and sensations that occur involuntarily in the mind during certain stages of sleep". The experience itself as it happens to the individual is not at all involuntary but is in fact a form of time travel carefully controlled by a tiny program within the sub-conscious mind. Yes "there's an app for that". It generally only functions when the imagination is allowed to run free, during sleep.

Very few people have ever learned to consciously control this dream program, or app. It takes an extremely creative mind to first be open to the possibility and second to mentally release conventional linear time thinking. Many believe dreams to be a form of out of body experience, and there has been much time and effort dedicated to the concept. Many books have been written on the subject of how to learn to become lucid within a dream in order to consciously manipulate the experience. This is not the same thing as time travel at all. The difficulty in teaching one's self to gain conscious control over a programmed (sub consciously controlled) experience is that the conscious mind is controlled by the sub conscious. The true art of time travel begins with learning to use a basic conscious function called imagination, which in turn enables us to transport our body through space and time. Imagination is the same energy that holds atoms together. It's the energy that can separate atoms from matter, move them at the speed of light and reassemble them in their previous form. Yes, there's an app for that.

There's one particular moment in time that naturally invokes the time travel app. It's a time when the brain is in a state that allows the imagination to control the app. and that is the exact moment when we are about to traverse from our normal conscious state to the sleep state. You know that one brief moment of time when your mind is slipping into sleep mode? Sometimes your conscious mind jolts you back out just as you were about to finally fall off the edge of the abyss. Your body suddenly jumps involuntarily as if you were just spooked by something. That moment, it turns out, is the one that is easier to control than the dream state because unlike during REM, it happens during a conscious state.

The best way to experience time travel is not by becoming lucid within a dream. The body of someone who is dreaming, lucid or otherwise will remain at rest. To experience time travel, you must consciously cause the mind to invoke the transformation of the physical being across space and time. The body of a time traveler moves to the location and point in time that the little program in the mind has been dictated to go to by the imagination. This sounds difficult at first, but if you had a dream last night while you were asleep, you already know how to do this...sub-consciously. To learn how to control this program from your conscious mind takes an athletic and competitive spirit, years of imagination training or meditation, and last but not least, someone to mentor you. Someone who has been trained and can teach you gradually to control this ability so that you don't accidentally alter the natural progression of our current time-line...A coach if you will...

- Excerpt from The Time Traveler's Handbook

Late Night Training
Part 2 - Harold

Harold awoke startled and in a sweat. Not as heavy a sweat as Sheila or Martin had that same night likely due to the fact that his participation in the game was as the coach, a much less physically demanding role. It had been another successful round of capture the flag, and Harold was smiling and invigorated. His students were coming along nicely and Harold knew he would soon have to tell the two what was really happening. He could sense their curiosity growing and figured that any day now they would realize that the three of them were in fact interacting together and with others in their dreams over the past two weeks. His time travel teachings were coming to an end for another year just like his hockey season was ending.

The Hockey season was nearly over with only one game left to play this being a varsity alumni-invitational a couple of weeks from now. Harold booked a 7:00 a.m. time slot for practice every week and this morning's skate was an optional final-fare-well to the season along with the seniors of the team. He scheduled this every year and without fail every single member of the team showed up despite it being an optional practice. It was viewed as a way to honor the coach, the seniors and to have one last work-out with the team. It was 5:27 a.m. Sunday morning and Harold was already wide awake. Partly due to the fact that today was the last ice-time he would have coaching Martin, and partly due to the great success he'd had coaching Martin and Sheila in their dreams. He knew he really should tell them today.

Harold lay watching the alarm clock as it struck 5:28 then 5:29 and finally 5:30. The radio came on as it did every Sunday morning to wake him up and get him out on time for practice. Today he heard 'More than a feelin….well give it a song babe…I begin to feeling…I see my Maryanne walkin' away….' The song by Boston was airing on the radio this fine crisp spring morning. Harold hit the off button and rolled to his left and gently out of the king size bed with a smile because this song was one of his all-time favorites. It reminded him of his training days and how he used to hear it so often way back then. At the time he was courting the girl who would later become his wife. He would often attempt to sing along to it while in her presence but it was far above his vocal range so his girlfriend would just smile and nod her head to the beat.

Harold's wife Maryanne was not affected at all by the early Sunday morning radio alarm made silent by the factory grade earplugs she lodged deep into her ear canals upon bedding down each Saturday night. He walked quietly to the bathroom, closed the door and turned on the shower. Harold thought about how he would eventually broche the topic of time travel training with Martin and Sheila. Worried about the emotions this could stir up and the potential repercussions that might spin-off from this situation, he focused hard on a tactful way to communicate the concept to the two. Neither Sheila nor Martin had willingly signed up for this training and the level of responsibility that accompanies such a powerful ability would require Harold to lay down some serious ground rules before allowing them to venture off in time without a chaperone.

In the shower he mentally worked through numerous approaches and tactics. Who should he tell first, Martin or Sheila? Should he tell them both at the same time? He finished his shower and shaved his face, brushed his teeth and went back into the bedroom to get dressed all the while pondering the inevitable conversation. Harold went downstairs to make some coffee and toast. As he finished his breakfast and was putting his dishes into the sink, Harold decided he would just sit the two of them down at the same time and put the cards on the table. He figured the chips would fall where they fall and that it would be better not to beat around the bush at this point.

Harold put on his jacket and locked the front door then sat for a moment warming up his car. He decided he would take Sheila and Martin both out for brunch today after practice. That's when he would tell them what was going on. Somewhat relieved by finally making the decision he shifted the car into reverse and backed out of the driveway. It was 6:35 a.m.

Harold's drive to the rink never took him more than ten minutes, but today he decided to take a short drive-through detour for coffee and especially to pick up a hot chocolate. Sheila would be there today and he wanted to get on her good side as early as possible. Harold placed the hot beverages in the cup holders and accepted his change from the attendant. He pulled out and turned left onto the street heading west towards a red light which was now about 100 meters away. The light turned green as he began accelerating on his approach to the intersection giving him no reason to think about slowing down. This was unfortunate because if the light had turned yellow or red as he approached the intersection Harold would have slowed his vehicle. Then he would have seen the pick-up truck approaching the intersection as the police chased it southbound, now just one block away to the north.

Harold, now traveling at 60 km/h, carefully reached for his coffee nestled in the cup holder between the passenger and driver's seat alongside his daughter's hot chocolate while his car entered into the intersection. It was 6:43 a.m. The driver of the pick-up truck saw Harold's vehicle about to cross his path and attempted to avoid the impact by swerving left to allow Harold to pass in front of him. Harold could hear the police sirens a few blocks north but at that moment was looking down at his cup holder to retrieve his coffee and didn't see the truck approaching. The truck was traveling at a velocity of 127 km/h which proved too fast to maneuver the thirty five hundred kilogram vehicle around Harold's oncoming path. The truck collided square against the passenger side rear door and hind quarter panel of Harold's car. Harold's vehicle was sent into a brutal spin which made one and a half revolutions before coming to a very abrupt stop against the traffic light post located on the south west corner of the intersection. The entire event took less than three seconds during which time Harold's only thought was the question why his coffee had flown out of his hand.

The driver of the truck, not wearing a seatbelt was thrown from his vehicle through the front windshield thirty feet before crashing head first into a parked car. He was pronounced dead at the scene. Harold broke several bones and suffered major head trauma along with some internal organ damage during the accident. He was brought by ambulance to St Michael's Hospital arriving at 6:58 a.m. in a coma and given very little chance of surviving.

Martin and Sheila had arrived at the rink at 6:50 a.m. Martin headed straight for the change room while Sheila walked out to the player's bench. Surprised that her father wasn't there, like he had been at this time every Sunday that Sheila had attended the morning practice over the past eight months, she began to wonder if he was in the dressing room or maybe he had stopped to get her a hot chocolate. He would surprise her once in a while with her favorite morning hot beverage when he wanted to get on her good side. She was wise to his ways but couldn't think of why he would want to get on her good side today. Sheila took a seat and waited in anticipation of her sweet hot chocolate that she hoped Harold would bring and that she knew would keep her warm for the duration of the practice. She watched as several of the players and eventually Martin came out and began skating around to warm up.

Sheila sat behind the bench watching Martin and the other hockey players warm up on the ice. She looked around repeatedly for her father and began to feel uneasy. It wasn't like Harold to sleep in and miss an occasion as special as this one. Sheila's cell phone rang at 7:05. She instantly felt a sense of relief as she read the caller ID display; the call was from her parent's house. But when she answered and heard her mother's voice she could tell right away that there was something very wrong.

Just a Little Weekend Get Away – Part 1

Devin and I just love to travel. We love to travel almost as much as Devin loves to decorate. Believe me she can take any space that looks good and make it look out of this world. I believe that when you love something enough to excel at it to the extent Devin does with interior decorating; you should do it for a living. They say "find something you love doing and find a way to get paid for it." They also say love what you do and you'll never get tired.

Did I mention we love to travel? The challenges we faced at this point in our lives like most people revolved around time and money. She had five weeks vacation time at her job and I only had four. She also traveled extensively for work which would on occasion include me so I would book off for vacation to accompany her on her business trip. This would leave her with an even greater surplus of available vacation time to take without me before year's end. She would usually spend a week or two with her friend Lisa in some European destination or another while I stayed home with the dogs. Now I didn't mind this so much once I had figured out the art of time travel. It was actually a welcomed time of year because it gave me some space to plan a solution for our future travel adventures. Why did I need this space you might ask? Well if you knew Devin you would know that the one thing she does as well as interior decorating is researching and planning travel. My main job in her travel plans was just to show up and bring a few ideas of what we could do while we are there.

I knew eventually I would confide in Devin about my ability to time travel and that I would some day be able to bring her along with me. This would open an infinite number of destinations to us. I knew I would be able to take her to places we would never dream of visiting, and that we could travel as often as we wanted and best of all, we could travel for free.

The idea I had in mind was to target destinations that were uninhabited at a very particular point in time. By that I mean the point in time just before the property was destroyed in some kind of disaster. It shouldn't be difficult to find a vacant yet well stocked villa or a resort hotel that had been for example completely destroyed in an earthquake. If we showed up a few days before the event and helped ourselves to all the amenities that would otherwise be destroyed, well what harm could that possibly do? It certainly shouldn't impact the present.

Devin wasn't currently away on vacation and with this time travel concept firmly entrenched in my head I didn't want to wait till she was away before I began researching on my laptop for possible vacation destinations. Once I narrowed down four or five great destinations I would start physically scouting them out to find just the right place and time. I thought "How dedicated a husband I am to put so much thought and planning into our vacation?" Well this was the first time I had ever planned travel for the two of us so I was pretty pumped about it. The only thing that made me nervous was the part about telling her that we were going to travel back in TIME. I didn't know how to approach the topic with her. Devin is a very pragmatic and realistic type of person. The idea of traveling through time and space would be as foreign to her as…well any sci-fi novel or physics theory or JAZZ music for that matter. See Devin is a very creative thinker in many other areas than I. Let's just say Devin is not one of those people that can focus on a mantra for more than ten seconds. Her mind just doesn't work that way.

There was a magnitude 7.1 earthquake in Lompoc California 1927 that looked good. Great location right on the Pacific Ocean but I don't know how much we would enjoy the era. The styles back then were awkward and everyone smoked. A couple other 6.6 magnitude quakes hit California in 1987 at Superstition Hills and Elmore Ranch, both located close to the Salton Sea. Perfect I thought we could spend our days at the beach lounging and boating. I just needed to find a place for us to spend our nights where we would have all the modern conveniences and wouldn't inadvertently affect the future timeline in any way by interacting with anyone who may survive the earthquake.

I found another possibility September 7th, 1999 near Athens Greece when a 6.0 magnitude caused widespread structural damage to several of the surrounding small towns. This sounded promising as well because being closer to the current time meant there was less possible impact we could have on the present. I decided to focus on California 1987 first and went about looking for suitable accommodations.

After a few minutes of searching I discovered that the Superstition Hills quake didn't cause enough property damage for us to move in and stay under the radar so I moved on to the Elmore Ranch quake. Sure enough, that quake November 23, 1987 at 5:54:15 P.M. caused very little damage as well. There were no major hotels or homes reported as being leveled. I thought, "What's a guy gotta do to find a devastating earthquake?" and of course typing a Google search "devastation caused by earthquake" or "Hotel leveled by earthquake" netted me significantly better results. I'm such a slow learner when it comes to research stuff like that. Devin runs circles around me in the online research department.

August 1994, Ellalong, in the Hunter region of New South Wales, Australia, one of the world's greatest wine regions. That's definitely on the top of the list. Next I found an earthquake in the province of Van in Turkey 23 October, 2011. A couple of hotels were leveled. I knew Turkey was on our list of places to vacation so I put that one on my list as well. It seemed somewhat morbid that I was researching locations where mass destruction and loss of life occurred for potential holiday retreats. Well I figured these disasters happened regardless and the result was a loss of property and contents the likes of which I was targeting a short term use of for our personal enjoyment prior to their demise. Again I justified to myself, what harm could this cause if the property was lost to destruction?

Next I came across an article about an earthquake that

struck May 29, 2010 at 9:00 A.M. in the town of Emilia Romagna Italy just outside of Bologna. This was after an earthquake that hit nine days earlier which forced 7000 people into temporary shelters. This second quake killed 16 and left 14000 people homeless while finishing off what was left standing from the previous quake. This sounded perfect for a quick weekend get away to Bologna and immediately went on my list.

Then I came across the one that I knew I should look into first, April 6, 2009 at L'Aquila in the region of Abruzzo in central Italy. This was a quake of 5.8 magnitude on the Richter scale that caused $16 billion in damages and left 308 dead, 1500 injured and 65000 homeless. L'Aquila being the capitol of Abruzzo would no doubt have several hotels and villas that I could scout for a holiday. On Google maps I found the locations of a few hotels that had been leveled in the quake and was adding Hotel La Compagnia Del Viaggiatore to the list I was compiling on my laptop when Devin walked in. It was 4:40 p.m.

        "Hey. What are you doing?" Devin asked nonchalantly.

        "Just a little research" I bounced back. "What do you want to do for dinner?

Devin was looking over my shoulder at the laptop screen. "Earthquakes, what are you researching earthquakes for?"

        "No reason." I sheepishly offered.

        "No really... why are you compiling a list of earthquakes? California, Turkey, Italy?"

        "Well I thought for our next holiday we could go to Abruzzo and visit the area where the earthquake hit L'Aquila in 2009. Maybe we could help out somehow by volunteering or something?"

As we spoke it dawned on me that the best way to break the news to Devin was to just show her rather than explain it. Explaining it would be far too complicated and I would get caught up in all the technical details. And scouting out a place? It would be far easier to just go there and find accommodations. I asked myself 'why explain how time travel is possible when you can demonstrate, right?'

"It's not my idea of a relaxing holiday but I like the sentiment." She asked with a questioning look, "Why all of a sudden are you thinking about helping out a community in need and so far away from home?"

"Sweetheart, what if you had the chance to experience the culture and the people before the tragedy occurred? Would you not feel some obligation to or at least a desire to help out in any way that you could?"

"Of course I would. But these earthquakes have already happened. So what the hell are you talking about? You haven't been to any of these places?"

"Sweetheart, you trust me right?"

"Yes, to a certain degree." Devin cautiously replied.

"Trust me enough to take my hand and close your eyes for ten seconds?"

"I don't know. What are you going to do?"

I opened my desk drawer and retrieved a small bill-fold of Euros. They were the older original printed paper bills and I knew they would come in handy where we were about to go. The clock on my laptop read 4:44.

I took Devin's hand… "Just close your eyes and shut the hell up for a minute."

In my mind I visualized the map coordinates and began

formulating the time travel equation; I set my sites on April 2, 2009 the Hotel La Compagnia Del Viaggiatore, Strada Statale 80 in L'Aquila, Abruzzo. I was at this point quite comfortable bringing certain "additional organic objects" with me into the past, I had brought Oliver back a few times and visited an off leash dog park. He would run around with a bunch of other dogs. There was one named Simon that he took to in a big way. Simon was a good name for a dog. I thought if we ever get a second dog we should name him Simon.

Here and now I was about to demonstrate to the love of my life that I had an awesome power that was way beyond most people's wildest dream. Oliver was lying on the couch looking at us with his big brown eyes and a curious face that seemed to say he was happy just to be a part of the conversation. I was so excited to share this gift and was feeling a little anxious because I was about to initiate a space-time jump that would bring the two of us to Italy four days before the most devastating event in the history of the region. I felt my imagination engage igniting my inner time travel app and felt instantly as if I was just about to fall asleep. We both saw a bright flash of white and then the gradual accelerating flicker effect as we reemerged April 2nd, 2009 in L'Aquila Italy. There we were now standing in the lobby washroom of the Hotel La Compagnia Del Viaggiatore. It was a single unisex water closet, quite clean and bright with extremely vibrant and conflicting patterned tiles in contrasting blue and orange.

"Where the hell are we? What just happened? What did you do?" Devin was freaking out after our re-entry.

I sensed the presence of only one person, likely the hotel clerk. He was Italian so I didn't fully understand his thoughts, however I could sense a bit of panic and anxiety in him as he approached the washroom. I quickly reached over and locked the door while I whispered to Devin, "Don't panic. Just calm down and listen carefully."

"What the hell, Victor! How did we get in here?"

"Listen to me carefully. We're in Italy, L'Aquila to be precise, it's in Abruzzo. The year is 2009 and it's my birthday, April 2nd."

"What are you talking about?"

Just then there was a knock on the door and the stern voice of a young man speaking quickly in Italian. "Ciao, c'è qualcuno lì dentro? Come hai fatto a entrare?"

Listen I said in a quiet whisper "Somebody either needs to use the washroom, thinks we are vagabonds off the street or maybe that we are having sex in here. Either way, please just trust me follow my lead and don't say a word for the next couple of minutes."

I grabbed a paper towel and placed it over Devin's nose, then tilting her head back I opened the door and lead her out. "Scusie, scusie, grazie paisano, grazie." We shuffled past a young Italian man who looked a lot like Marcello Mastroianni in Fellini's La Dolce Vita. "Scusie mille grazie".

The Hotel clerk was caught off guard by the site of us, having not seen us enter the lobby let alone the adjacent washroom, and now assumed that Devin had a nose bleed so proceeded to lead us to a couch in the lobby just beside the check-in desk. After many words in Italian that came out too fast for me to understand, 'Marcello' walked around the corner of the desk and down a stair case. I suppose he was going off to get an ice pack or some first aid supplies from another area of the hotel. By the sounds of his shoes on the steps I could tell he was walking down at least three flights. I knew I would hear his approach as he returned.

"Devin, stay right there. Hold this on your nose and don't move an inch."

I stepped behind the counter and looked at the computer screen. What I saw was pretty easy to interpret. I was looking at the hotel occupancy calendar in a simple spreadsheet. At a glance I could see that there were several available rooms on the top floor. Room 943 had been vacant for a while and there were no reservations due to arrive for six more days. I took this opportunity to book our room into the ledger by adding the name Mr. and Mrs. Ray Romano to room 943 for yesterday April 1st through to April 7th. OK I thought…Ray Romano? Everybody loves Raymond? I probably could have come up with a slightly less conspicuous name but under the circumstances it was all that came to mind. So I finished the entry, grabbed the room key for 943 (yes many hotels in Europe still use actual physical keys…go figure) and was about to go back to Devin who was now sitting up watching me with 'That Look'…You know the look that say's "Whatever it is you *think* you are doing right now, well it is NOT gonna fly with me Pal, so I'm just going to let you continue to screw up until I get my chance to tell you I told you so." The time on the computer was 6:39 a.m. as I began to step out from behind the counter I also noticed another board with about a dozen hooks on it. The board had a set of car keys on each hook along with a license plate identifier attached. I took one set of keys and got out from behind the counter.

I said quietly but in an urgent tone, "OK come with me. We are officially checked in."

"What the hell are you talking about?" Devin asked in a not so quiet voice.

"Just trust me and come on, hurry up Marcello will be here any second. Keep quiet, not a word till we are in our room."

I could hear the faint footsteps approaching from down the staircase. Marcello wasn't moving as fast on the way up as he had been going down.

"Let's go this way, not the elevator we'll walk up the stairs.

Devin was confused and somewhat annoyed. "What the hell."

"Shush, zip it, and try to not to make any noise with your shoes." I whispered grabbing on to her hand and leading her silently up the stairwell and onwards towards our room further and further away from the lobby from where Marcello was quickly approaching.

The entrance to the hotel lobby was on the south side at street level. Having been built into a steep cliff the lobby was actually on the sixth floor of the hotel which we learned on our ascent up the three remaining floors to the ninth. Once on the ninth floor we turned left, walked down the hall and found room 943 which was the last room on the right. I opened the door and we walked into a beautiful suite with a walk-out balcony that had an incredible view of the sun rising over the Abruzzo landscape. I put the 'Do not disturb' sign on the outer door knob. The clock in the kitchen read 6:42 a.m.

The suite had a bar that was well stocked with wine from the local region. I quickly grabbed a bottle of red and proceeded to open it and pour two glasses while I explained what had just happened. It was a 2003 Montepulciano D'Abruzzo (Emidio Pepe). A very good wine in fact this bottle sells today for $249.00 in the LCBO.

Somewhat shocked and in a state of disbelief Devin took the glass of wine. Her hands were shaking a little as she took her first drink.

Taking a sip of my wine I launched into a bit of a speech to console her.

"Listen carefully. Remember when I told you how some people who have practiced Transcendental Meditation for a long time had developed abnormal abilities like levitation and the ability to read minds?"

"I remember." Devin replied quivering a bit while she sipped her wine.

"Well about a month ago I stumbled upon the fact that I have the ability to travel back and forth in time and space. I can place myself at any time or place I want to."

"A month ago, you've been able to do this for a month? And you never told me? Thanks a lot Victor." Devin said as she turned her head quickly away from me.

"Well it's complicated." I explained, "I knew I would tell you eventually but I needed to understand more about it, how it works and such. I only recently discovered I could bring other living things with me. I started trying it with a couple different plants and then moved up to an earwig, and a frog, then Oliver."

"Oliver? You took Oliver on a trip?"

"Not really a trip. Just a couple quick jumps to make sure it wouldn't affect him at all. Then I figured it would work for you as well and I started to get excited about the possibility of taking vacations whenever and wherever we wanted."

"And you took Oliver on a vacation before me? So how often do you and Oliver go on vacation? Is it a daily event?"

"No not daily. Every now and then I just feel like looking back at our past or getting a glimpse into the future." A little uncomfortable now with the conversation I was beginning to think I sprung this on her too abruptly.

"And at what point did you decide to take me along on what ever it is you call this? And why are we in a hotel? I have to work in the morning. Hey this wine is exceptional."

"Ah, actually you don't have to work in the

morning. We are here to enjoy Abruzzo Italy for the next four days. It's April 2nd 2009 and this hotel is going to be completely leveled in an earthquake on April 6th. So from now until then we can help ourselves to anything in this hotel room. And when we return home we will have only been gone about five seconds. So we don't need to worry about feeding Oliver or working in the morning."

"Only five seconds? How is that possible?"

"I'll explain that to you later. Just drink your wine and let's watch the sun rise while you digest what I have just told you. It's a hell of a lot to take in all at once. Hey it's my birthday!"

Devin was starting to feel the effects of the wine. She was definitely less concerned about how we got here and more concerned with the view. It seemed a bit strange drinking wine at sun up but for us it was pretty much 5:00 o'clock.

"Good idea, great view. Happy birthday, cheers. How did you find out you had this ability?"

"Through meditation the first time, then I trained my mind to take me where and whenever I think of. Just drink your wine and I'll tell you all about it later. I wonder what's in the fridge. We have a rental car so we can see the sites later today."

"It's *your* birthday. I'm good with whatever you want to do as long as you get me back in time for work." Devin said with a smile.

"No problem there, happy vacation. Cheers"

We watched as the heat of the sunrise over the hill tops to the east began to burn the light fog off the valley in front of us. We both just inhaled the calmness of the moment savoring the wine and the early morning song bird melodies. It was 5:00 in the evening for us back home in real-time but here we were experiencing a

Tuscan sunrise. Marcello the clerk would be wondering who we were and where we went. I could picture him getting back to the lobby standing there with an ice pack or a towel looking around for us. Checking the washroom again and finally giving up the search. I supposed he would be going off duty soon, probably at 7:00 a.m., and hoped he wouldn't clue into the missing rental car key or the additional entry on the computer log before he left his shift. Mr. and Mrs. Ray Romano didn't want to stir up any suspicion for the next couple days.

The suite was surprisingly large and well stocked with an abundance of fruit, snack food, water, wine and even a variety of procciutto, olives, cheese and chocolate in the fridge. We sat on the balcony, drinking the exceptional wine and nibbling on a variety of goodies. The view was spectacular; we were on the top floor with a balcony that looked out over the countryside and down nine stories to the courtyard and swimming pool. There was a staircase at the end of the hall just outside our door leading down to the common area poolside with an alternate exit on the sixth floor which walked out onto the street from the east end of the hotel. I was relieved to know we had entry/exit points from the building alternate to the lobby because I wanted to avoid Marcello-the-clerk at all costs.

"So let me get this straight, we can do this anytime we want, for as long as we want and then go back to our present time without taking vacation time off work?" Devin was getting louder and more excited, an obvious side affect of the red wine.

"Yes we can. Does that please you my queen?" I said in a bad medieval accent indicative of the effect the wine was having on me.

"Please me? It's friggin' awesome! What the hell took you so long to tell me about this?" Devin practically shouted as she slapped my chest.

"Well you need to realize the potential impact that going back in time can have on the present situation."

"Yeah, yeah whatever just tell me again that we can go anywhere we want and for as long as we want and we don't need to take time off work?"

"Yes we can, but there are precautions we need to take."

"Screw the precautions, I want go to Hawaii next and I've always wanted to check out South Africa. How are we going to pay for this? How could you check us in without our passports or reservations?" Devin asked her usual string of questions so quickly that I lost track of what I was supposed to answer.

"That's just it, we didn't reserve or check in and we aren't going to pay for the room. This hotel is going to be leveled by a 5.8 magnitude earthquake in a few days. Everything you see here is going to become rubble. We are here to consume what would otherwise be destroyed, wasted. And that guy at the front desk, well chances are he is either going to perish in the earthquake or become homeless on April the 6th."

"So the research you were doing on earthquakes was to target vacation destinations, NOT to volunteer our services after the fact?" Devin was sounding a bit harsh now.

"That's right. Sorry for the deception and of course we could always come back here afterwards to offer assistance in the rebuilding of the town." I said in a charitable tone.

"Well let's see how things play out. Maybe we can give back after the fact. It would be the right thing to do." She added with a slight matter of fact.

"Sweetheart, one thing you need to know and respect in a big way is that any interaction we have during an adventure into the past can have a huge impact on our present." I looked at Devin's face to see if she understood the message. "I know you don't want to hear about the precautions we need to take, but if we ignore them we could do some serious damage to our 'Real Life' time-line."

"What do you mean?" Devin looked at me with questioning eyes. I knew she was listening and ready to hear the important details that had the potential to destroy us if ignored.

"Well, let's say we accidentally caused the outcome of a situation to be altered from its intended course. That could cause a chain reaction over time which could make our present day life much different from what we know it to be now. Like say we went back in time and for whatever reason it caused you and I to never meet. That would mean when we went back to our present time we wouldn't be married or even necessarily know one another. So our house and life as we know it would be entirely different. That's why we need to keep to ourselves and not get involved in any way, socially or otherwise, in the local community here over the next few days."

"So we can't even talk to anyone?" Devin asked quietly.

"Preferably no, but realistically we should keep it to a minimum. Like ordering food from a server in a restaurant shouldn't have any impact, but getting to know and exchanging contact information with other tourists could do some devastating damage. Don't ask me how or why, but interaction with anyone who survives the coming earthquake could have a ripple effect that changes everything in our current lives."

"OK so what are the ground rules?" I could tell by her corporate tone that Devin was trying to sound interested.

"Tell you what. Best thing is to not speak with anyone other than me and if you need to, assume an alias. I registered us at this hotel as Mr. and Mrs. Romano. So as far as anyone knows I'm Ray and you are Debra."

"Are you serious? Everybody love's Raymond? Couldn't you come up with a better name?" Devin laughed a bit at my choice of alias' names.

"Hey I was under pressure. I put in the first name that came to mind. Just go with it if it comes down to that. Besides we are in Italy, do you think many folks here would recognize the name of those characters?" I asked defensively.

"Oh man you are brutal. OK I'll go along with it but what if we run into the clerk from downstairs? Or what if they realize we didn't have a reservation and are squatting for a few days in this awesomely terrific suite totally stocked with amazingly wicked wine."

"Not to worry my darling, as long as we are together there is nothing stopping me from bringing us back to present day. It only takes me a few seconds to do it." I felt a little like a super hero on one hand and a little dumb about the choice of names still. Regardless I felt relieved that I had now come clean to Devin. I knew this was going to open many doors that would help our relationship in a big way.

"That was a pretty amazing trick you did getting us here. I trust you, and I promise I won't make a spectacle of myself. Can we go shopping now?" Devin asked with a batting of her eyelashes.

"Ughhh. Tell you what. Stay here, I'll be back in a few minutes and we can go shopping or do whatever you want." I stood up and headed for the door.

"Where are you going?"

"I just need to find the car that belongs to this." I held up the stolen car keys and jingled them as I continued, "Then we can venture out and explore the town. Just what ever you do, do not leave the room, please just stay right here and enjoy the wine."

The clock in the kitchen read 7:30. I walked out our door and turned right. Walking through the exit door at the end of the hall I took the stairs down to the sixth floor level and looked out the south window to the poolside. There was nobody, it was too early in the morning. I turned around and exited out the sixth floor onto the street where I could see a delivery truck had just pulled up to the front door of the hotel and was coming to a stop about thirty meters to my left. I stood in the doorway half hidden as the driver got out of the truck and went inside. When he returned Marcello was with him, apparently not off duty yet. They went to the back of the truck and talked for a minute while the driver unloaded a few boxes onto a two wheeled trolley. As the two of them went inside I hurried over to the driver's side door. Looking through the truck's window and into the hotel lobby I could see the men inside the hotel. The clerk Marcello was counting the items that had been delivered and was reconciling against an invoice that was on a clipboard furnished by the driver. The driver was smoking a cigarette and talking on a cell phone while nodding to Marcello who was speaking a mile a minute during the entire interaction. Making my way up the street past the hotel to the corner I could hear the two exiting the hotel, Marcello talking loudly as the driver got back into the truck. I didn't look back at them for fear of being recognized but I'm certain they didn't notice my presence. I walked around the corner where I found a long line of small cars parked against one side of the street. Sure enough after inspecting a few vehicles I found the car that matched the plate number on the key tag in my hand. I tried the key in the lock and it worked.

Making my way back up to the room I stopped briefly to count the Euros that I had brought with me. As I counted I realized that the driver and the clerk would not likely survive the week. A strange feeling came over me. Knowing what their fate was and that it was coming soon made it hard for me to relax. I kept getting flashes of anxiety feeling that I needed to get out of here before the earthquake, even though I knew the exact time that it would hit. I felt guilty for being in the midst of this beautiful place with the knowledge of what was about to happen. I looked around at the beautiful town soaking in the morning sunshine and knew full well this was all going to be buried in a few days and that there was nothing I could do about it. My selfish desire to capitalize on and consume what was to be destroyed was now turning into empathy for the massive loss that was imminent. I made my way back to the hotel on foot being careful once again not to be seen by Marcello.

When I reached the room I felt a twinge in my stomach. A housekeeping cart was parked outside the room and the "Do Not Disturb" sign was gone from the door which was now wide open.

I quickly stepped inside wondering what Devin's reaction to the housekeeper would have been. There was a woman cleaning up the wine glasses and nibbles we had helped ourselves to earlier but no sign of Devin.

"Debra? Debra. Bon giorno." I called out.

I greeted the woman but tried to avoid eye contact as I scurried out to the balcony to see if Devin - Debra was still out there. Of course she wasn't. The time was 7:38. I was away from the room for eight minutes and she was already missing in action even though I explicitly said….

I looked out over the balcony railing I heard voices and then spotted some people by the pool. There she was talking with a young couple. As I left the room and headed down the stairs to the pool I was steaming mad. Eight minutes…Don't talk to anyone, just stay here please. My word, eight minutes, imagine if I were gone for twelve. I tried my best to regain my composure as I approached the three of them standing next to the pool. They were laughing in unison now and it was obvious that Devin had made friends in freakin' record time.

"Hi Baby, these guys are from Toronto too. This is…"

"Hi I'm Steve and this is my wife Jamie."

"Hi I'm Ray, nice to meet you two." I said quickly and had to bite my lip as I greeted the two. I shot Devin a look and she could tell I was pissed.

"Hi there, Debra and Ray, like, 'Everyone Loves Raymond'.

"I know we get that all the time." I chirped with as much charm I could muster along with a fake smile.

"Debra here tells me you just arrived today. Did you fly in from Toronto?"

"Oh no we drove down from Arezzo and are working are way south over the next week. How about you guys? How long are you staying here in L'Aquila?" At least she had stuck with the naming convention we agreed on, although I did feel dumb once again that I had picked those names.

"I have family here," stated Jamie, "my cousin is getting married next weekend. So we are just touring around this neck of the woods for ten days and going back to Toronto after the wedding. What do you guys do in Toronto?"

I knew I needed to cut this off now. "Awesome, listen sweetie we gotta get moving if we're going to make it to that thing. Sorry guys we really gotta run."

"But we just got here." Devin objected, "Hey Jamie where is all the good shopping?"

"Not far, just a couple blocks that way. Actually, see that church? That's where my cousin's wedding will be. Right on the other side of that church is where all the shops are. Hey why don't we meet up for lunch?"

"Yeah, that sounds great. Or dinner." Devin piped back.

I quickly jumped in with "Wait a second. Sorry to rain on the parade but I have a special day lined up for our tenth anniversary, and we're already late."

"Tenth anniversary," Steve asked, "Well you at least need to let us buy you guys a drink later on at the hotel? Maybe a bottle of proseco to celebrate?"

"We'll see, maybe if we are back early enough." I offered, "Listen it was nice meeting you and we'll talk to you later, Have a great day."

As we walked away, more like as I dragged my wife by the arm away from the pending danger of intermingling with strangers from the past, I began to describe to Devin what was likely about to happen to this couple from Toronto that she just befriended.

"Why are you being so rude? Can't we just hang out and get to know them a bit? I wanted to hear more about the wedding. I want to see the dress."

"There isn't going to be a wedding. Remember there is going to be an earthquake in a few days? That couple is going to be seriously injured or killed on Monday if they are within five miles of this town. That's why we are here having a freebie? Today's Thursday and all of this will be rubble on Monday."

"But they're so nice we can't let them get caught in the earthquake! We have to tell them to get out of here before Monday and take their family with them."

"Sweetheart, I've been telling you how important it is that we don't change the course of events. Come on let's get our rental car and take a drive."

I Hate Hospitals

Martin and Sheila arrived at St Michael's Hospital at 7:45 a.m. and found Sheila's mother Maryanne, now a complete wreck but composed enough to brief them on Harold's condition. He was in surgery for four and a half hours before being moved to the intensive care unit where his doctor gave the family an update.

"Hello Maryanne, I'm Doctor Proctor."

"Is he going to live, Doctor?" Maryanne was shaking and wavering a little on her feet. She stared at the doctor anticipating the worst.

"The surgery went well. However in cases like this, there is no way to predict the outcome. "

Seeing Maryanne was starting to shake more violently, both Sheila and Martin moved closer in behind her and embraced the woman so she could withstand the impact of the news head on.

"Harold is still in critical condition, there was some organ damage and internal bleeding which we took care of. He is stabilizing nicely but I want you to understand that there was trauma to his skull, the extent of which we don't know yet. He was in a coma when he arrived and is still in that state. The coma likely helped him through the surgery but no one can suggest how long the coma will last or if he will even come out of it at all."

"You mean he might never wake up?" Maryanne asked as she quivered even harder.

"It is a possibility. He could wake up in a day, a week a month, a year. No one knows. The scans we took show no major damage or bleeding in the brain so we just need to keep monitoring. You will be able to sit with him this afternoon once the team gets him settled. I'm really sorry. I need to get to my next surgery but I will check in later on and let you know what we find. We will do everything we can."

"Thank you, doctor." Maryanne seemed a little relieved now that the news had been delivered. It wasn't good news but at least there was still hope.

Sheila consoled her mother and Martin consoled Sheila. They sat down in the waiting room. A nurse approached and told them that they would be able to see Harold in room 414 in about an hour.

The afternoon passed slowly for the three visitors sitting in room 414. Harold on the other hand had no sense of the passage of time. In his coma he was physically stifled but mentally he was devoid of any time constraints. The blow to his head had virtually no negative impact on his brain functions. The coma was his way of self-preserving so that his brain would not react to the internal damage nor interfere with the body's natural healing process. Present past and future all melted into one existence of being for Harold now in his coma, and he used this opportunity to mentally visit his younger self. With a window into his past he looked in on his life activities of long ago and learned how certain circumstances had shaped the man he later became.

His first camping trip was a great lesson in outdoor survival and teamwork. He had learned how to pitch a tent and the proper way to build a fire. There was fishing and cooking and poison ivy, marshmallows and hot dogs and best of all Harold's father was there. This was one of the few memories that Harold had of his father and it was a good one, camping and fishing and building fires to cook over and stay warm near. His father and Uncle Mike exchanged late night stories around that camp fire while Harold listened intently with increasingly drowsy eyelids. Harold was nine years old at the time and had never stayed up this late before. It was an exciting time for him. A time of new experiences that he would cherish always because Harold had no way of knowing that this would be the last weekend he would ever spend with his father.

Afternoon slipped into evening and as night fell on the hospital, Maryanne, Sheila and Martin returned from eating dinner in the cafeteria to see no change in Harold. Sheila and her mother talked for a while as Martin leafed through a magazine. Eventually Martin dozed off in the corner chair with his head against the wall. Sheila was not far behind Martin. She lay down on the vacant bed next to Harold's and was asleep within five minutes.

Harold's imagination took him fast forward to a time when his mother was hospitalized after having triple by-pass surgery. He was twenty at the time and recalled a discussion he had with his mother while standing next to her hospital bed.

"Mom, I hate hospitals." He said as he held her hand.

Harold reflected on his Time travel Mentor, Uncle Mike who camped out with him and his father all those years earlier. Uncle Mike had come into Harold's dreams around the time of his Mother surgery. Uncle Mike had taught him in his dreams to play the game. The same game that Harold was now coaching Sheila and Martin to play. Harold was suddenly engulfed in a light foggy haze. He could see that he was lying on a hospital bed and from out of the fog there were two figures approaching that he thought were his Mother and his Uncle Mike.

Harold, thinking he was dead and about to be taken away began to panic. "I hate hospitals." Harold shouted. "I hate hospitals. I hate hospitals." He shouted again as the two figures approached Harold in the bed. The white haze receded and as the fog drifted off of the approaching couple Harold heard his daughter's voice.

"Dad? Is that you?" Sheila asked.
Martin joined in the line of questioning.
"Harold? Are you OK? How are you talking to us?"
"Martin, Sheila! Wow I thought you were -

nevermind."

"Dad, we hate hospitals too. Is this a dream? How are we all having a conversation?"

"Listen. Guys, I know that you have started wondering about your dreams the last couple weeks. We've been together all three of us playing capture the flag each night. Running and diving through the portals. You wake up in a sweat and can't figure out why? You're not sick, you don't have a fever and you can't understand how the three of us are in the same dream every night?"
Martin came back with "Uh yeah. I've been wondering lately but…"

Sheila cut in, "Me too but I just figured it was a really vivid recurring dream. So what are you saying Dad?"

"I'm saying that it isn't really a dream. It's more of a different dimension. It's impossible for me to define it exactly so let's just say yeah, it's in our dreams."

"So we've been hanging out in a different dimension in our dreams at night learning to play capture the flag?" Martin stated.

"Essentially, yes." Harold replied.

"Why is this happening? And what exactly have we been jumping through?" Sheila asked with a puzzled look.

Martin ventured, "I know the slits are portals of some sort and we jump through them to follow the other team or try to shake them from following us. But what are they?"

"OK, this is the whole point of the exercise. What I am doing is teaching you to time travel.

"Time travel?" Sheila spouted.

"Time travel?" Martin followed suit.

"Yes time travel. I learned years ago from my Uncle Mike. He was my mentor and now it's time for me to pass it on to you."

"Time travel? You're teaching us time travel?" Sheila was still very confused.

"Yes my daughter, time travel. The slits in the game that you jump through are actually time travel portals that have been carefully set up to facilitate your training. Each one has a specific location associated with it so that you will reach a pre-intended destination. The training requires close supervision because as you pass through one of the slits you can accidentally change the intended destination by focusing on another place or time.

"You mean if I jumped through one and I was thinking of the year 1829, London England I would suddenly be there and then?" Sheila mused.

"If you had that thought firmly in your mind during the entry to the portal, I mean vivid and clear then yes it could possibly happen. You need supervision so that we can return you to the game from whatever place and time you wonder off to. The training has a specific function to allow you to become comfortable teleporting while keeping you contained within a small set of pre-configured time-location coordinates. This is sort of the sand-box for you to play in until you become comfortable with the idea of bouncing from place to place and time to time. The next step is to move on from the supervised sandbox and teach you to travel with a little bit of assistance. I will take you to places like London in 1829 and eventually teach you how to do it without my assistance. As a matter of fact my goal is to train you well enough to accurately hit the month, day, hour, minute and second of your landing and to pinpoint the exact area of London you wish to land on within a square meter."

"Dad, come on, really?" The two protégés were not convinced.

"Really Sheila, it will take practice to master that level of accuracy but now that you two have the fundamentals down, it's time to teach you both how to apply them outside of the game. I was going to tell you all of this at brunch after the final practice today but I don't know what happened. I was on my way to the arena and the last thing I remember was hearing police sirens and seeing my coffee flying out of my hand. Do you know what happened? Was I in an accident?"

"Dad, your car was totaled. There was a police chase and you were hit by the pick-up truck that they were chasing. The other driver didn't survive; you arrived here at the hospital in a coma. After hours of surgery to stop internal bleeding and tests and everything you are now laying in the ICU room 414 and you are still in a coma. Can you feel your body at all? Could you hear us talking around you earlier?"

"A coma huh, I hate hospitals. No I can't feel my body, no pain at all. I did hear Maryanne and you two blabbing on about where to eat. How is the cafeteria food?"

An orderly was now entering the room which made just enough noise to cause Sheila, but not Martin to wake up. Martin required a little more disturbance than Sheila to be brought out of slumber. Harold and Martin watched as Sheila vanished back into the fog.

"Martin, I'm sorry I didn't get to tell you two in person today. Please let Sheila know we will pick up the discussion again tonight after you two are asleep."

The Orderly having entered the room was asking the group, "And how is everyone in here?" As the Orderly began to speak Martin faded out of Harold's sight and awoke in the hospital room. He wiped the saliva that had drooled down the side of his cheek in his sleep.

"Doctor Proctor sent me to check in and let you know he is on his way. He will be here in a couple minutes to give you an update."

Maryanne was awake and responding to the orderly's question. Sheila and Martin's eyes met with a mutual understanding of what was going on. The questions about their dreams had been answered and a wave of emotion was now flooding over the two of them that was difficult to contain. Sheila's fear that her mother would grow suspect of the current tension was quickly broken when the Doctor walked in.

"How we doing, folks?"

"We're holding up fine. How is he doing?" Martin offered.

"I have some good news. The test results show no major damage to the skull and his brain activity has been increasing rapidly. We think he will stabilize to normal by morning. I don't want to get your hopes up but if his vitals remain strong I will move him out of ICU tomorrow night and I would not be surprised if he wakes up within two or three days. You are welcome to sleep here in the chairs tonight, but I suggest you head home and get a good night's rest. There is nothing you can do for him tonight or until he comes out of the coma for that matter."

With that the Doctor took his leave. The three said good night to Harold and left the room. Not much was said as they made their way through the hospital corridors and out to the parking lot. It had been a long day and Maryanne was ready for bed as soon as they reached the house.

Sheila and Martin were eager to talk about the experience they had in their dreams state today. The conversation with Harold in the ethereal sub-conscious world of slumber had them both perplexed. They promptly put Maryanne to bed and retreated to the kitchen where Martin opened a couple beers.

"Martin, what the hell was that dream all about? Was Harold really talking to us? I know you were there I could see it in your eyes when you woke up."

"I know, and the last few weeks we've been having the same dream like he said."

"The game…"

"Exactly, the game…"

"Time travel, Marty do you really buy that?"

"Well if you think about the dreams. There are only a couple things that change each time. One, the people we play against…and two, the places we land after going through the portals."

"Right, so I remember one night there was a beach and a forest and a cornfield. And coming back is always easy."

"Yeah just jump back through and you're home."

"But who are we playing against? They all feel familiar but I don't recognize any of them from our normal lives.

"And each night it's a different team."

"Not each night. There have been two or three players that I'm sure have played on more than one team against us. And I think one or two teams have played us more than once."

"It's weird Sheila because I don't usually register faces in my dreams, just emotions around any people present. Maybe that's why I haven't identified with any one individual."

"I have. And I think maybe some of the players are guardians to help make sure we don't stray off like my Dad said, you know into a different time zone."

"But why is your Dad doing this and how did we get brought into it? Who volunteered us to be trained as time travelers? Don't we even get a say in the matter?"

"Are you mad Martin? You are. Why are you angry?"

"I'm not angry I just, I don't know that I want the responsibility that comes along with this."

"What are you talking about?"

"It's Time Travel Sheila. Time Travel...Do you know what that means? Going back to 1829 merry old London, or anywhere in the world at anytime for that matter means we can alter the present. It means we can see the future and change the natural course of history. That's a pretty big thing to be able to do and I'm not sure I want that ability."

"Well I think it's awesome and I can't wait to learn more. I'm sorry that you think my Dad is imposing this on you."

"Listen, I'm sorry about the car accident and that your dad could have died. I don't see why he doesn't just go back in time and avoid the collision with the truck. I'm sure he will be out of the hospital in no time. Oh he asked me to tell you that we would continue the discussion tonight after we go to sleep."

"You have to admit, it's pretty cool that we can meet in our dreams and transport around the world any where we want."

"...and to different points in time. Yeah that is

pretty amazing. I just get a funny feeling about this. I know I seem skeptical but I'm sure Harold will teach us all the safety rules and regulations before we go and do too much damage."

"OK as excited as I am, I'm also friggin tired. I am ready for bed. Do you want to stay over?"

"I do, but I have to work in the morning and my stuff is at home."

"That's OK, see you in my dreams. Good night Mr. Mc Dreamy."

They kissed and Martin walked through the front door, off the porch, down the stairs and got into his car. As he drove off Sheila turned off the lights and readied herself for bed. She was in bed and asleep ten minutes before Martin reached home.

Sheila came through the fog and approached her farther who was lying on a hospital bed just as she had left him earlier that evening. She stopped suddenly in her tracks when she realized that he was not alone. There was a women standing next to the bed with her back to Sheila. The two were laughing completely unaware of Sheila's presence. The thought of meeting people in this new dimension was not a possibility that Sheila had even pondered. It took a few seconds to regain her composure and accept the fact that she would need to interrupt the two and socialize with this unidentified person who was obviously a close acquaintance of her father. Sheila crept up on the two slowly with a slight uncertainty in her heart. As she approached the women slowly turned around. Astonished, Sheila's uncertainty quickly receded as the words came from the women's mouth.

"Hello Sheila."

"Mom?"

Beam Me up Scotty

Do you remember the original Star Trek TV series? If not then perhaps Star Trek the Next Generation? Or maybe you are too young to remember either and have only seen one or two of the Star Trek movies. If you didn't, then I recommend that you do. You'll be going back in time and getting a glimpse of the future. If you have seen an episode or one of the movies then you'd remember their ability to teleport from one location to another. The concept basically is about converting matter into energy, beaming that energy to a specific target location and converting the energy back into its original form at the destination. In the Star Trek series, whenever Captain James T Kirk was transporting back to the ship from a planet he would usually say "beam me up Scotty", Scotty being the teleport technician who was usually manning the controls.

So what's the difference between time travel and teleportation? Well the short answer is not much. The two are nearly identical with the exception of moving ahead or back in time. Time travel, like teleportation includes a transformation of mass into energy and back into mass again however, time travel may or may not involve beaming the energy to a new location prior to reorganizing it back into its original form. Teleportation on the other hand always involves a departure location and a destination and occurs within a linear timeline the length of which varies depending on the distance. Time travel is teleportation ahead or back through time with or without changing location.

The processes involved in teleportation can be broken down into three components. One; the conversion of matter into energy, two; the transportation of the energy packet from point A to point B, and three; the reorganization of the matter back into it's original form. The time it takes for the conversion process of matter to energy and then back to matter depends on the density and amount of matter being transformed. The time to transport from point A to point B is usually short because energy travels at the speed of light. So unless the beam needs to travel an extremely long distance, the time to transport is short.

To give you an example, at the speed of light a beam will travel around the world seven and a half times in one second. It takes light a little over eight minutes to travel from the sun to the earth. The distance from the sun to the earth varies based on where the earth is currently positioned in its elliptical orbit around the sun, but the distance is roughly ninety one million miles, so the speed of light is roughly eleven million miles per minute; give or take a quarter million miles.

It took some trial and error to realize that time travel was a natural extension of teleportation. In fact the time travel founders stumbled on it quite by accident and during these initial trials they inadvertently caused some serious true timeline deviations which required considerable cleanup. But that's a whole other chapter of this handbook. Maybe even a whole other book.

You can think of time travel as a "Beam me up Scotty" that takes you to a different place at what ever date in time you have in mind...quite literally. Only you don't need Scotty to beam you up, it's controlled by the time travel app that's embedded in your mind, the same app that's at everyone's disposal ignited naturally each night when we dream; or in your case soon to be ignited consciously by your imagination. The main purpose of this handbook, and the focus of the next few chapters, is to teach you the methodology, and how to stimulate and train your imagination to enable you to invoke the conscious ability to teleport your body to other times and locations.

- Excerpt from The Time Traveler's Handbook

Game On! Part 1

Brent entered the washroom of the hotel about thirty seconds after I had heard the gun cock behind my head. The concern on his face, serious at first became far more than just concern. His look was now borderline panic mixed with anger when he saw his partner come out of the 3rd stall, gun in hand. He knew I had come there for a reason. He knew I had escaped his grasp, for now. He also knew I was a time traveler like him. By the time he had reached the stall from which I so hastily departed Brent suspected the reason for my visit had everything to do with the kidnappings.

Looking into the stall, Brent could see the rip in space that had been left by my jump back to present day. Brent was a seasoned time traveler but hadn't learned entirely how to properly read the aura of the portal left by a jump. Brent didn't have the benefit of a late night training ground or mentor.
He could see the reddish orange fringe around the outer edge like little northern lights shining in toward the center of the gash. He knew the red color was indicative of a jump forward in time and that a small fringe meant that the jump was not covering a large gap in time, maybe a month or two.

His partner on the other hand was a complete novice. Brent had been teaching him the art of jumping for only a few weeks now and he was not yet able to see portals let alone read them. One day he would be as good as Brent who was now trying to determine where and when Victor had come from. The fluorescent light in the washroom was distorting the fringe details enough that it was nearly impossible to read so he couldn't tell how far away or long ago or ahead the jump was from.

Brent spoke quietly to his counterpart, "I'll be back in a moment." and walked into the stall then disappeared through the portal, emerging in my powder room only a few seconds after I had flushed and rejoined my wife and guests in the dining room. The toilet was almost finished refilling when Brent arrived, the powder room door was slightly ajar. Once the tank completely refilled the water stopped running and Brent could clearly hear the conversation from the dining room. As he listened to us talk about the future of decor and possibilities in new material technologies it confirmed his suspicions about my motive for appearing in Buenos Aires. Brent turned to face the mirror and then realized his suspicions were further warranted. He could see in the mirror that there were two portals present here in the confined space. One rip had a blue fringe meaning it was a jump back in time and the second rip had a reddish fringe. In the darkness of the powder room Brent could see clearly that the destinations of both portals were Buenos Aires. Knowing now that I had gone forward and back gave Brent cause for alarm. He couldn't allow me to mess with his timelines. The conversation in the dining room made it obvious that I was wise to his caper, but Brent needed time to formulate a strategy to take me out of the picture.

Oliver stuck his nose through the door and began sniffing the dark air. Upon smelling Brent's presence he gave a low warning growl. Brent caught off guard by the dog stepped back and inadvertently caused the lid of the toilet to crash down on the toilet seat with a loud clunk. Oliver began barking wildly and Brent left through the portal back to the past.

As I walked to the powder room I could tell by his barking that Oliver was protecting the house from some kind of danger. It was the type of bark he would use when he saw another dog while out on a walk, vicious and determined to attack. When I reached the powder room Oliver was excited but the intensity of his barking had subsided to that of a happier sort of yelping. His ears were back like he was in a playful mood. I turned on the powder room light and looked in as a familiar scent came across my nose. I thought maybe he just saw the portals in the dark room had mistaken them for a stranger.

"Good boy Ollie, that's enough." I said as I picked Oliver up and turned to go back to the dining room when I became aware of a familiar scent in the air. The scent had caught my attention but was not something I focused on at the time. I walked down the hall with Oliver in my arms and rejoined the party.

We said good night to our guests and soon after they left our house I returned to the powder room to brush my teeth and get ready for bed. I reached down to put my tooth brush back into the vanity cupboard when I realized two things; A - that the lid of the toilet seat was down, and B - that one of the two portals in the powder room had been traversed by someone other than me. After returning from Buenos Aires tonight in such a hurry, mid-stream as it were and having accidentally urinated on the toilet seat, I clearly remembered cleaning said seat and furthermore remembered that I definitely did not put the lid down. Since no one else had used the room since, I suspected that I had been followed by Brent or his counterpart. As for the portal, the fringe around the edge takes on a unique pattern for each individual. When you become accustomed to seeing your own fringe it's almost like looking at yourself in the mirror. You can easily identify your own aura on the fringe. When someone else travels through your portal, on the other hand, the pattern reconfigures to reflect the aura of the last person who traversed it. Like a finger-print, the fringe of a portal always morphs to the unique pattern of the last traveler who has passed through it.

A cold shudder went through me thinking that Brent had been here. I knew I could smell him earlier this evening when we heard the thud and Oliver had a freak-out. My heart raced and my blood pressure climbed quickly. I thought for a moment that I was going to black out with anxiety. I had a terrible feeling knowing I had put Devin and our guests in danger. I had no idea what extents Brent would go to in order to protect his interest in this technology venture. I had no idea what his employer would do or how invested either of them were. I only knew I needed to take care of this and now.

"Game on, Brent, game on." I spoke under my breath as I spit out my toothpaste and looked in the mirror at the man I knew had altered the true time-line as we knew it.

I needed to go far into the future to gather intelligence on Brent's scheme. I had to understand the scope and breadth of this whole plan and how many stakeholders were involved. I needed to uncover who Brent was working for and how high the stakes were. I knew there was no way he came up with a concept like this by himself.

I set my sights for Paris, France in the year 2212, September 30, 11:00 a.m. at the Four Seasons Hotel. This property was notorious for being one of the most expensive hotels in Paris so I figured it should have the most state-of-the art amenities and would likely still be in existence 200 years hence. I wanted to land at 11:00 a.m. because check out is generally around that time and I could likely gain access to a room that was being cleaned.

I emerged in the second stall of the lobby washroom. Funny I thought how I always seem to land in a washroom. I could hear that I wasn't alone in this washroom and I wanted to give the illusion that I had actually used the facility, but I couldn't figure out how to flush the toilet. I decided to forego the flush and just leave the stall. As I opened the door to the stall, a rush of light pink colored smoke flowed down the walls from the ceiling on all four sides of the cubicle. As I walked out of the cubicle into the washroom I heard a light hissing sound similar to that of a high-powered central vacuum cleaner sucking air through its tubes. Turning around to look back into the cubicle I could see the toilet was flushing itself and sucking the thin layer of pink smoke off of the walls and down the drain. There seemed to be no water at all used in the process.

I noticed there were men and women present in the washroom and as I crossed the expansive room to the hand sinks I could see there was no water being used here either. I placed my hands under what looked like a faucet that was shaped more like a mini rain shower head which began to emit the same pink smoke that I saw in the stall when the toilet flushed. This pink smoke was highly attracted to my skin as though I was a magnet. It was like a fine powder that felt silky smooth as it coated my hands and wrists. I was concerned it would stain my shirt but as the sink drain began to emit a very light hiss the powder quickly slid off of my skin and shirt cuffs. As it left my skin I thought it felt like egg whites at my body temperature dripping off of my hands and leaving my skin completely dry. I looked at my hands and was amazed how clean they were even under my fingernails. My skin felt exceptionally soft and smooth as though I had just moisturized.

It was a little disconcerting to be in a unisex bathroom, but I guess that was part of the future advancement of the Parisians or maybe mankind in general. I also noticed that everyone was wearing sunglasses. In a washroom I thought, that's weird.

I left the room and was further amazed at what I saw in the lobby. I had come from a time where nearly everyone had a smart phone or tablet with them. Most people in public were not watching their environment; they were engaged in games or social media. Teens would be playing games, adults sending texts and posting on twitter and Facebook, adults playing games, teens twittering and sending SMS and posting on Facebook, occasionally you would see someone reading an e-book. The most common sight was that of people with their head down focused on the electronic device they held with both hands with their thumbs typing a mile a minute. I figured by now mankind would have evolved massively strong thumbs to manage all the typing required to stay in touch with their friends. I took a seat in the lobby to observe and learn what I could about the current times.

In the lobby there were several people checking in and

at least a dozen people sitting on the plush furniture scattered throughout in various configurations like mini living rooms. Nearly everyone had sunglasses on and there was not one person typing on a tablet or smart phone. I didn't see anyone on a cell phone even though there were several conversations going on which at first seemed like people talking to them self. I realized that the conversations they were having were on telephones which were built into their sunglasses. I just didn't know how they could dial the numbers without a keypad or speed dial button. I suppose it was all voice activated now.

The couple who were not wearing sunglasses seemed to be the only people in the lobby actually speaking to each other. I couldn't understand what anyone was saying because the French that they were using had evolved dramatically from the language that I understood of two hundred years previous. It was first of all way too fast for me to catch more than a few syllables here or there and it had a much more Arabic quality to it.

At this point a young woman carrying a coffee cup sat down on the sofa across from me and continued having a conversation in an impossibly fast French dialect. She placed her coffee on the table between us and I immediately became uncomfortable. Wishing I had a newspaper or magazine so I could pretend to read while I observed, I became aware that there were no newspapers or magazines anywhere in sight. Not one magazine, not one newspaper in the entire lobby, how odd. A server came around a couple of minutes later to refill the woman's coffee. He motioned a refill gesture to the woman who raised her head and smiled pleasantly at the server and gave a little nod of approval. I noticed something interesting about her sunglasses at this particular moment. When she looked up to acknowledge the server's presence and accept the refill, her sunglass lenses lightened up from a very dark tint to no tint at all just for the brief moment that she made eye contact with the server and then quickly tinted back to dark as she resumed her conversation. It took me by surprise because I had never seen photosensitive lenses adjust that quickly. They went from dark to clear and back to dark within a half second. And it appeared they did this on demand as though the woman had intentionally willed them to go clear and then back to dark. The only light sensitive glass I had seen went darker as the environment became brighter, and conversely the lenses became clear in darker situations. Looking around I could see that everyone's sunglasses were quite dark.

While I was coming to grips with the realization that she had somehow controlled the tint of her sunglasses, the server turned to me and asked me something in French that I just could not understand. I replied in English, the man responded with a smile and asked me in plain ole English.

"Would you care for coffee, tea, juice and perhaps a pair of house lenses while you wait?"

"House lenses?" I queried.

"Very good sir I shall return momentarily."

I had meant it as a question not a statement. "House lenses..." what were they? Was he getting me a pair of sunglasses that belonged to the Hotel?
That's exactly what he did. The server returned with a pair of sunglasses in a cloth pouch that had the Four Seasons logo on one side. I thanked him and promptly opened the pouch to put on the glasses. I was about to ask the server how they worked when I realized he had already left.

I placed the glasses on my head and was amazed at what happened next. My entire field of vision now became like a movie theatre. The Hotel lobby was blocked out and what looked to be about twenty feet in front of me was a curved wall approximately sixty feet high by a hundred feet wide. My entire field of vision was covered by this screen which had a series of boxes each with a language listed within. As my eye moved slowly over each, the box that I was focused on lit up. I lingered on one which began to flash so I skimmed across each until I found English and kept my eyes on the box as it lit up. After a second it flashed a few times and the screen gave me two options: English YES – English NO. I kept my sight on English Yes, which then flashed and brought up another screen. I was amazed how the glasses could read where I was looking and allow me interact and make choices. It took less than a minute to complete the configuration of these glasses which involved a number of choices that drilled down to map out a number of my personal preferences.

Once the "house lenses" were configured I was seeing content that was relevant to a thirty year old man who enjoys food, fashion, fitness, cars and jazz. The big curved wall faded away and I was left with a much smaller menu across the top 10% of my field of vision. This menu was a bit confusing but it appeared that it would let me participate in video phone calls, research products and services and make purchases among other things.

Through the rest of the lens a series of labels began to materialize, floating in a 3D virtual space. The labels were similar to roadside mile markers that pointed in various directions but sort of just hovered off the ground around 4 or 5 feet in the air like tethered helium balloons. As I moved my head, the labels also moved in relation to my perspective of the room and surroundings. Each label had a main heading and a distance; Concierge 15m; Business Services 28m, Health Club 33m; Pool 43m, Starbucks 20m; Café St. Germain-Des-Prés 331m; Rolls-Royce 25m; Limousine 45m; Peugeot 93m; Porsche 236m. As I had discovered when configuring the lenses, as I looked at each label it would light up and if I let my eyes linger on a label for more than one second it would flash. The label would expand to reveal additional info about the product or service with options that would allow you to quickly place a video call to the location or simply send your contact info to request a reservation.

I couldn't believe how easy it was to use these glasses but I was brutally aware that I was procrastinating. My motive for coming here, the need to see a room and the technology used inside was now my focus. I stood up and began to walk towards the elevator. As I did the labels moved according to my perspective on things, and the numbers on each label changed to reflect the actual distance to the destinations. They were somewhat translucent and would move out of my way as I attempted to collide with them or walked past by the ninety degree mark of the designated route to the location.

Before I reached the elevator I noticed a label titled "Model Suites 10m". I followed the direction this label pointed to down a short corridor just off the lobby where I was greeted by a pleasant young lady standing behind a wooden podium. She appeared to be in her late twenties and there was just something about her that seemed instantly familiar.

"Hello." I offered in a level tone.

As soon as I looked at her and spoke the tint in my glasses lightened. I took the lenses off and put them in my shirt pocket.

"Ah English, hello, my name is Zia and I will be your guide today. Are you interested in a condominium for yourself?" The young lady bubbled.

"Pardon me, condo? Isn't this a hotel?" I asked, somewhat confused.

"Oh yes it is a hotel, but we also have twenty floors of condominiums most of which are now occupied. We still have a few on the upper floors ranging from thirty million for a standard two bedroom unit up to sixty million for the four bedroom penthouse."

"Sixty…million?" I gasped, with a bit of a swallow between the second and third syllables.

"Yes I know, very reasonable and the fees are the best in Paris, only four hundred thousand per month."

"I um, I'm just passing through and wondered if I could take a look at the decor and entertainment systems you have in the units.

"Listen, I'm not supposed to show these to anyone unless they tell me they are in the market for a condo." Zia said with a slight whisper.

"Oh, I just wanted to take a look at the decor and entertainment. I don't really want to…"

"Even if you are just *thinking* of buying a condo….know what I mean?" She was interested in showing me but somehow was looking for me to grant her permission. I was confused.

It took me a few seconds to catch her meaning but eventually I clued in and said, "Oh, right OK yes. I am thinking of buying a condo for myself, a two bedroom unit. Can I see what you have?"

"Of course it will be my pleasure Mr...?"

Again my killer instincts kicked in and I answered "Barone, Call me Mr. Barone."

Zia responded with, "Right this way, Mr. Barone."

We proceeded to a series of doors each with a six inch by six inch touch screen on the wall next to it located on the wall approximately five feet high. Zia had a grin on her face as she keyed in a security code and that I didn't pay attention to. There was also a fingerprint identifier and retina scan that followed. She asked me if I prefer above or below the fortieth floor and if I would like one or two washrooms. I answered that my preference would be above the fortieth and with two washrooms.

It wasn't just her long red hair and big blue eyes but something in Zia's personality reminded me very much of Devin. Her grin became wider as she typed and her fingernails clicked on the touch screen in a way that reminded me of how Devin composes a clever email. It was like she knew what was coming soon and was having a hard time containing it. I always knew the sound of Devin's clever email because the typing seemed steady and calculated, never rushed or frantic. The velocity of Zia's fingers attacking the touch-screen keyboard reminded me of Devin typing on a computer keyboard, the kind of keyboard that has a moving button for each letter like an old type-writer. And it made me think of times when I could hear Devin's email-typing whip up into a frantic and aggressive tone. I remembered the loud clickity-clack of fingernails on keyboard that left me no doubt that there was deliberate emotion in the words being composed from her mind to her fingers to the screen where her email was being crafted and poised like an arrow in a drawn bow ready to make its journey to deliver damage to the intended recipient.

Zia finished with her retina scan and flurry of fingers-on-touch-screen then as the last deliberate click sounded on the touch screen, the door opened up to reveal the most expensive condo I had ever seen in my life. I was escorted into a thirty million dollar two bedroom condominium, apparently the least expensive of the current offerings here at the Four Seasons Hotel Paris.

The view was stunning and the furniture looked futuristic. The design looked warm, plush and comfortable, not at all what I expected which would have been a much colder sterile feel than what I actually encountered. Twelve foot ceilings gave the space an airy feeling. The unit was sparsely, however more than adequately, furnished.

Zia launched into a well rehearsed, but somewhat canned spiel about all the features and benefits of the unit. Most of which I tuned out because my attention was on the pleasing visual appearance of this place. A minute or so into the tour I got over the initial impact and re-engaged in the dialogue.

"Nice view!" I offered as an opening for Zia to elaborate on.

"Yes every unit has seventy interchangeable views. This one is one of my favorites."

"You mean I can change the view?"

"Of course, this view of the Eiffel Tower can be changed anytime you like. Here I'll show you on the control tab."

Zia picked up a thin rectangular glass tablet and held it so I could see the surface.

"See here is the exterior view menu. We have Paris-Eiffel Tower selected. Here is the list of other views we just touch any one that we want and the outside view changes. You can drill-down through different cities or various categories as well.

We walked onto the balcony which was enormous and wrapped around to the other side of the unit. Zia touched three or four different options each immediately replacing the previous outside view, each equally stunning and realistic. The air smelled fresh and sweet like the countryside we were witnessing, not at all like I would expect in the middle of Paris. The views were amazingly realistic. I could see no other condo units from the balcony and there were no obstructions anywhere. Of course there would be no obstructions the scene wasn't real. We must be encased in some kind of very large view screen. This reminded me of the lenses I had in my pocket and the way my surroundings disappeared from view when I put them on.

"Do you have any views of Toronto?" I asked of Zia who was now in a state of elation for some reason. Perhaps the ability to present virtual visuals of certain locations beyond her current physical reach gave her sense of empowerment.

"Toronto Canada, yes there are four! Here is the city skyline from the Toronto Island. You can adjust the time of day in the view to be the same as the current time in Toronto. The sun rise, sunset and weather can also be configured to accurately reflect current Toronto conditions if you wish."

Zia seemed just a little too enthusiastic about her job. Maybe it was a passion for Toronto that was shining through, but something about her seemed to be too energetic.

I asked, "And you can adjust those options for any of the views?"

"Absolutely, the climate outside will also adjust accordingly based on your selection and preferences including temperature wind and smell.

"So I can have summer by the sea on my balcony all year long?" I inquired.

"Yes if you wish. You could loop your exterior view to continuous sunset or dusk indefinitely if you want. Anything is possible, within the seventy views available."

"Only seventy views?" I asked sarcastically.

"Additional views will be automatically loaded into your controller tab and are included in the fees. We expect a dozen or so more at the end of this month."

"End of the month? Do you know who supplies them to you?" I asked.

128

"I'll find out for you right after the tour. Please sit here and I will show you the audio-visual system controls."

I was intrigued now that Zia had promised to give me the name of one of the suppliers. I was curious if the same company that supplied the external views supplied the rest of the audio-visual technology. I sat on one of the oversized chairs and sunk right in as if the cushions were meant specifically for me. It was the most comfortable seat I had ever sat on. Zia requested a movie which began playing on the wall. At first I thought there was a hi-def projection but I couldn't see where it was coming from.

I asked Zia, "Is that a rear-projection or is the screen built into the wall?"

"Neither." She replied, "The paint on the wall is displaying the video."

"The paint? The paint is displaying the video?"

"Yes, it's the newest technology for video display. You define the display size and position with the controller. See you can pinch it down or expand it easily. The variable zone setting will track your position within the space and allow the video to follow you as you move around. It's great for getting ready to go out. You never have to miss a thing. Come with me I'll show you the rest of the unit."

I was so comfortably situated I didn't think I would be able to get up but as I leaned forward the cushion under me began to stiffen as if it were assisting me in my endeavor to elevate. Brilliant, I thought, intelligent furniture. We walked from the living space through a dining room area into a wide hall that leads to the first bedroom. The video image that was on the large living room wall followed down the hall beside us. As we walked it kept up with our pace, moving along always in sight and the sound didn't seem to change really at all. We walked into the bedroom and the video moved along ahead of us and took up what seemed to be a logical position on the main wall across from the king size bed. Zia continued to deliver her pitch.

"There are three dozen speakers hidden in the walls and ceiling throughout the unit allowing the system to maintain the proper intended surround sound audio mix for the video presentation regardless of where you are. The video will settle in a predefined zone within each room as you move from area to area. This is the master bedroom. You'll notice there is also a balcony here and the view is consistent with the living room but you can vary the two as you like. Here's the walk-in closet and over here we have the ensuite spa."

We walked across the master bedroom and into the spa. The room was massive about fifteen feet wide by approximately twenty feet long with an enormous multi-head shower built into a glass encased marble room at the far end on one side with a soaker tub next to it that could probably bathe six people simultaneously. The lighting gently faded up as we entered and seemed to come from inside the walls. The movie that was playing on the bedroom wall now followed us into the bathroom and locked into position on the big wall across from the vanity above what appeared to be a massage table.

Zia continued her dialogue, "There are several configurable amenities within the spa including floor, room and water temperature, light levels and scent. The automated massage unit can be programmed for intensity, routine and duration. You can fill the tub from anywhere within the condo using one of the tab-controllers enabling you to assign water temperature and level as well as selecting bubble bath and the controller will indicate when the tub is ready. It usually fills within three minutes."

"There is no faucet or drain. How does the water

get in and out of the tub?" I asked.

"Come here and I will show you."

A couple of clicks on the tablet and the tub began to fill with water from all sides as though the inside surface was made of cheesecloth. Zia continued. "The tub has a permeable membrane that can be controlled to let water in or out. The tub has built in heaters so the water temperature will remain consistent at the temperature of your preference give or take one degree Celsius. Touch this panel to open the bar which is stocked with your preferred beverages. Replenishment is automatic and is included in the fees. Here we have the steam room and over here we have a drying chamber."

Zia walked around the room and touched a small panel on the wall which caused a door to appear where there was just a tiled wall a second before. This was the steam room which I could now see into. She continued to walk and talk and as she touched the next panel another door appeared as if out of nowhere. The steam room door faded away leaving the tiled wall in tact as it was before.

"The drying chamber?" I echoed.

"Step inside Mr. Barone. Please allow me to demonstrate." Zia referred to me as Mr. Barone which kind of threw me off but nonetheless I still obliged her. I stepped into the room which was about three feet by three feet. When the door was closed I was engulfed entirely with pink dust, the same dust that I had encountered in the lobby washroom. Then a draft began to create a slight wind that began pulling the dust off of me. The wind intensified for a few seconds and then stopped. Zia opened the door and I stepped out. My clothes felt as though they had been cleaned and pressed and my skin felt really smooth.

"How do you feel Mr. Barone?" Zia asked calmly.

"Clean and dry thank you very much." I

responded.

"Then on to the dining room." She proclaimed.

"Lead on, Zia, my guide."

Zia turned and walked out of the spa, through the master bedroom and across the hall. The movie followed us as we walked.

"Here is the dining room my favorite part of the tour.

"And why is that may I ask?"

"Because this is the part of the tour where I have the privilege of demonstrating the most impressive features our condominiums have to offer; most impressive because these configurable decor materials were invented by my Great-Great Aunt Devin. You will notice that the controller can change the wall color, the table surface, the material on the chairs and the curtains. Each component can be adjusted independently, and there are dozens of pre-configured style sets to select from. Here we have the 'Barkin Suite' of tasteful preconfigured city look, 'New York Urban Chic' I will now change to 'French Provincial'."

With a click of the tablet Zia had changed the entire look of the room. The table surface morphed from a sleek dark charcoal finish to a medium brown oiled grainy wood with dark exposed knots. At the same time the material on the chairs morphed from a light grey to an even lighter cream color that had a soft scroll pattern in a darker beige tone. The drapes changed from an off white to a medium grayish blue while the walls faded up from medium brown to a light aqua tone.

I inquired, "Zia, who was your Great Aunt that came up with this? Devin you say?"

"It was my Great-Great grandmother's sister.

She became an interior decorator in 2015 and developed a virtual showroom application to quickly change materials and colors within a photo so that prospective clients could visualize a number of styles before making a purchase decision. She further developed the concept for model homes to actually map materials over physical objects using thin television projection film, the same stuff they used for wallpaper years ago."

"Try-before-you-buy?" I piped in.

"Exactly, and it evolved into the video projection paint that we use today on these walls. Recent advancements allow us to coat fabrics and nearly any other object to appear as any kind of material imaginable. To the human eye it appears real but in actual fact it is a coat of paint that can change its appearance depending on the video signal sent to it. So based on user preference, these surfaces can resemble well pretty much anything."

"So a receiver connected to the painted area reads the material map information transmitted from the controller and then displays it over the surface of the object. Your Great-Great Aunt was a bit of a genius wouldn't you say?" I asked.

"Yes I would say the "Tracker-Mapper" was the best invention of the past two hundred years. The consumer version is used on clothes, watch this."

As she spoke the words Zia touched a button on her blouse causing it to change from white to denim through a full range of browns and finally stopping on a light grayish-green.

"Well now I've seen everything, Zia."

"Actually Mr. Barone you haven't seen the second bedroom yet but if you wish to stop the tour short that is your prerogative."

There it was again, that Devin grin and sort of "smart-ass-attitude" coming through.

"I meant that thing you did with your shirt. That material colour changer video paint is amazing. Why is it called the 'Tracker-Mapper' Zia"?

"The Tracker-Mapper was derived from my Great-Great Aunt Devin's nick-name 'Tracka' coined by her Australian friend Lisa. Lisa called her 'Tracka' because she was really good at tracking down places and things, so the original version of this app, created by her husband was called the 'Tracka-Mappa' which later became known as the 'Tracker-Mapper'. The 'Barkin-Suite' available here, is a set of 12 of her most famous and successful interior design projects which include complete bedroom, dining room and living room material configurations available instantly at a touch of a button."

As Zia spoke she also quickly changed the look of the dining room over and over, scrolling her way through the various sets of décor plans apparently designed by my wife. There had to be a reason for the familiar way Zia carried herself, and now I knew. I was stunned by the realization that I was visiting with one of my relatives 200 years into the future. Zia was obviously offspring of me and Devin, although she bore far more of Devin's traits than mine.

"Zia, I would like to thank you very much for the tour. You have been most helpful and I couldn't think of a prettier more knowledgeable tour guide to have shown me the space, and to discover that some of this great technology was invented by your family made the tour that much more exciting."

Zia blushed again reminding me of Devin. We walked towards the exit where Zia engaged a wall panel to unlock the door to the lobby.

"The pleasure was mine, Mr. Barone. If you will

place your lenses here against this panel you will have all of the technical information on the condo unit itself plus the contact information for all suppliers, technical and building trades involved in this project including the exterior view as you requested."

I took the glasses out of my shirt pocket and held them up to the small glass panel just inside the exterior door. The lenses glowed green for a half second and then went dark. The download of information was complete.

"Thank you for taking the tour and we hope to be of service in the near future."

Zia opened the door back to the hotel lobby and walked with me a few meters out to the podium where we first met. We said goodbye and I put the lenses back on as I walked back into the lobby.

The lenses powered up and resumed where they had left off showing floating labels for everything relevant to my preferences within 300 meters of my location. There was an additional icon at the top left of the screen labeled Model Suites. I walked back to the lobby lounge where I sat down to read the contents of the file I had acquired. There it was, the supplier I was looking for jumped out at me immediately: Kruder-Schuhmacher Technologies Corp. Koenigsallee 58, Düsseldorf, NW, 40215 Germany.

Mind Travelers - Chapter 3

Just a Little Weekend Get Away – Part 2

Somewhat relieved after putting the Toronto couple behind us, I held Devin's hand tightly as we walked up the hotel stairs and onto the street. The town was starting to come alive as mothers walked their children to school, business men in suits met on the sidewalk kissing each other on both cheeks, numerous delivery trucks sputtered up and down in both directions and shop keepers were outside sweeping the sidewalks and setting their offerings out on display. The town was bustling and the scene was beautiful.

As we walked up the sidewalk and around the corner to the rental car, I kept Devin close to me to avoid another potential timeline mess. Who knows what impact the interchange at the pool was going to have I thought to myself. I opened the car door for Devin and got her settled in on the passenger side. We drove out of the town into the incredibly beautiful countryside where the April morning air was fresh and the early morning sun was beginning to burn the dew off the low lying vineyards. As we reached the peak of one hill and began our descent down the next valley, we could see a thick haze of fog down below us. The bright orange luminance being cast from the sun now peaking over the distant hills was meeting with the dark shadow now deep in the haze below us. I thought about how this fog, which at the moment seemed so much an integral part of the landscape, would soon evaporate to reveal row upon row of grape vines that made up the vineyards we were driving through. How each molecule of H_2O that made up this cloud of vapor which filled the valley soon would be forced by the sun's energy to transpose into its base atomic components and disperse. It was amazing to me that billions of hydrogen and oxygen atoms were gathered together here to witness the sunrise only to start their day venturing off to find a new place to witness the sunset and tomorrow's sunrise. Who knew where they would each end up today and where the journey would take them tomorrow?

The beauty of the landscape was exactly what we both needed to take our minds off the morning activities. I was a little concerned about Devin now having knowledge of my ability to time travel and how she would react once the knowledge truly sunk in. Where would this ability actually take us? Devin was worried about the Toronto couple she befriended in my eight minute absence this morning, and wanted desperately to save them from the pending disaster about to descend on the city of L'Aquila. We drove in silence for many miles up and down the beautiful hillsides, twisting and turning in through densely wooded areas and out again to the open fields, zipping past row after endless row of old world grape vines. Soaking in the awesome beauty of the landscape, we didn't need to talk about it. We just felt the same deep appreciation for the history and culture of the environment that we were experiencing. The slight buzz from the wine certainly did add to the ambiance.

We'd been driving for about two hours, the sun was high now and we were beginning to feel hungry. I could see off in the distance a medieval town up on a hill surrounded by a stone wall that perhaps eight or nine hundred years ago was the protective perimeter. I drove the rental car up a winding road to the entrance of the town, over a short bridge and through a large arched door in the stone wall. We wound our way through the town and approached the main piazza. I parked on a side street just off the piazza where a row of shops were located about a hundred meters or so from the square.

"Let's get out and stretch our legs for a while." I said quietly as I turned off the ignition. I looked over and saw that Devin was crying. "Sweetie, what's wrong?" I asked with genuine concern.

"I'm sorry I just feel bad for the people who are going to die in the earthquake on Monday."

"I know but listen we can't make friends or get into any meaningful conversations with people while we are out of our time. It's just too dangerous — especially in the past because of the affect we may have on our present."

"I know but I can't help thinking about how we can save so many people. I just feel helpless knowing that we could help but we won't."

"I know but look at it this way, you and I are both going to die at some point, that is a given. The one sure thing about life is nobody gets out alive. Do you agree?"

"I agree."

"So if you knew the time and place that it was going to happen to you would you try to avoid it?"

"Probably. I would want to live as long as I could."

"Well that's my point, if your life is pre-destined to go from point A to point B, what right do you have to mess with destiny and change point B to point C? If it is to be, then let it be. We all make choices that extend or shorten our life expectancy but you can't outright change an event without repercussions. There is a grand universal plan that is carried out by God, destiny or whatever natural or supernatural force you want to believe is at the center of it all. This universal plan moves forward regardless of what you and I do in our every day lives and while it's alright to question the plan it's a bad idea to change it. Come on let's get out and walk."

We got out of the car and began walking slowly towards the square.

"So you wouldn't try to avoid your death even if you knew when it was going to happen?" Devin was drying her tears as she blurted out the question.

"I already do know when and where I am going to die. After all I am a time traveler. Of course I won't try to prolong my life beyond that predetermined point. The time and place of my death is meant to be and I really don't want to cause a major disruption in the universal scheme of things. The true time line needs to remain true. People are not meant to know when they are going to pass along to the next incarnation. It's part of life's mystery. This is why mediums will never tell people when they are going to die. They would have to take on the responsibility of possibly changing destiny and that is too great a burden for any one person."

As we walked along the cobblestone street talking about life and death and the limited time we have on earth, I sensed Devin was beginning to relax and gain a better appreciation of the incredible gift I had been given. We walked from shop to shop buying wine and bread and cheese and walked some more up and down the side streets and then out into the main piazza.

"I was given a gift that could extend our lives indefinitely. With the ability to stop the present time while we travel and experience the past or future, I can prolong the inevitable for quite some time but not infinitely. Eventually, life moves on and death is the last part of the cycle of life."

"Life moves on." Devin echoed, "Life moves on. Baby, take me home?"

"Home home? Or back to the hotel home. Tell you what, let's go have a picnic and then see how we feel?"

"I'd like to go back to the hotel. Let's have the picnic tomorrow. We can stay a couple days right?"

"Of course, today's my birthday and we have two more days here.

We walked back to the car and drove along the country roads nibbling on cheese and bread as we made our way back to the hotel in L'Aquila. The sun had receded close to the horizon by the time we reached our hotel.

When we finally made our way back up to the room Devin was tired and decided she would lie down on the bed and take a nap. After all, it was approximately four a.m. for us in real-time even though the sun was still visible in the sky here in our displaced time in Italy. I kissed her on the cheek and went to the living room couch to meditate. I was thinking how remarkable it was that while we adventured around in this recent past, our present time was at a stand still, our bodies here and now were fatigued from the day's activities and we required rest just the same as any normal day.

I sat comfortably on the couch. The clock showed 8:21 p.m. I closed my eyes, and after thirty seconds or so I began repeating my mantra. In a few seconds, my mind and body began to transcend my current state of consciousness and I found myself standing in a light fog watching from a distance, a man in a hospital bed talking with his wife and daughter.

Welcome to Dreamland –
Time Traveler's Training Ground

"Hello Sheila."

"Dad, how are you feeling?"

"I don't feel a thing. That's the beauty of being in a coma. My body is healing fine, no permanent damage. I'm going to be alright."

"And does Mom know about this time travel thing? Mom did you know Dad was training Martin and I to be time travelers?"

"Yes sweetie, your father and I decided many years ago that this would be the best time in your life for him to mentor you."

"So you time travel too?" Sheila asked her mother.

"Of course, that's how your father and I first met."

"I thought you met in high school. I thought you two went to high school together?"

"We did meet in high school, actually, well not at the same school."

"And not exactly at the same time, but we did go to high school together, so to speak." Harold added with a grin.

"I'll tell you more about that later on but what's important right now is your training."

"Of course mom, whatever, shall we wait for Martin?"

"We shall." Harold answered, "We shall."

Harold was the name of the man in the bed. I could tell

he sensed my presence at the edge of the fog, and I knew somehow that he was aware of me. I waited there watching, intuitively knowing that the family needed time to catch up on a recent turn of events. A young man named Martin appeared out of the fog not far from me and approached Harold, Sheila and Maryanne at the hospital bed. I remained at the edge of the misty fog, watching the interaction between them. They looked familiar but I didn't know why.

"Dad why on earth would you let this car accident happen? You must have known that it was coming."

"It's all part of God's plan my sweet pea, part of the grand scheme of things. I knew it was coming but not exactly when. I also knew that I would recover quickly and it would afford me the time to devote to you and Martin at this most important phase in your development."

"But you could have avoided the whole thing altogether." Sheila was emotionally charged. "You could have avoided the pain and our anguish, and the guy that died, he could still be alive."

"I didn't want to know exactly when it was going to happen because I feared that I may have tried to avoid it. I'm sorry that I scared you all. The man who died was supposed to die when he did. If I avoided the crash he would have escaped death and the natural order of things would be set off balance. The man who died was a fugitive and if he'd lived because I avoided the collision, well who knows what he would have gone on to do."

"Harold, I want to understand something." Martin stepped into the conversation now at the bedside.

Harold could sense Martin's frustration with the whole situation and launched a pre-emptive defense.

"Martin, please don't be upset. This is truly the best gift anyone could receive."

"Gift?" Martin asked abruptly. "I didn't ask for any gift. Especially one that is as bizarre as this. I didn't sign up for this. I just want to play hockey."

"Martin, listen I lost my father when I was nine years old. This gift has allowed me to spend several additional years with him. It's enabled me to visit him many times before he died and allowed us to get to know each other during the time before I was even born. I've followed him through high school and parts of university."

"Well that's great but I don't see how it's going to help me."

"The best way it can help you is if you help others. You can go back in time and use what you learn from the past to help people along the way in the present so that your path to hockey stardom will be paved with positive endorsements. You should never manipulate the past to influence the future, but it's alright to take advantage of the occasional opportunity especially when it comes from the heart and it helps someone out for no other reason than to help them out."

"Well I don't understand it fully, but I guess if I can help others along the way I can live with that for now."

Harold rose up on one elbow and waved at me and beckoning for me to approach the group.

"Welcome Victor," Harold shouted to me, "thanks for waiting in the wings and giving us some time to talk through all of this family business."

"You knew he was there?" Martin asked," How long was he been watching us?"

"You look familiar." Sheila said with a puzzled look.

"Victor, come closer I would like you to meet my wife Maryanne, my daughter Sheila and her boyfriend Martin. Everyone this is Victor. Victor has been training with us for some time now. He has been helping from the side lines and was instrumental in setting up the portals the last few weeks. But wait, Victor you are visiting us from another time than your own real-time correct?"

"That's right I guess. I am on an adventure with my wife right now. We jumped back a few years for a little weekend getaway. Have we met before? You all look so familiar but I don't remember you or any kind of training."

"That's why you have a puzzled look on your face." Harold continued. "You don't remember the training sessions because you haven't been through them yet. It's a bit of a paradox that happens here in the fourth dimension. You went back in time from your current present real-time and then time jumped again to get here. You are 'twice removed' so to speak, your present being would remember the training but here and now for you, it is before the time we met. Your memory is not in tact here because, in a way, it hasn't happened for you. Welcome to dreamland, my friend."

"Dreamland? Man, I am confused."

"Yes dreamland, the time traveler's training ground. In this environment you will only remember things in order of their occurrence. Do you remember watching us play Capture the Flag, and the time you visited your high school baseball game?"

"Yes I remember that and there was something or someone that brought me out of the dream and back to my couch where I was meditating."

"That someone was me. You had come here to our training ground and sat on the sidelines for several nights. Finally you got the notion to get in the game and that's when you jumped through one of the portals. I was aware of your presence but didn't engage you until you took that leap of faith. By the time I got to you quite a few people had already seen you materialize on the pitcher's mound."

"So you hit rewind then brought me back to my present time?"

"Yes but I wasn't able to completely rewind the clock so there were likely a few changes in your life caused by that episode. I hope the experience didn't throw too much out of balance?

"Well actually there are a couple things that I am still trying to correct." I was thinking about my boy Simon and nemesis Brent. It was interesting that here I remembered Simon, but in real-time I had completely forgotten him.

"I know the outcome of that time jump to the baseball game had a big effect on the natural timeline." Harold continued, "Trust me when I say you will work out a solution eventually. But before you do, I want you to join in the remainder of Sheila and Martin's training. This will help you learn the art of time travel as well, and these two here will eventually become your greatest allies moving forward. I want you all to know that I'm going to stay in this comatose state for a while, until you three are trained and my body is completely healed."

"How long do you think that will be?" Sheila asked.

"Seventeen days, six hours and thirty four minutes.

"Really?"

"No, I'm messing with you. It'll take as long as it takes. My insurance will cover the medical costs and my work can wait a few weeks. Besides, right now is the most crucial time in your training. We need to really focus on honing your skills and getting you to understand proper conduct. Also the amount of time it takes is irrelevant because when you are finished training, time will be in your control. For the next seven nights I want the three of you to meet me here. We'll see how it goes and hopefully by then your abilities will be up to code."

Martin chimed in, "O.K. I'm ready to get started but tell me a bit more about how I can influence my hockey career by helping others?"

"I'm in, let's go." Sheila added.

That night Harold had us warm up with a few basic techniques before introducing a couple of new concepts to the three of us. What seemed to be an awkward beginning between the team members quickly turned into a very familiar exercise. Sheila, Martin and I had no trouble taking verbal instructions from Harold laying in his hospital bed and no problem executing them flawlessly.

In the hours that followed we became quite a fluid team. We seemed to naturally motivate each other and feed off of one another's energy and drive. Martin of course was the most energetic and aggressive which seemed natural, he being such a strong athlete while Sheila and I were more subtle. The usual "Capture the Flag" game that we practiced over the past few weeks had now become familiar to me and was turned into more of a game of hide-n-seek. Harold had me create two portals then while Martin was looking away Sheila would choose a portal to go through. Martin would then have to read the pattern to determine which portal Sheila went through. If he was correct he would see her and chase her till he could strip her of the flag, then the two would return back through the portal to the starting point. If he was wrong, he would have to return back through the portal he chose and then traverse through the second portal and try to find her prior to the two of them returning.

We each took turns at the three positions in the game and to increase the level of difficulty we gradually put more and more portals into play and varied the time between traversing through and coming back. We learned that the patterns around the edge of the portals varied depending on which direction in time the person traversed. So "going" patterns look different than "returning" patterns. As well the "feathered" edges were different for each individual. Mine had less blue in it than Martin's and less yellow than Sheila's.

By the end of the first night's practice Harold had made things interesting by introducing as many variables in the game as he could. Eventually we were at a point where the "hider" would take one portal out and another back then yet another out again and back through the first then out through a fourth. We all became so familiar with each other's portal patterns that a complex path of this sort traversed by the "hider" would take no more than four or five seconds for the "seeker" to identify correctly in order to uncover the whereabouts of the "hider".

Harold knew it was time to take us all to the next level but that this new level would begin tomorrow night.

"That's enough for now. Good work all of you. Tomorrow we tackle some new ground."

I had an urgent feeling that it was time to get back from this ethereal fourth dimension plane to our earthquake-doomed hotel room in L'Aquila Italy. After all I was still just meditating during a weekend getaway with Devin.

Martin asked Harold, "Why do we need to come back tomorrow? If we are time travelers can't we just do all the training in one session and end up back at the same time we started? Couldn't we learn everything in one second of real time even if it takes us a couple weeks or months here?"

Harold took on a very serious look and starred directly into Martin's eyes as he answered, "No, absolutely not. Knowledge actually changes the chemistry and physical composition of your brain. It normally takes time for new information and experiences to be processed and become a new memory in your brain. Your brain physically changes as it accommodates all new information. If you were to learn too much at once it would place a dangerous amount of stress on your brain. It would likely prove fatal to try and accept the changes of a week's worth of information in a split second."

Harold had a small paperback tucked under the blanket that covered him in his hospital bed. A part of the book was exposed and I could just make out a portion of the title '…veler's Handbook…' He noticed that I had become aware of this book as he was speaking and gently covered it up without a skip in his delivery and before Martin or Sheila could become aware of it.

"See you guys tomorrow night." I said as I walked out to the edge of the fog clearing where we had been training, with Harold barking directions from his hospital bed. Somehow I doubted that he needed to stay in that bed here in this 'dreamland' as he called it. I wondered why he was hiding the book from Martin and Sheila but had been careless enough to let me to see it.

The fog was dense but as I approached the fringe I could see what looked like a number of people moving slowly just out of visible sight within the thick mist. I felt somehow very familiar with these surroundings and suddenly a voice spoke my name. It was an unmistakable voice that I had known since early childhood. It was my Aunt Dora who called to me from the fog. I stepped a few feet toward the direction of her voice and as I did the fog quickly dissipated in front of me and there she was. My Aunt Dora stood right in front of me looking like she did when I would go visit her as a

151

young boy. She was probably forty years old at the time and oddly she looked exactly the same age now. I knew she had passed away at age eighty three a few years ago, so how was it that I was seeing her here and now and as a younger version of herself?

 As soon as the questions about my Aunt Dora entered my mind I found myself meditating back on the couch in L'Aquila. I slowly opened one eye to look at the clock. Eight twenty four p.m. Three minutes had transpired since I closed my eyes. My head began to hurt as it sometimes does after a lengthy time away. Having briefly emerged after only diving three minutes into my meditation, I consciously deliberated on what had happened in my mind while I had been in the dreamland training zone. Dreamland… I continued meditating.

Just a Little Weekend Get Away – Part 3

I had spent seven hours in the training zone with Martin and Sheila and we had all learned quite a bit from Harold. Harold was right about the brain's capacity to change dramatically in a short time frame. If my head hurt that much from seven hours of learning crammed into less than five minutes, I can imagine how a week's training would have affected me. I finished my meditation which helped my head dramatically, and got up to check in on Devin. She was sleeping soundly. It was 8:45 and the sun had now set over the Tuscan hills, presenting a canvas that transitioned in colour from brilliant orange on the horizon to a dark purple and navy blue at the furthest visible point from the apartment balcony.

The rest of our Italian getaway was thoroughly enjoyable and relatively uneventful in terms of real time line impact. We drove around taking in the countryside and had two more afternoon picnics on a blanket which we laid out in the mid-afternoon sun and where we consumed wine and nibbles that we purchased in the shops. At night we ate dinner in the local restaurants and then walked around the town soaking in the culture and architecture. We saw Steve and Jamie, the couple that we had met from Toronto, a few times while we were out on these after dinner strolls but managed to avoid being spotted when we did encounter them. Devin now understood the need for us to keep very much to ourselves and was reserved to the fact that the earthquake may or may not claim their lives on Monday, and as such was not so inclined to engage them in conversation. I was relieved that she finally knew about my ability to traverse time and space and that she was becoming mindful and respectful of the guidelines associated to such ability. She was just really happy knowing that we could get away any time we wanted to without much to worry about.

We left Tuscany and returned home to Toronto on the evening of April 5th, the night before the earthquake. Now home, we were feeling refreshed but sad knowing that the hotel we had just stayed in and much of the city we had come to love was to be destroyed by an earthquake the next morning. Well to us, now in present day it technically had happened three and a half years ago. Still, having been there just prior had imparted a strong sense of appreciation for the beauty of the region and for the immense loss of life and devastation to the area. We both felt a profound obligation to somehow assist in restoring the area back to the normal life that existed there during our visit. It was 4:40 p.m. and Oliver lay on the couch looking at us curiously. I couldn't help thinking he knew what just happened to us and was happy we were back. To him, we had been gone less than five seconds. To Oliver, we would have appeared to flicker out of vision in about two and a half seconds and then flicker back into vision over the next two and a half second. He likely would have thought he was hallucinating.

In the days that followed, the feelings of dread, doom and obligation to assist in helping the tragic displacement of normalcy in the L'Aquila region gradually dissipated, giving way to a renewed sense of adventure and playfulness. We had come to grips with the idea that having the power to change the course of humanity did not mean that we should exercise said power. Sure, we could have saved hundreds, even thousands of people by evacuating them from L'Aquila but having knowledge of the earthquake in advance would have made us seem suspect and any number of scenarios could have spun off from that suspicion. The earthquake was meant to happen and it did happen.

Instead of dwelling on the inevitable we began focusing on the future and that's when our adventurous curiosity took over. We decided that we would limit our getaways to the weekend. We would finish off the work week and spend Friday night discussing where we would go over a bottle of wine and some nibbles. We'd wake up Saturday, get cleaned up and take off to a new destination for a few days, maybe a week or sometimes even a month and then come back to finish off our weekend doing what was required to keep our household running. Oliver never missed us because he was only left alone for a matter of seconds. It was odd for us to return home and not receive the usual joyous greeting from him. On occasion we took Oliver with us but only into the future as I didn't want to risk him running off and changing the world.

Entertaining guests had taken on a whole new meaning. We used to be tired and often cranky by the time our guests arrived on Saturday nights. Now we were in the habit of getting everything ready Saturday morning and taking off for a few days or a week to laze on the beach before returning to our present time relaxed and ready for the next chapter of our social schedule. In the past we would open the door to our guests with a detectable level of tension in the air, but now that tension was gone. We would greet our guests upon their arrival and it was apparent, obvious in fact that we were completely stress-free when they arrived. Our guests began to question our amicable nature which was a departure from the norm, and frequently commented on our stress-free demeanor. Devin's sister, Suzanne, went as far as accusing us of having sex just before their arrival. Truth of the matter was that we did have sex minutes before they arrived except that it had happened while on a getaway in a place far away and years before we opened the door to her and her husband Paul.

One Friday night, Devin and I debated back and forth on a number of points mainly around the topic of interior and exterior design, interior decorating and how technology within the living space would advance in the future. Armed with first-hand experience in the matter and having met one of Devin's sister's descendants who proudly proclaimed her ties to the family technology, I was eager to share what I knew. The problem was that what I experienced had been within a time-line that needed to be corrected. I really wanted to share my experience of the future with Devin but I knew I couldn't because the present needed to change and this may have a big impact on the future. Telling her what I knew of the future would be a lie because what I had witnessed, particularly the walk-through that I took with Zia, may not ever have come to be true. The conversation I had with Devin that night sparked intrigue and adventure which resulted in the plan for our next getaway. Tomorrow, Devin and I would go forward 300 years into the future to settle our little techno-debate to gain insight into the new science of luxury living.

We also had Buenos Aires to look forward to. That trip was a real-time trip where we would actually have to bring our luggage along and check it in, and actually get on an airplane with other people for a nineteen hour flight. We had all but forgotten what the true linear-time travel experience was like. It was coming up on us real fast, we were leaving next weekend. Both of us had somewhat lost interest in going through with the trip but it was way too late to cancel. We hadn't booked cancellation insurance and neither of us was willing to forgo the three thousand dollar expense that we would incur if we cancelled. We agreed that it would be a very strange experience compared to our new-found instant mode of transportation which we had enjoyed immensely over the last several weekend adventures. The 'beam me up Scotty' approach was far more convenient than the airports check-in, security, immigration, etcetera approach to travel that everyday people were forced to endure. We also agreed that this would be a great opportunity to enjoy spending some quality time with a couple of our travel friends, Lisa and James.

Effect of Light-Speed Travel on Matter

Matter itself cannot reach a velocity equal to that of the speed of light. It's a physical impossibility that was theorized by Albert Einstein and which has never been disproved. Light is a form of energy and as such has no mass. It has been argued that photons which make up light have mass because they have momentum and energy which has an impact when it strikes a surface. As energy cannot be created nor destroyed but only converted from one form to another, it stands to reason that for matter to reach light speed, it would need to first be converted into energy. That would seem true if light were strictly a form of energy. It turns out however that light behaves as a wave as well as a particle, making light an energy form that contains mass, or at least acts like it does. Light is affected by gravity so it must contain mass, right?

The wave particle duality of light was a key discovery that invited scientists to look deeper into the energy associated with various matter and eventually ask the question "We know that gravity holds us on the earth and causes the moon to stay in orbit around the earth; planets around the sun. But what exactly is the energy that holds atomic particles in orbit around the nucleus of the atom?" Newtonian physics gave way to quantum physics as we turned our gaze away from how visible objects relate to one another and began to investigate what holds matter together at the atomic and sub-atomic level.

Einstein viewed the entire physical world and all matter in the universe as energy vibrating at a variety of different frequencies. Associating the vibrational frequency of matter directly to the frequency and wavelength of energy or electromagnetic spectrum was a major scientific breakthrough which helped open doors to developing time travel.

It was through later experimentation of focusing energy through the space that existed between the atoms within crystals and gemstones that the laser beam was created. It was determined that the smaller the distance between the atoms, the stronger the intensity of the beam. Diamond, for instance, creates a much more intense energy beam than emerald, for example, because diamond is a much more dense material. So it was discovered that the distance between the atoms in a diamond which is made of carbon atoms packed really, really close together, coincidentally matches the distance equal to the frequency and wavelength of gamma rays. This is the most energetic and destructive part of the ultra violet spectrum. Emerald on the other hand matches with a visible part of the UV spectrum that appears green to the human eye and carries much less energy and is virtually harmless. Ruby, as another example, used as a laser is consistent with red light and has properties associated to that frequency.

When we time travel, we convert our matter into energy and then back into its original form. When we are in the pure energy state we travel at the speed of light. Short distances and short time jumps have minimal impact on atomic structure but after many of these jumps there is a negative cumulative effect notably a gradual deterioration in short and long term memory. Contrary to old beliefs, not all brain functions are confined to certain fixed locations. As such the brain's ability to change throughout life not only allows us to time travel but it also acts as an impediment. The brain learns to accommodate, changing gradually over time to successfully handle all the functions and requirements and especially new memories from all the experiences we have. When we time travel, we have many experiences that our brain needs to make adjustments for in order to accommodate. When we return to our original time, we bring all of those experiences back with us as memories, so when we rematerialize our current brain adjusts to accommodate the new memories and experiences. Over the course of many time jumps this will cause our brain to overload on memories, sort of like a computer hard drive that is reaching its capacity. The human brain has a limit to the amount of information it can retain, and generally the more recent experiences are given priority in the memory department.

One other level of complexity is that of sorting memories from various times. The brain's natural instinct is to chronicle experiences into memories that exist in a linear timeline. When we travel back and ahead in time, the brain is somewhat challenged as to when the experiences from the past and future actually happen. In your mind's reality they may have happened today, but your brain is conflicted trying to file them according to when they happened in the past or even harder on the brain is filing experiences from the future that haven't happened yet.

Our brain has an ability to accept change quickly but despite its neuroplasticity we are conditioned to deal with linear time lines. The speed of light has no real impact on us and transporting around the planet in real-time will not harm you. Conversely there are dangers associated with the physiological changes that may have occurred within our brain during an extended period away. This often presents itself soon after returning in the form of a headache. The intensity and severity of the headache is directly proportional to the amount of new knowledge you return with, and this is usually a result of an extended time away. In the next chapter we will look at neuroplasticity but it is always advisable not to extend your time away nor participate in activities that involve in-depth learning.

-    Excerpt from Time Traveler's Handbook

Late Night Training
Part 3 – Back to Dreamland

On the second night of training I made it a point to arrive early for two reasons. One, I was curious about having seen my Aunt Dora and needed to understand if she was an apparition, maybe a bi-product of the stress from learning so much in a short time? Perhaps the vision of her was a memory that short-circuited in my brain while I was mentally heading back to the meditation couch. And the other reason, I wanted to know what was so important about Harold's book that he didn't want Martin or Sheila to see.

It was five minutes to ten o'clock when I went to the loft to meditate. Oliver by my side and Devin reading in the living room I settled in, closed my eyes and began repeating my mantra. Soon, I was back at the foggy fringe of the clearing looking in at the hospital bed that Harold lay propped up on, reading. As I approached Harold acknowledged my presence and closed the book without hiding it this time.

"Victor you're here early. I didn't expect anyone for at least another hour."

"I came early for a reason, Harold." I said as I approached the bed."

"I know. It's this..." He held up the book he was intently reading. "...and your Aunt Dora."

"How did you...?"

"How did I know?" Harold finished my question for me. "I know you saw the book and Dora last night and both made you curious. Thanks for not mentioning the book in front of the other two."

"O.K. but why? And my Aunt, how did you know I saw her? And what do you know about her?"

"Well first let's start with the book. This is my favorite book of all time. It hasn't been written yet so I shouldn't be exposing it to anyone, especially the

164

author's Grandparents."

"Do I want to know?"

"No Victor, you aren't the author's Grandfather and you have to promise you'll keep this between us for now. Its Sheila and Martin's future grandson's book, he publishes this book seventy two years from now." Harold held the book up so I could read the cover.

"Time Traveler's Handbook, a simple guide to traversing space and time. And sure enough Martin Saunders III is the author. Your favorite book?"

"This book is my favorite because when you get to know my Great Grandson you will see that he is not a scientist. He's not an author either, but this book came from him. It's a book that describes the science of how time travel is possible, and the practical side of how to become a time traveler including all of the universal rules and regulations required for safe time traveling. The thing I love the most about the book is that it's written in terms that the average person can understand. Not all pure scientific terms and physics mumbo-jumbo. Knowledge pulled together from experiences he will have and books that he will read eventually will lead him to write this break-through piece of literature that eventually becomes the absolute all-time best selling book on the subject of time travel."

"Wow that's great news for Martin Saunders III, and yes I will keep that information to myself. We don't want Martin and Sheila to find out the name let alone the gender of one of their future off-spring. Thank you for explaining why you need it kept secret, now what can you tell me about my Aunt Dora?"

"Ah, yes your aunt passed away quite some time ago, as did your grandmother and many other relatives. They're all here."

"Here? What do you mean here? Are we in

heaven or something?"

Harold chuckled at the word heaven. "Heaven's no. Or hell no, we aren't in heaven or hell. There is no heaven or hell, just this. This is what I call dreamland. It's more of a universal plane that all energy is connected to. Some call it the cosmic consciousness; some call it the ethereal plane, some call it the fourth dimension or spirit-world."

"So this isn't heaven or hell. Is it more like purgatory?" I asked.

"This is where our spirits go after they leave our body. This is where are souls go after death. This is where we go when we dream. This is where you come apparently, when you meditate."

"So everyone who ever lived, every deceased person in the history of mankind is here?"

"Yes exactly, but not in the way you vision it. When a person is finished learning what they have set out to learn in the physical plane as a human, the soul leaves their body and comes back here to plan for its next incarnation. Sometimes the wait is long, and sometimes its short but at some point the soul is ready to go back to the physical plane for another round. While here, the soul undergoes, for lack of a better term, 'training' for the next incarnation. This can involve time spent in what you would refer to as hell and it can involve time spent in what you would refer to as heaven. In many cases it involves some time spent in both areas.

"Isn't hell a place we go to as punishment for our sins?"

"The reason souls are exposed to the bliss of heaven, and the tortures of hell, has nothing to do with punishment or reward. It has everything to do with the reconditioning required for the soul to embark on the next incarnation in the physical world. Reconditioning in

166

order to prepare for learning a new set of lessons and grow to a higher level in the next life-time. The Catholic religion teaches us that Jesus forgives all our sins and takes us into his home for all eternity. So if that were true, why would there need to be a heaven or hell. There would just be a very big house with area for all the souls of every person that ever lived. And there would need to be a perpetual expansion project going on in order to accommodate the ever growing number of future habitants in said house. No, death is not a permanent condition my boy, it's simply a transition. The soul is a form of energy that was created by God and cannot be destroyed by anyone but God. It can only be converted from one form to another. In human form the soul combines with mind and body to make up a person.

A simple more anecdotal interpretation of this cycle would be a rain drop. Think of an oxygen atom as the soul of a water molecule and the two hydrogen atoms being the mind and body. They combine with other water molecules like a family to form a rain drop. The drop lands in a large lake to hang out with many other water molecules like communities. Here it can encounter several billion other water molecules in a single lifetime. The molecule hangs out in the lake until one day near the surface of the lake, it gets struck by lightning. The lightning causes the molecule's oxygen atom to break the bond with the hydrogen and go its separate way. As the soul of this water molecule ascends up to the sky, the oxygen atom mingles with a variety of other atoms, some of whom he may recognize from the lake, some he may recognize from previous life-times, maybe they were snowflakes together. So the soul of the molecule, the oxygen atom, hangs out in the sky for a period of time until one day the oxygen atom decides he needs a new purpose and joins up again with a couple of hydrogen atoms to form another water molecule and become part of a rain drop that falls to earth to go through another life-cycle."

"I get it, when a rain drop lands in the desert, it lives a pretty short life, and when it lands as a snowflake on a mountain it may have a longer go-round, say till spring when it melts and either evaporates or becomes part of a stream; if it lands in a lake it might live to be hundreds of years old. Between each life-cycle there is a time of reflection and regrouping with God or the universal energy. What if you don't believe in God?"

"You don't have to believe in something in order for it to be real. You don't need to understand gravity to know that exists. You can't explain how your brain can calculate complex mathematical equations, even though you are able to. All religions revolve around a faith that there is life after death. The tragic thing is that cultures argue over who's religion is the 'right one' and even go to war over their beliefs. The reason for atonement or reconditioning in 'Dreamland' or 'heaven and hell', call this what you will, is to ready the soul for its next visit to earth in the physical plane. Another way to look at it is that every soul is a part of a larger spirit – God; (we are created in his image) and when we live in a human form our spirit always resonates with the higher spirit (God is always with us) and when we die our spirit returns to it's higher form as part of the larger spirit (God prepares room in his house for each of us). A raindrop returns to the cloud to get ready for its next trip to earth. Humans return to the original universal energy source to get ready for their next trip to earth. The need for each individual spirit to recondition is based on what the soul is setting out to achieve during the next incarnation."

"It makes sense to me. I've read somewhere that life is just a series of lessons that we are here to experience and learn from in order to reach a higher plane."

"Exactly, each incarnation is a pre-determined set of lessons that the spirit has decided to learn and teach in order to help elevate itself and other souls to a higher ground so to speak. One of the greatest lessons we need to learn is that a good teacher is also a good student. We tend to learn so much from other people that we forget that we are actually influencing as well. Few of us realize how much knowledge we impart onto others in the course of a lifetime. That is one of the biggest contemplation points in planning an incarnation. Our souls don't always come back in a human form depending on the lessons we are setting out to learn and especially those that we are planning to teach.

Some souls believe it's more of an honor to incarnate as a domesticated animal like a dog because you get to teach one of the most basic but important lessons of life, unconditional love. That unconditional love is a difficult yet fundamental lesson that all souls eventually come to learn and yearn to teach. I personally agree that this incarnation is most honorable because it focuses far more on helping others progress rather than on ones self. An incarnation as a domestic pet can tend to be rather unfulfilling if your owner does not engage you as much as you would prefer.

But I've strayed way off track now. I wanted to explain the dynamic of this plane, and that is no matter where the soul currently resides, there is always a connection to this universal consciousness here, right where we stand now. Your Aunt, your relatives, you and everyone you have ever met has passed through this area many, many times. This is merely a rest stop between lifetimes where you get a chance to reconnect with your higher self, reflect on your past incarnations and plan out your next life. Your next set of lessons that will help the universal consciousness evolve and elevate.

"Has my Aunt Dora's soul reincarnated yet, how about my grandmother, Philomena, or her brother, Angelo?"

"Actually Dora has not gone back yet but your grandmother has incarnated into the person you know as your niece, Celeste. And your Great Uncle Angelo, he is Oliver your pet Havanese. From what I understand he is quite happy this time round. You and Devin are very good dog owners and are learning unconditional love from him. Angelo was a dog lover last incarnation and chose for this life-time to, I could go into much more detail but I think you get the general idea."

Harold tucked the book under the covers and looked over my right shoulder. I turned and watched as Sheila appeared out of the fog and approached us with a puzzled look on her face. I think that her arrival was the main reason Harold cut the discussion short and definitely why he hid the book.

"I think I just saw a ghost." Sheila said in a quivering tone.

After hearing the details of how Sheila had just run into a recently deceased relative Harold began to explain the fact that we were not alone here in the fog, and continued the story again from the beginning after Martin had arrived. Hearing the description over and over helped me understand the meaning of life in general and how we as humans fit into the universal scheme.

As Harold spoke I felt a calm come over me that I had never felt before. It was a vibration that resonated with my soul as I thought about my life and what my purpose might be or could be for this incarnation, this lifetime. I thought about the evolution of mankind and how the current state was not just a cumulative effect of a bunch of different tribal behaviors or interactions over thousands of years. How all of mankind was part of a common higher energy interconnected through this ethereal plane.

I thought about what made up my life to date as I knew it. I truly believed I was now here in the place where the meaning of life, each life and every lifetime had been carefully reviewed and planned before and after its soul lived and had died. This was the home of our souls and it felt great to be home.

The training on this second night and each of the several nights to follow was as productive as the first. We started off reviewing the key takeaways from the night before, how familiar we became with each other's portals created when we traversed time, and how quickly we learned to identify each other's patterns, coming, going, distance and depth into the future or past. We could now easily identify for each other, the direction of travel through time and the coordinates that the person came from or went to anywhere on the planet.

On night number four, Sheila experimented setting a very interesting portal for me to follow her through. We were all accustomed to, and often entertained by, the creative destinations that we picked for each other to land, such as under the head table at a wedding reception; the outdoor observation deck of the CN Tower; an underwater landing in a public swimming pool that nearly drown me; or even atop Mount Everest in a snow storm. But this night as I jumped through a portal approximately one second after Sheila, to my surprise I landed on a fast moving subway train. When I landed I was facing the back of the train and completely lost my balance as my full mass materialized and was now subject to the momentum of the train and the speed of the floor moving under me. I rolled through three summersaults before my body got up to speed with the train. Each time my head came around I could see the portal that I had just traveled through moving away from me and pass through the back of the train car I was on. I stood up and watched it shrink away in the distance out the back window of the train hovering in space above the tracks. I was shocked that we were able to land on a moving object. As I turned around to face in the direction the train was moving I saw that Sheila was in the car ahead of me looking back through the window. Sheila came through the doors between the train cars and approached me laughing. Luckily the train was completely empty apart from the two of us.

"Good one Sheila! How did you ever come up with that?"

"I've been waiting to pull that off for a while. This train was one my Uncle took me on a few times as a kid in Toronto. We got off of it at the station around sixty seconds ago. It's on its way to the yard to be parked for the night. I wanted to see if the portal would move with the train or stay fixed with the earth."

"I guess we found out the hard way." I said as I rubbed the back of my head.

"Are you O.K. Victor? Sorry if you got a little banged up."

"I'm alright. Here let's head back. I'll drive!" I reached out my arm and Sheila took a hold of my hand while I jumped us back to Harold and Martin in Dreamland.

Training in the 4th dimension also afforded Martin the opportunity to get reacquainted with some people from his past along with some ancestors that had moved on before he was even born. A few nights after training Martin spoke with his grandfather and uncle — both of whom had died in World War Two. They usually discussed war strategy together and tactics of combat though sports sometimes came into the discussion. Martin had a sincere curiosity about the life and times of people living in the late 1930's and early 1940's and developed a whole different outlook on humanity by listening to the stories that these old timers shared. Martin wondered how two men who looked so young could have experienced so much. They both appeared to be in their early thirties, but had stories enough to fill several lifetimes.

Martin discovered that the two men had lived several life times together in various relationships, brothers, sisters, cousins and father & son just prior to World War Two. As they continued their conversation it was revealed that the form in which the spirits presented themselves here were that of the intention of the beholder. In other words, Martin had sub-consciously chosen to speak with the spirits of his Uncle and Grandfather in their thirties. They could have just as easily been Martin's Great-Great Grandfather and Great-Great Uncle living in their teens or forties because these spirits were all synonymous. They were all part of a greater universal spirit which, like all energy, is influenced by its environment and undergoes transformation. In this case the appearance was influenced by Martin's intention or expectation.

The time that he spent here with his ancestral spirits inspired Martin to share the ether world or 'Dreamland' as Harold liked to call it with others. One day Martin confided in a close friend Warren, his ability to travel through time and space. He had described this dreamland as a place where souls went to rest and plan for their next journey into the material world. His friend Warren, of course, couldn't believe the story was true so in order to prove it Martin took his friend's arm and jumped to the ether world where he and the others had been training. The first visit included an introduction to Harold and a discussion with Martin's Grandfather. The friend was now a true believer, but to put the icing on the cake Warren had an encounter with his own Mother who had died less than a year before.

The emotion of this experience had touched Warren deeply and brought much needed closure to the incident of his Mother's passing. This prompted discussions which lead Martin to develop a time travel holiday service where he offered to take people into this dimension to connect with their deceased loved ones. 'Past Time Travel' was born and in order not to disrupt the space-time continuum, 'Past Time' visits stayed within the 4th Dimension or 'Spirit World' allowing travelers to speak with the higher spirits of friends and relatives with no possible repercussions to the space time continuum. There was no way to affect the present real-time line by going in and out of dreamland.

Over time, this travel concept proved to be a success among the elite travel set however when it fell into the wrong hands and became commoditized, 'Spirits' began to come out of the shadows and rebel. But that's another chapter altogether, perhaps even another book.

On the sixth night, after a couple hours of rigorous complex portal pathway training and through a number of time zones and back again we felt we had truly become a strong team. We were about to wrap up for the night and gathered around Harold's bed to talk. Martin was growing tired of the low level of challenge present and asked Harold about once again inviting others to join in and compete against us in the Capture the Flag game as we had initially played in our dreams. Harold told us that 'The Game' was just a 'Crawl' step in the overall process of training and that we were now already passed the 'Walk' stage but had not quite made it to the 'Run' level yet. Harold went on to further describe the dynamics of the environment we were training in.

"The ethereal plain hosts the human dream state and this environment is shared with the spirit world. Mediums have a strong connection to this ever present but seldom seen dimension where our souls live before and after incarnating in human body form. This is a great training ground for time travel mainly for the reason that time is not linear in this environment, and as such the environment is conducive for matter to traverse time. Second, the environment morphs to reflect the intentions or wishes of the observer. Similar to the dream state, objects appear and change and disappear at the whim of the dreamer.

It was discovered in the 1980's that matter, for the most part, behaves in a way that is consistent with the intentions or expectation of the onlooker. Scientists used particle accelerators to move tiny particles towards each other at a velocity approaching the speed of light. When they crashed into one another the resulting behavior of the fragments was at first unpredictable, but after further observation it was discovered that the behavior was consistent with the expectation of the observer. The link between behavior of matter and the energy associated with intention or expectation had now been discovered. This became the basis for how we now understand mass and energy and the workings of everything within the universe.

The universe as we know it is mostly a product of our individual intention and our collective expectation. In short, the universal collective conscious shapes the world we see based on our outlook. You've heard the phrase 'perception is reality'? It is a true statement that the world looks different to each of us. That's because we each have our own perception, our outlook on the world around us."

Suddenly, while Harold was speaking, a strange and negative vibe fell over us that made me feel like I needed to run and hide. In the fringe of the fog I could sense someone looking in at us. I wasn't sure but I felt the same emotion that I had felt in Buenos Aires when I had been followed into the washroom by Brent's bartender and kidnapping accomplice.

"What the hell is that?" Sheila asked the group.

"You feel that too?" Martin added, "It's weird isn't it, like we are being watched."

"Guy's hang on a second," Harold closed his eyes for less than a second, opened them and then said "Come in here. Come close."

Harold whispered, "Listen we are all in serious danger. I know you feel it, so listen carefully and don't ask questions. Sheila, bring Martin and Victor to our house right now. Talk to you mother immediately and she will help you three work this out. Don't any of you come back here until you have Maryanne's green light to do so. All our lives depend on it. Now go quickly, that way, and don't stop to talk to any dead relatives."

We quickly shuffled off in the direction that Harold had pointed, somewhat confused but confident that it was the right thing to do. We all felt there were eyes upon us that belonged to someone who had really bad intentions. I was certain it was Brent.

175

As we scurried off into the fog to make our escape, I chanced a glance back towards Harold and saw two male figures in the fringe at the far side of the fog. As I looked back I couldn't help thinking about that damn first jump where I messed up everything. I had brought this on myself, I know, but I still had very little knowledge of how I could fix it. Brent was after me now, of that I was absolutely certain. And somehow I had inadvertently dragged Martin and Sheila and Harold into this mess.

Neuroplasticity –
The Ever Changing Brain

As a young athlete begins to learn a new sport they require extensive practice in order to build and strengthen the muscles and coordination needed to physically perform the required tasks. At the same time that the body is repeating this and gaining motor skills, the brain is creating a long-term "muscle memory" for that task, eventually allowing the athlete to perform it without conscious effort. This process decreases the need to focus attention on the task and enables maximum efficiency within the motor and memory systems. Examples of muscle memory are found in many daily activities which become automatic and improve with practice, such as playing scales or a melody on a musical instrument or typing on a keyboard. The brain's ability to change or mold its neural pathways and synapses due to changes in behavior, environment as well as changes resulting from injury to the body has proved to be the foundation of many studies and experiments including the development of time travel.

In Post Traumatic Stress Disorder cases the event that caused the disorder was so overwhelming that the brain was not able to file the experience in a normal way. As such, the sufferer keeps experiencing the emotions and memories over and over again as everyday life events continue to trigger the memory. And the more these triggers happen, the deeper the emotion becomes for the sufferer. In order to correct this problem, the memories need to be brought back and filed where they belong, in the past, so that the brain can move forward from the trauma. One successful experimental treatment involved writing the account of the event in great detail and then reading it out loud once a week. It was found that this technique caused neurons that linked the emotion to the memory of a traumatic event to become disconnected from each other so as not to affect the person in such a deep emotional way. Eventually most or all of the old emotion from the trauma were removed.

This technique of reading one's own personal account of the event was referred to as the "Impartial Spectator" as it involved viewing oneself from a different perspective.

In effect it teaches one to not always believe what you think. For treatment of Obsessive Compulsive Disorder, for example, deliberately focusing on the cause of the desire to compulsively repeat a task is a way of mindfully separating oneself from the compulsion. The "Impartial Spectator", also known as self-directed neuroplasticity, can be used by an individual to help relieve the suffering.

In the next chapter, we will learn how to put into practice the "Impartial Spectator" by employing self-directed visualization during a lucid super-conscious or meditative state. This is Lesson One and the first step to becoming a time traveler.

- Excerpt from Time Traveler's Handbook

Let's Solve a Puzzle

As we entered the fog at the fringe of our training ground, Sheila hooked arms with both Martin and me and quietly said "I'll drive." We arrived a moment later at Sheila's house. It was midnight as the three of us landed together in the living room. The furniture looked surprisingly sleek and futuristic.

Maryanne wasn't the least bit startled when we woke her up, nor was she surprised to hear that we were in danger. Maryanne asked us to tell her what we experienced including what we heard, smelled, saw, felt physically and especially the emotions that we felt. She asked that we take turns starting with Sheila then Martin then I, and that no one speak while the other is relaying their story.

It seemed as though it was an everyday occurrence to Maryanne, who calmly listened to Sheila, and gave the occasional nod of acknowledgement while filling the kettle with water and putting it on the stove to boil. Either it was an everyday occurrence or she had been speaking with Harold within the last half hour. Sheila spoke for about five minutes and when she finished her account of the events, Martin gave Maryanne his version of the story. Maryanne listened intently, nodding acknowledgement as he spoke but never interrupting to ask for clarification. Sheila and I sat silent while Martin spoke. The kettle boiled and Maryanne poured the water into an old fashioned tea pot along with some herbal tea from a ceramic container on the counter. She placed the tea pot on the kitchen table and reached up into the cupboard for some tea cups then placed them around the table for us while Martin finished his story.

Once Martin finished Maryanne looked at me and calmly said "Victor, now it's your turn. Take as much time as you like and try not to leave anything out."

Martin & Sheila sat in silence through my whole story which took about six or seven minutes to convey. Maryanne acknowledged only with nods and not any verbal cues at all. It felt odd to speak for so long without any interruptions or questions. I felt anxious at first to get all my thoughts together and tell them in chronological order as they occurred without leaving anything out. But what I found was that it was impossible to chronicle my emotions, sights, sounds and smells into a time line. So I felt that what came out was a mumbo jumbo of words describing the encounter rather than any real coherent story. Maryanne's nods were reassuring me that she understood what I was saying, but I felt as though I was missing several bits and pieces of the overall story. I wanted to tell them what had happened in my past and why I thought these two guys were after me, but I stuck to the one encounter tonight from the fringe of the fog by Harold's bed.

When I finished Maryanne looked at all of us and put a finger in front of her lips to silently tell us not to speak. She closed her eyes for a few seconds and then opened them, took a deep breath in and out. Next she poured the tea for the four of us and returned the teapot back to the placemat in the middle of the table.

Maryanne began to speak softly and slowly. "Based on what I am picking up from the three of you, I get a strong sense that the true harmony of the world was set off balance some time ago, and that this somehow is a side effect. Some people are after you Victor because of something that you know and they fear that you will stop them from achieving their goals. Now from what I understand there have been some situations that have caused the natural space time continuum to be altered and in order to set the present and future back on its proper course, we as a team will need to go back in time and make a few adjustments. Much of our present day has been changed due your first attempt at time travel Victor. We've known about it since it happened, and Harold was unable to reverse entirely the effect of your miss-step because ultimately the miss- step needs to be corrected by you.
   As a result of that episode, the company take-over and the kidnappings in Buenos Aires, countless millions of other events since the baseball game so many years

ago have happened in ways that weren't meant to occur. Changing it back in a single step right at the point of the game would be too much mental adjustment for quite a large number of people. It could be devastating for everyone in your life, Victor. Now I believe the time has come to correct your miss-step and we are all here to assist and enable you to do it. The approach we will take must be systematic. We need to dissect this down and plan a series of maneuvers back through time in order to allow us and everyone you know, Victor, to mentally adjust. Without these gentle adjustments we could possibly cause varying degrees of brain damage to hundreds or even thousands of people.

 The team needs to work in concert to divert and restore timelines working back to and around the original kidnappings. Afterwards, the root cause will be addressed where the distraction at your high school baseball game will be revisited and restored. What we need is a point sometime in the future that we can engage the kidnappers, allowing us to distract them long enough to do our work."

I interrupted with "I think I have the perfect occasion."

Messing With Timelines
Part 3 – Time Out

The flight to Buenos Aires was difficult for Devin and I having experiencing many vacations without the need to cram into a confined space with hundreds of other people. Being able to travel at light speed to and from any destination and time of our choosing had spoiled a part of our passion for travel. They say it's not the destination but the journey that is important. With our new found mode of transportation, the destination had become the only part of the journey. So the flight from Toronto to Santiago, Chile, and connection to Buenos Aires felt to us like nineteen hours that we could never get back. We agreed it would be quite some time before we traveled in a conventional way again.

The ride from the Buenos Aires airport to our hotel downtown was uninteresting. We were driving through a large city with a lot of traffic and exhaust, and the sites were what you would usually see in a large city. There were large buildings, many people, much graffiti and garbage everywhere. The scene was a little bleak and after the flight it made us feel even more drab than the scenery. We were accustomed to arriving at our destination instantaneously. This was far too much time out for us.

The hotel was clean and bright with all the trappings any tourist could hope for. It wasn't at all what we were craving but it was exactly what we had expected. In fact it was what we decided on many months ago, so we had no one to take issue with regarding the non-descript nature of the accommodation. If you dropped someone blindfolded into this place they would never be able to guess where they were. It could have been anywhere in the world. There was nothing to indicate the local culture or history of the region let alone the country. The pool area was the typical tourist resort type set-up with a bar and loungers with umbrellas, servers walked around in tight black pants, white shirts with bow ties and serving trays.

So far it was everything we didn't want in a vacation, and yet we were here and loving the warm sun and cold drinks poolside with our music and books and our two friends. It seemed surreal to me that we were paying an arm and a leg to do what we could do for free and within seconds of a jump from our kitchen. I could see that Devin felt the same way and was putting on a good show of high spirits despite her true feelings. It took us a few hours and a few drinks to get over ourselves, but once we did, we actually began to really enjoy our holiday. Perhaps the effort required made us more appreciative on this trip.

We spent the next few days shopping and dining and exploring the downtown core of Buenos Aires. We took in some jazz and began to get a good feel for the vibe within this enormous city. In particular, the neighborhood called Palermo Hollywood, which was where most of the artistic types had come to set up shop.

It took some time but we settled into a great groove which involved far too much eating and drinking. We justified every meal by stating the estimated distance walked that morning or afternoon. Some days we actually did walk a great distance, maybe even twelve or fourteen kilometers, however judging by the tightness of my clothes, the caloric intake for the day undoubtedly exceeded the output. Afternoon walks generally ended poolside where we would cool down with a swim and chill out with wine or cocktails.

The mood on the last day was a bit melancholy as most holidays tend to get towards the end. We were looking forward to heading home and reminiscing about the good times we had here. We talked over lunch at a nearby cafe which served local cuisine and decided we would travel together to Italy next year. The conversation was easy and the chardonnay was flowing as easily for the ladies as the beer was for the boys. We wrapped up lunch and headed back to the hotel to enjoy a relaxing afternoon poolside before we had to pack to leave the next day.

The pool area was void of all tourists so we had no problem enjoying ourselves to the fullest. The staff had become familiar with our little party of four and was now rather quick to replenish our drinks. They knew that Canadians were great tippers and scrambled over each other to serve us.

The sun was hot and the atmosphere was jovial. I stepped out of the pool and was drying off with a towel as an overwhelming sense of déjà vu came over me. I knew it was caused by my past self popping by for a visit from a couple months ago. I finished drying off and asked James if he was ready for another beer, then I excused myself to go to the washroom.

As I walked into the washroom I could see the reflection of my past self looking out from behind the shower curtain. I couldn't quite make eye contact from this angle of approach but I knew, having been the person behind the curtain, what was going to happen in about two seconds from now. I timed my breathing quietly inhaling deeply as I crossed the threshold of the washroom. I turned towards the toilet and closed my airways in anticipation. The man stepped out from behind the door and quickly came up behind me crossing his left arm in front of my chest as his right hand came over my right shoulder placing the ether soaked rag against my nose and mouth. I struggled for a moment as the man held my body tightly with the rag pushed hard against my face. Eyes closed and breath held, I reduced my efforts after about three seconds and gradually allowed the man to take my weight and guide me to the floor as I let my legs give out entirely. I opened my mouth and dropped my head for effect as the rag came away from my face, carefully holding my breath and keeping my eyes closed as I was gently situated on the cold bathroom floor tiles with my back against the wall.

Fully conscious still, I was starting to feel some effects of the ether despite not inhaling any. My skin felt the cold evaporation of the liquid as it quickly transformed into a gas state. Fumes were rising up my nostrils so I exhaled gently and slowly a little air out through my nose being careful not to give any audible or visual indications that I was awake. I thought about how gentle the intruder had been with me, careful not to let me fall over and hurt myself. It made me think of the article we had read over dinner several weeks ago. I wondered if I was going to get sushi.

A little anxiety began to set in as I heard the speed dial tones of the man's cell phone. "Zee package is ready"

Within only one or two seconds Brent arrived. He pulled a black laundry bag over my head and shoulders down to my forearms and pulled the draw string snug, my hands and lower body still exposed to the air. The bartender left very quietly through the front door of the hotel room. Brent time jumped me out of the bathroom. The past version of me lingered for a short moment behind the shower curtain in the bathtub then returned through time to several weeks previous reemerging in the powder room of our house and back to the dinner party with our guests and Oliver.

Five seconds later, a version of me arrived from the future, landing in the main part of the hotel room next to the bed. He removed his clothes, packed them up in my suitcase and pulled on some short pants and a tee shirt. He slipped into my sandals and went to the bathroom. A faint smell of ether was still there as he turned on the sink faucet and cupped some water in his hands then proceeded to wet down his hair to give the appearance that he had just come out of the pool only a few minutes ago.

He returned to my lounger at the poolside and sat down where my present self had just left the wet towel. Our beers had arrived so he kicked off my sandals and swung his feet around and reclined. He took a swig from the frosty beer and returned it to the table between him and Devin. Then he caught sight of the compression marks that his socks had left on his lower calves and quickly covered up his lower legs with the wet towel. Somewhat embarrassed but certain that no one had seen them, he rejoined the poolside conversation and enjoyed the rest of the afternoon and evening in Buenos Aries.

Mind Travelers - Chapter 4

Game On! Part 2

My present self arrived with Brent at his predetermined destination. I assumed it was some sort of holding tank by the way sound reverberated. I envisioned a rectangular storage container, or the back of a semi-trailer used for shipping long haul loads by truck. I had started counting to myself as soon as I hit the floor in the bathroom, one-one thousand, two-one thousand and three-one thousand. It had been about ten seconds now since the ether had been applied to my face. I could feel that the cooling sensation of evaporating ether was beginning to subside. I knew I should wait until the bag was off before I dare take a breath for fear of feeling the full tranquilizing effect of the anesthetic.

Twelve one-thousand, thirteen thousand. I also was aware of Brent's presence and did not want him to think I was holding my breath so I made my chest rise and fall slightly to imitate a person breathing slowly while asleep. Eighteen thousand, nineteen thousand. With the bag over my head I was able to open my eyes but when I did I felt the sting of ether fumes so I quickly closed them again and kept then closed. I knew if I stayed calm I could hold my breath for over ninety seconds. Anticipating that the ether may have some short-term effect on me, the team agreed that ninety seconds would be the optimum length of time to wait before trying another time jump. This would allow the ether to evaporate entirely off my skin. What we hadn't planned for was the rising emotion caused by 90 seconds of oxygen deprivation. In a state of anxiety with a bag over my head, counting to myself while I kept still and pretended to breathe every ten seconds so my kidnapper would think I was asleep, well it was kind of difficult to keep calm. I was now beginning to question whether I could hold my breath for the full ninety seconds. My heart was pumping harder than normal and I could feel my body begin to crave oxygen.

Thirty one thousand, thirty two thousand, thirty three thousand. I opened my mouth and began to exhale a quarter-breath slowly. The warm exhaust from my lungs circled my face inside the bag. I began to inhale a first short breath gently and could taste the still present evaporated ether fumes. My head instantly felt light so I stopped right away. Had I waited long enough? Was I going to pass out if I took in more fumes? I held my breath for another ten seconds and tried again. The laundry bag had trapped a large portion of the fumes within, and I supposed I would either pass out from lack of oxygen or from the fumes, so I took my chances and began to breathe again. Lucky for me, I didn't pass out although I now felt on the verge. Fifty one thousand, fifty two thousand, fifty three thousand. The heat from my exhaled breath must have helped dissipate the fumes through the top of the bag. I could feel cool air coming into the laundry bag up and along from where my arms protruded out from the bottom. My mind automatically went into calculus mode attempting to determine the volume of remaining space surrounding me within the laundry bag. I tried to estimate the rate in which fresh air was permeating the material of the bag, along with the possible ratio of ether to exhaled carbon dioxide to fresh air; and with all these variables what would the concentration level of oxygen be in the mixture now reaching my lungs. I knew I wasn't getting enough fresh air and began to breathe faster all the while keeping my chest heaves at a normal ten second pace, maintaining a steady count and continuing my calculus visualization because for some reason, my mind needed to know if I was going to pass out. I would never be able to calculate the amount of oxygen I was getting in the present situation, but my mind had gone into auto-drive perhaps as a survival mechanism. My mind was focused and it helped to reduce or slow down the anxiety from welling up further, causing any number of other possible outcomes of the situation.

I was aware of Brent's close proximity and knew that if I ran now he would catch me. I could hear him about ten feet or so to my left rummaging through what sounded like a tool box. I became very alert the moment I heard Brent slam an ammunition clip into a pistol and cock the chamber.

Ten feet away meant I would have a head start of no more than two or three seconds. My mind was foggy from lack of oxygen and the ether fumes but I knew what I had to do and how fast I had to do it. I only hoped that when the time came, I would be out of his line of sight enabling me to maximize my lead. Seventy nine thousand, eighty thousand, eighty one thousand I opened my eyes slightly and was able to see Brent's shadow through the bag with no stinging effects from the ether. I thought I saw him disappear around a corner and my ears confirmed it as the sound of his footsteps began to reduce in volume. I had repositioned my arms so as to allow air flow into bag. The fresh air was sweet as it reached my nose and mouth. My brain was clearing up and shifting out of calculus mode. Thank you Brent for wearing hard leather soles. Thank you also for walking seven, eight, nine paces from your previous location at the tool box. Brent's footsteps had stopped somewhere around a corner in another room approximately twenty five feet from my current position. Ten paces times one point five feet, plus the original ten feet gives me about twenty five feet. My mind apparently was not yet out of math mode. It was now eighty five seconds since I had hit the floor in the Buenos Aires hotel bathroom. Five seconds early for what I had to do next, but I didn't care. I knew this was the best opportunity to escape and so I set my sights and jumped across time to the pre-arranged coordinates on a roof top where Martin would be waiting.

Messing With Timelines
Part 4 – Time to Fly Home

On the flight home from BA there was going to be a noticeable change in the environment. By that I mean a hard shift in the time line that had a significant impact on present day. Most of the passengers were asleep now at the three hour mark into the flight, but I was wide awake and watching for the signs. I knew the team was at work making the first set of time line corrections, distracting Brent and the bartender in order to stop the kidnappings from happening. This would allow the original technical team to develop their relationships and meet their future investors then agree to form their company as was supposed to have happened at the two day conference in BA.

I waited and watched intently for the signs, thinking that they would likely be subtle to me and knowing they would be imperceptible to everyone else on board. I knew I was about to undergo some changes just like many of the other passengers, but for me there was a difference. The difference was I had experienced enough of these shifts that I was able to identify them when they happened. I had also become accustomed to the headache that a shift of this magnitude would cause. When it finally did happen this time, I was surprised to observe more details than I originally thought I would. I was aware of much more than just the headache and this may have been caused by the altitude or the cabin pressure or maybe the fact that I was from the past.

The flight attendant was suddenly a completely different person. The cup of coffee I was drinking was now a glass of red wine, actually a very nice Malbec. Lisa and James who were seated directly behind us were now sitting two rows ahead of us. Another change I noticed immediately was the screaming child that was sitting close by had suddenly stopped crying, and Devin who had been fast asleep sitting on my left leaning against the window was now awake and sitting across the aisle on my right watching a movie on her iPad. The window seat next to me was now unoccupied.

The kidnappings must have been prevented I thought, and for something that had only happened a few months ago, the correction did have a significant impact on the present. My head instantly began to ache, so I took the Advil which I had stowed in my pocket in anticipation of this event. Seven or eight people pressed the flight attendant service request button within a matter of seconds. I knew they were all going to be requesting pain relief of some kind.

"So Victor, why did you sub-in back at the hotel?" Devin asked in a quiet voice from across the aisle.

"Huh?" My future self asked.

"Why did you sub in? My husband went to use the washroom and you came out and took his place, why the sub-in?"

"Oh, 'Sub-in' you say. Why did I, sub-IN...?"

"Stop stalling. Why? I saw the marks on your ankles and sock lint between your toes when you came out, and your tan was nearly non-existent."

"Oh you saw my ankles did you? I can't tell you right now why, but I can tell you one thing, before we get home, I am going to go back where I came from."

"What do you mean 'where you came from'?"

"I came from the future to fly home with you and go through customs and all that. A future version of me was needed to stand in today at the hotel and to take the flight back from BA. The other me, the one that flew down to BA with you was delayed coming home. He will arrive at our house, your house at approximately six thirty tonight, five minutes before you get home, provided everything goes as planned."

"What do you mean 'as planned'? What was the

plan and why is there one?"

"I told you I can't say anything now, its best that you don't know what is in the works. Let me just say that the purpose for me subbing in was to maintain a seamless experience for you, Lisa and James, the airline, Immigration and Canada Customs. Victor had to take care of some important business. I, your other husband, will fill you in tonight before you go to bed."

"You friggin kill me. All the secrecy and dire consequences crap. He better have a good excuse. I'll bet he just didn't want to go through the eighteen hours it takes to get home. I bet he just wanted the extra time to get stuff together for the guys tomorrow coming over to watch the big game."

"Trust me, its better that you don't know until tonight."

The rest of the flight back to Toronto was uneventful. It took a short while for Devin to calm down about the secret but afterwards we talked about the accommodations in BA and what the creature comforts of the future might evolve into. Having experienced first-hand some of the new technologies, I was at an advantage in speaking to the subject. Devin, in her inquisitive way, got some of the information out of me but wanted to see for herself what accommodations would be like a couple hundred years from now. I agreed we could have a look anytime she wanted, and told her I was pretty sure that her true time-line husband would likely agree too.

We landed in Toronto, went through customs and picked up our luggage before exiting the airport with Lisa and James. Waiting in line for a taxi, I made certain that James and Lisa were ahead of us. We said our good byes and acknowledged that we would see each other tomorrow at our house. Lisa and James got in the taxi ahead of us and departed. When it was our turn to load into a taxi I packed the luggage into the trunk and kissed

Devin before saying goodbye.

"I'll see you at home." Devin said with a bit of an edge in her tone.

"I know." I replied. "Been there and done that."

She got in and closed the door, then shot me a cold look as the taxi pulled away.

I went back inside the airport and bought a coffee. I had twenty minutes to spare before the present-time Victor would arrive at the beautiful home that I shared with the love of my life and our dog. I mean dogs...I'd almost forgotten about Simon even though here in the displaced time he was still a part of my memory. I missed Simon so much now. It was amazing to me how this alternate time line could exist where Devin and I didn't have two dogs and there was no memory of the little brother we got for Oliver. I wondered if Oliver had any memory of Simon here within the alternate reality that I had caused. I wondered why I remembered him. I suppose the neuroplasticity memory effect was not a hard-fast rule for a seasoned time traveler. Maybe the amount of time traveling I had done reduced the effect and I was able to retain memories from other timelines.

I sat and enjoyed my coffee watching the linear-time travelers come through the big sliding doors arriving home from various destinations. I thought about the joy that travel brings to so many people and how it is like a little time capsule that people get to experience whenever they take a trip for a week, or two. And then they go back to work or school and it's down to business for another chunk of time until they get to do it again. How lucky am I to be able to travel anytime I please, and to any time and destination.

It was time to go. Just like all the vacationers I watched returning home from holidays, I needed to get back to work. I got up from the bench I was seated on and walked to the men's room. There was a person in the first stall and no one else present. I walked down to the fifth stall and went inside. After the man left the men's room I traveled back to Maryanne's kitchen where and when we had just finalized the plan.

"So, how was the flight?" Maryanne asked as Martin and Sheila sat watching.

"The flight back was fine, long and uneventful except for the shift in time-line which altered some things and caused a few headaches. Oh, and thanks again for the Advil." The tea in my cup was still hot as if it was just poured from the pot. I took a sip as Maryanne continued.

"Well I'm sure the flight there will be just as uneventful. When do you leave?"

"We leave in ten days." I answered.

"O.K. lets all go over the pattern again. You'll take no more than three seconds to make the first portal and then its right, right, center, left, right.

Just a Little Weekend Get Away – Part 4

The weekend before going to Buenos Aires, Devin and I had decided to settle a bet. She wanted to prove that her predictions for the future would be closer to reality than my predictions. Of course I already knew that we could affect any future that we wished, and having seen the future, I already knew what was in store. Really I just wanted her to see the future of where technology and interior design had merged together. I knew she had the potential to be extremely successful so my goal was to inspire and motivate her enough to get her interior design career going. I thought "mission accomplished" as I brought coffee and toast back to her in bed on this bright Saturday morning.

"Here's your breakfast. We need to discuss a few things before we go."

"I know, don't talk to anyone; do as I'm told."

"Pretty much but one more thing, we are going a long way into the future. The knowledge we bring back can have a great impact on how the future actually evolves. So I need you to promise you won't speak at all about what we experience to anyone and you won't write down anything you see or hear. I need you to look at this as if it were a movie that only you and I will ever see. This movie may not ever be produced and if it is produced, it may have any one of a million different endings."

"O.K., I don't really understand why, but I promise I won't tell anyone about what I see on our journey. If anyone asks we were on just a little weekend get away."

"You don't need to know why but please understand that if you don't abide by the rules, there will be extreme consequences for everyone you know; and not necessarily good consequences by the way, extreme and dire consequences most likely."

"How far into the future are we going to go?"

"We're going to New York City, three hundred years from now. Let's get dressed."

"What ever should I wear?"

"It doesn't matter, but put on a long coat. We're landing in January so it will be cold and we can hide our ancient clothes under our coats till we can get some up to date threads. This way we shouldn't raise too much suspicion."

"We're going to buy some new clothes after we land?" Devin seemed joyful that shopping for clothes would be one of the getaway's activities.

"Of course, but I can't promise they will be nice clothes." I added.

We got dressed and put on winter coats and scarves. When we were ready I put out my hand and Devin took it. We landed on a hotel roof top January 24th, in the year 2312, at 10:43 a.m. in between what looked like a couple of very large air conditioning units. There were no witnesses but I did notice surveillance cameras in the area. I'm sure we were recorded by one or more of them however no alarms went off and I'm sure either no one cared we were there or nobody was watching the rooftop in real time. We would likely have been approached soon after landing if we were a security risk.

We immediately began to loosen our winter clothes mainly due to the fact that it was eighty-five degrees outside.

"I thought you said it would be cold?"

"It should be cold, it's January."

"Are you sure this is New York?"

I pointed across the roof top to the Statue of Liberty at which Devin acknowledged that I had at least landed us in the right city. The buildings in New York and taken on some interesting shapes over the last three hundred years. Some even appeared to defy gravity which indicated to me that new materials used in architecture were either incredibly strong or mankind actually did devise a way around the force of gravity.

We walked out from behind the air conditioning units and saw that the roof top was extremely large, probably the size of a football field. We could now see a portion of the roof was used for an indoor outdoor recreation centre which had trees, a swimming pool and tennis courts plus a mini putt course and indoor volleyball courts. There were a few people present which I noticed were wearing clothing not all that different from what we were wearing underneath our coats. We removed the coats and tucked them into a safe corner next to one of the extremely large yet very quiet air conditioning units and began to walk towards the activity center.

"Good to see denim is still in style." Devin observed the jeans worn by the people we were approaching.

"I know. I half expected some crazy futuristic George Orwell spandex and plastic uniforms to be all the rage."

As we walked towards the recreation area we noticed the sky looked different than we were used to. There didn't seem to be a sun or any clouds at all. I could feel the warm ultraviolet light all around and a slight cool breeze that wafted over us every ten or fifteen seconds. I wondered how it was possible that there was no single source of light outside.

"Look, we have no shadow. Look at the ground, why are there no shadows?" I pointed to the ground and spun three hundred and sixty degrees looking for a shadow.

"I know, look there isn't a sun either, or clouds or blue sky. It's like we are inside a white plastic dome."

"Maybe we are in a dome. It does seem strange to not see shadows or any source of direct light."

We were approaching the main pool area and blended in quite well despite our having come from three hundred years in the past. Other couples were walking hand in hand, some in jeans and tee-shirts of various colors, some in plain white shirts. There were no brands or logos anywhere, none of the tee-shirts had been silk-screened or printed on. Everyone was wearing fashionable but generic clothes. There was not a Calvin Klein logo or YSL bag anywhere to be seen. We also noticed the lack of bowed heads. We were accustomed to seeing most people head down in their mobile device. Everyone here had their heads up high and fully aware of each other and their surroundings.

As we reached the pool-side bar we agreed we should get a cocktail and perhaps look for somewhere to have lunch. Lunch was one of our favorite pass times on weekend getaways. It gave us the chance to observe from a situated place rather than on the move. People-watching was always easier from a café table. We sat down at the far end of the long bar on very comfortable tall bar stools. Within two seconds a little blue orb about the size of a golf ball appeared out of nowhere and hovered silently over the bar in front of us. A voice from the blue orb asked…

"Greetings, would you like to experience the beverage of the day?"

"That depends, what's in it?" Devin inquired.

"I'm sorry. I don't understand the question?"

"The beverage of the day, what is it made of?"

"I don't believe I am able to answer the question. The beverage of the day is constructed specifically to suit the biological needs of each individual guest, based on your current physiological make-up, and is designed to offset any chemical imbalance that exists within the individual. Each one is unique. If you wish to know the particular ingredients for your unique beverage I am required to submit a formal request to the central beverage dispenser and await approval."

"But what if I don't like it?"

"I'm sorry I don't understand the question."

"What if you bring me the beverage of the day and I don't like it? What if, after I taste it, I decide that my preference is for something other than this so called beverage of the day?"

"I don't believe I am able to answer your question. I have never had a guest claim that they prefer something else. I can submit a formal request to the central beverage disp…"

"Two beverages of the day it is!" I quickly interrupted the banter.

"Thank you, please blow into the orb."

As the orb flew close to me and hovered a few inches from my mouth a small funnel protruded out towards my face. I exhaled towards it, and noticed the orb also had a tiny lens that had focused on my eye. The orb flew over to a position about 3 inches from Devin's face, hovering there it repeated the request to blow into the orb, Devin obliged then the orb disappeared under the counter of the bar.

Devin turned to me with a puzzled look and began to say, "I hope the drink of the day isn't lame."

Before she finished her sentence, there appeared on the counter in front of us a couple of beverages. Uncertain where they had appeared from, we were both a little startled. The orb appeared again for a moment to tell us that our drinks had arrived and that it hoped we enjoyed them, and then hovered away.

My beverage was contained in a tall pilsner glass and appeared to be lemonade. Devin's beverage was a large red wine glass filled with a dark blue liquid. Both beverages were the absolute perfect temperature for consuming on a day like today. Eighty five degrees outside and these drinks were around forty degrees; not frosty cold and yet not warm, just right.

"Bottoms up, I hope yours isn't lame." I said, "I see they at least got your glass right."

We took a sip of our drinks. To my surprise it tasted rather neutral. It wasn't sweet nor tart or bitter. It seemed to almost taste like nothing at all. It tasted like what my mouth already tasted like, just wetter.

Devin commented on her beverage, "It doesn't taste like anything I can think of. I can't quite put my finger on it."

"It tastes like my mouth?" I added, "Like the taste that I already have in my mouth? Like nothing."

"Yeah, what's with that? Why the bland taste?"

After a couple more sips, I started to feel a strange sensation coming over me. Gradually at first and then I could really feel it intensify. It was a sense of alertness that I hadn't felt in years. I felt like I did back in high school while playing volleyball. My muscles felt responsive, my eye sight seemed sharper than usual, and my hearing became very acute, my heart rate and breathing seemed to slow right down as if I was meditating yet my body and mind felt super oxygenated and awake.

"Sweetie, do you feel that?" I asked in a whisper.

"I do. What is it? I feel kind of a rush like I'm drinking vodka and red bull, or espresso."

"So do you want to send your drink back now?"

"Shut up. How about I kick your ass at mini-putt?"

"Yeah right, 'kick my ass' my ass."

With that we burst into a fit of laughter. The effects we felt from consuming only an ounce or two of our drinks had been much more than we had expected. Another swig and something else began to kick in. This felt more like amphetamines than alcohol. I was feeling a tingle over my scalp and in the pit of my stomach. The taste of the beverage also seemed to change the more that I consumed. It became sweeter somehow.

I caught a hold of myself after a few moments and was able to contain my laughter. I needed to look away from Devin to maintain my composure, and it helped her not to look at me as well.

I suggested, "We'd better slow down on this stuff. Whatever's in this is having a much stronger effect on us than anyone else here. Maybe people in this time have built up a tolerance for these cocktails."

Maybe it was just exactly what we needed and we were reacting to the immense balancing effect this concoction was having on us. Either way I didn't want to lose my faculties to the point where we could get into trouble. We knew nothing about the current day consumption laws or regulations about intoxication in public here in New York, 2312.

We took a few deep breaths and calmed down as we watched some people take part in the nearby activities. Two couples were playing doubles tennis at an advanced level. They looked semi-professional and took the game very seriously. For some reason this made us laugh pretty hard. A few other couples were swimming and chatting around the pool. The mini-putt course was on the opposite end of the bar from us, approximately two hundred feet away. I doubt we could walk that far without buckling over in laughter.

A man approached us from behind the bar.

"Good afternoon. My name is Walter. Are you enjoying your beverages?"

"Yes very much." Devin had a big smirk on her face.

"A little too much in fact." I said with a snicker that was contagious.

Devin attempted to hold back her laughter but after a second she burst out uncontrollably and was tearing up as she turned away from the man and I to let out all the air from her lungs along with several tears of laughter.

I was more subdued and able to control my giddiness. But I still couldn't look her in the eye without having the same reaction as her. With a long deep breath Devin came back to the conversation that the man had struck up.

The man was wearing a uniform of sorts, was definitely an employee and was on the business side of the bar. The vest he wore had an emblem on the left side with the letters **KS** embroidered on it. The bar itself seemed strange due to a lack of alcohol or bottles in general. There weren't even glasses or ice or fruit visible, but it was undoubtedly a bar with stools and music and drinks that instantly show up after a retina scan and breathe analysis by a strange hovering blue orb.

"I'm sorry, Walter, yes we are enjoying the beverages."

"Please sir, there is no need to apologize, I am here to serve you and make your stay as pleasant as possible. I apologize if I am interrupting something. I would be happy to return later."

"No, Walter please, you are not interrupting. I understand what you are saying and we haven't checked in yet. Would you tell me, where is reception?"

"Mr. and Mrs. Stephens, I know you have not checked in as of yet and I am here to assist in the process. When you wish to check in I can accommodate you from any location. I am 'reception' to coin your term. May I ask what year did you arrive from?"

"How did you know our names?" Devin asked, now able to control the effects of her blue wine.

"Breath analysis and retina scan tell us everything we need to know about our guests with one exception. Date of Birth is not an attribute we can read from someone who has time traveled here."

"Do you need my date of birth?"

"Not exactly, but we would prefer to know what year you currently live in. We have accommodated many time travelers from the past and the future, and wish to customize your visit by filtering out any potential experiences that may significantly impact the true time-line. Knowing what year you come to us from, your true time line that is, will allow us to protect you from hearing or seeing much of anything that could influence for or against certain concepts in the distant past. We want to protect you from yourselves and protect humanity in general. It's actually a law now within the industry."

"Before we get too personal," I added, "we would love to have a look at some of your rooms, and then we can decide on one we would like to stay in."

"I assume by your language and reaction to our beverages that the time you are from predates the year 2100?"

"Yes, it does." I confirmed.

"Great, I will be happy to show you our accommodations. We will either place the appropriate filter on you both which alters the experience of the room and your visit, or you will agree to a memory cleanse at the end of your stay. This is standard for all time travelers who come from the distant past."

"I guess it's like signing an experiential Non-Disclosure Agreement." I commented to Devin, "We will take the memory cleanse at the end of our stay."

"And how long will you be staying?"

"A couple of nights should do it." I answered.

"Very well, please follow me and feel free to bring your beverages with you."

We followed Walter, the employee with the **KS** logo embroidered on his vest, through a set of doors that slid silently apart in front of us and then silently closed behind us. A short walk down the corridor off the main recreation area placed us in front of a door with a retina scanner and finger-print reader. Walter placed his hand on the plate and looked into the small camera which activated the door latch. The door automatically swung open for us to enter.

"Please, after you." Walter stood aside and motioned with one arm for us to proceed ahead of him.

"This is nice!" Devin offered as she wandered around the main entrance that led into a great living space. We visually took in the fifteen hundred square-foot suite with awe. Walter had walked over to the glass patio doors which spanned the entire width of the main room, pushed a button on the wall-mounted tablet which engaged a motorized system to draw back the curtains.

"I love the view," Devin chirped, "it looks like California. Isn't that the Golden Gate Bridge? Aren't we in New York?"

"It is, and we are. Would you prefer Paris at night?" Walter asked as he activated the tablet panel on the wall which instantly switched the view to Paris in the evening. The lighting inside the room faded up automatically to compensate for the drop in natural light outside. There were no lamps or light fixtures anywhere, the luminosity was radiating from the walls and ceiling. The ambiance had switched from day to night in a matter of three seconds.

"How about Colorado in the winter, here is one of my favorites." Walter touched another pre-set on the panel which caused the external view to change to a wintry scene of a snow covered mountain with people skiing down it. The lights inside the unit adjusted to the daylight as Devin and I walked out onto the balcony to get a better look at this magnificent ski resort view, complete with real snowflakes falling and melting as they landed on us. The air was cold and crisp we could see our breath as we exhaled. I noticed there was still no direct sunlight, clouds, blue sky and strangest of all, no shadows.

We savored this magical moment, watching as skiers traversed the mountain in front of us. Then we went inside and marveled at the technological wonders that were the amenities within this incredible hi-tech hotel room. Devin witnessed first-hand the furniture, wall and window coverings that changed at the touch of a fingertip; television that followed you from room to room; the robotic massage table in the spa and the pink drying powder.

We noticed there were no appliances in the main room or kitchen. There was no mini bar fridge or microwave, no stereo or television controllers. Of course, this far into the future I knew paint would deliver video signal to configurable coordinates on the wall. And those video images would move around from room to room with you without skipping a beat. Walter had turned on a news feed which delivered an ongoing account of headlines for today. With the volume set low, I could just make out the events being reported by the newscasters as we made our way around this incredible fifteen hundred foot hotel suite.

Computers or robots would likely be used to do practically everything by now. There was a gadget on the counter that resembled a blender but it was more of a glass cylinder attached to the backsplash. Walter pushed a button next to the cylinder and within two seconds refills of our drinks arrived inside the cylinder. Walter reached towards the cylinder which rotated to allow access to the beverages. He took them and offered them to us with a smile, explaining basically that this micro biotic concoction was the only sustenance we would need during our stay and that it contained all the nutrients, enzymes, fiber, bacteria cultures, minerals and vitamins that our bodies required. In fact there was no need to consume solid food as long as we drank a litre of this per day. He showed us an under counter mini bar for those guests who wish to consume alcohol and snack food, but that was mostly a thing of the distant past. I supposed that by now farming would have changed drastically. Crops were either scarce or maybe there had been some global contamination that reduced farming. Either way I assumed that solid food was obtained at a premium in this new age.

The experience was similar to my earlier tour with Zia of 100 years previous. Many of the features here were similar to the Paris unit plus there were several new features. Devin was fascinated with the configurable decor. The ability to change the materials on the sofa, chairs, curtains and wall colors all with a simple touch of a button on a hand held tablet simply blew her away. I was blown away by not only the ability to change the view outside but with the level of detail and how realistic it appeared with temperature and light. And this was customizable for each unit, which meant we could have Paris by Night outside our balcony and the people in the next unit over could have Hawaii by day complete with sounds, sights and smells. So if they had mastered replicating environments why couldn't they mimic foods? Perhaps a big steak for dinner was more appropriate than a glass of silly-juice, although the silly-juice did make me feel good.

Walter continued the tour of the unit with the bedroom and bathroom. I suggested to Devin she try out the bathroom sink and when she did the pink drying agent surprised her. She immediately began looking for a hand towel and seeing there was none, she began trying to shake and wipe the pink powder off. After a minute she finally gave up trying to remove the powder from her hands and asked what to do. I took her arm and held her hands close to the sink where the air could draw the powder off. Devin smiled when she realized how easy it was to clean up. No towels, no water and the pink agent left her skin feeling silky smooth.

Walter finished the grand tour back in the kitchen where he presented us with the rate card. "Here is the nightly rate card. This unit is available also by week, month, year, or if you wish to purchase the unit outright it lists as is for forty three million, five hundred thousand inclusive."

"What does inclusive include?" Devin asked.

"Included are all communication requirements in and outbound, video and audio communications, housekeeping and all cleaning, laundry, beverages, food, nuclear power everything."

"Nuclear power: fission or fusion?" I interrupted.

"Fission." Walter quickly answered.

"Fission. I knew it." I chimed.

We were amazed and awed by what we saw here and then as we read the rate card reality set in hard.

KS Hotel Rates:
Nightly Room Rate $29,800
Energy Rates - @ kilowatt/minute $1800 per kwm
Air Treatment - $650 / cubic meter

Mini-bar:
50 ml Liquor $160
500 ml Beer $190
750 ml wine $900,
Cashews $175
Pringles $90

Kruder-Schuhmacher Technologies Corp.
Koenigsallee 58, Düsseldorf, NW, 40215 Germany.

Walter continued to speak as we read the card. "The **KS** Company owns most of the tourism industry around the globe directly and indirectly."

As Walter spoke I could also faintly hear the news feed coming across the video channel. "Thousands of protestors gathered today in Düsseldorf outside the offices of 'Past Time Travel' company, a division of Kruder Schuhmacher Enterprises which specializes in fourth dimension destination travel. The demonstration was in protest of the side effects many travelers have experienced since patronizing Past Time Travel service which advertises the service of 'Connecting customers to their deceased friends and family through ethereal plane travel.' In many cases the experience has caused a permanent bridge between the physical and spiritual planes of existence and patrons are complaining that the service, if used incorrectly, will break down the natural barriers between the two worlds, exposing entities from the spirit world long after the service has concluded. Brentcliff Schuhmacher the author of The Time

Traveler's Hand Book and current CEO of 'Past Time Travel' was unavailable for comment.

I excused Devin and myself from Walter to discuss something in private.

"Listen, Devin we have to leave right away."

"I always know it's serious when you start a sentence with "Listen" Why do we have to leave, we just got here?"

"I can't explain right now but trust me, this time and place is not on the true timeline. This place isn't stable. There are initiatives under way to correct this timeline and if things change while we are here, there could be..."

"Don't tell me, dire catastrophic consequences."

"Well yes, but much more serious than the way you just said it."

We explained to Walter that we would return some day to enjoy the property but had decided we were not going to stay at this point in time. Walter graciously bowed his head and said, "Very well, thank you for considering KS for your next destination. If you will follow me I will take you to the exit."

"No need Walter, I believe we will take our leave directly from here." I replied. With that I took Devin's hand and brought us back to present day. After explaining the danger we were currently in I went upstairs to meditate and visit Harold to see if he still had the Time Traveler's Handbook. My guess is that he didn't but if he did have it, it would likely have a new author credited on the cover. Oliver followed me up the stairs as usual and took his position next to me on the couch.

I closed my eyes and took three slow breaths before

beginning to repeat my mantra. Within the next thirty seconds, I was at the edge of the fog walking into the clearing where Harold was laying in the hospital bed reading the handbook. He greeted me questioningly as I approached and I could sense the anxiety in him well up. He knew that my presence meant danger and that there would soon be someone following; someone who would be closely tapped into the universal energy source, listening for such a meeting as this to occur.

"Victor, why are you here? I told you not to..."

"Harold, who wrote that book?"

"What do you mean?"

"Quickly Harold, look at the author. Who wrote it?"

Harold turned the book over so he could read the front cover. "Martin Saunders III..." I read out loud as the words hit my eyes.

"Why do you ask?" Harold looked at me questioning my motive.

"I heard on the news in the future that Brentcliff Schuhmacher takes credit for authoring this book. I think it's time you come out of your coma. It's been three weeks."

"Victor, I can't come back until you set the time line right. Maryanne tells me your plan is in motion and will be complete soon."

"It will be complete the day after we are back from our trip to Argentina. Same day I'm hosting the big game."

"Well then go and finish what you started. Carry out your plan and I will see you then."

I was relieved to speak with Harold and knew that he was coming back to the land of the living soon, but I was afraid for his life given the fact that the credit for the hand book will eventually be assumed by Brent's lineage. Certainly Brent at some time knew that Harold was my time travel trainer and that he had a copy of the book. He would know that Harold had a relationship to the real author. Perhaps he was being cautious not to approach Harold for fear of certain unknown repercussions.

I returned home and opened my eyes from my meditation. Only two minutes had transpired so I continued for the next twenty. Afterwards, I came downstairs and spoke with Devin about our trip to Argentina. Devin and I were not entirely looking forward to our BA trip, knowing the extent of the travel and amount of effort involved in getting there and back. The day after we return would be the final game of the World Series and I had reservations now about hosting the guys the day after such a long journey home and with Brent most likely in pursuit.

Game On! Part 3

My head was foggy. It had been eighty five seconds since I'd taken my last full breath of fresh air. I hadn't dared to inhale too deeply with a bag of ether fumes over my head. I couldn't quite calculate the concentration of ether present or the volume of air contained within the bag, but figured it would knock me out if I inhaled too much. Attempting the math helped me stay alert and focused on the task at hand but not as focused as the sound of the bullet clip slamming into Brent's pistol. The game was on. He was around the corner and I was now leaving his holding tank. The game was most definitely on!

I landed at the correct coordinates on the Toronto rooftop and knew I had next to no time to get through the five sets of portals that Martin had carefully created for me to traverse. There were twelve that he set up as part of an elaborate maze which Brent would be required to navigate through if he was going to attempt to catch me. Sheila had set up ten portals which linked off of one of Martin's adding an additional three levels of depth to the maze. Many of these portals were carefully designed so that a person attempting to return through one would be redirected to a completely different location. The game was now real. This was no training match and I knew if Brent caught me, it would cost me my life. I needed to get away and stay away from Brent until tomorrow afternoon.

"Man, my head hurts." I said while Martin helped me to my feet. I exhaled hard as I pulled the black laundry bag off my upper body like a t-shirt then inhaled a big breath through a wide open mouth. The city lights from the tall buildings around us threw a light yellow glow across the rooftop where we were standing. It felt good to open my eyes and take in some real air.

I could see the two portals in front of me and recognized

the fringe pattern. They were both created by Martin within the last two minutes. I exhaled while Martin reviewed the directions.

"One deep breath between each portal," Martin spoke in a succinct and sport-coach-like manner, "three seconds max. Right, right, center, left, right, just like we planned now GO!" Martin gave me a push as I started towards the first portal. I had been on the roof-top for five seconds.

With my second breath on its way into my lungs and Martin pushing me forward, I stepped through the portal on the right. Martin stepped through the left portal as we had discussed with Sheila and Maryanne before my trip to Argentina. I knew Brent would be roughly three seconds behind me at this point, but had no way of knowing which of the portals he would choose to take from the roof-top. If he acted fast and took the right one, he could catch me. The faster I got through the maze the better my chances were, but I still needed oxygen.

I was now in a semi-state of anxiety because my body craved air and the time travel was making things seem to drag on. It had only been ninety seconds and although I had taken nearly a full breath and a half of air between jumps, it seemed like an eternity since I had fallen to the floor in Buenos Aires and begun holding my breath. The mental perception of oxygen deprivation was my current reality. "Right, right, center, left, right, just like we planned" I thought of Martin's words and began to question if I was recalling the order correctly now. 'Don't panic' I told myself.

I landed and finished taking in the second half breath I had started on the roof top, then exhaled and took another. The three deep breaths helped and I was feeling my head begin to clear. I was now on a sand dune near an ocean in the tropics. It was warm and inviting, however I knew time was tight. I completed my second breath in and began to exhale as I stepped towards the next portal, the one on the right. I was glad I didn't have to think about my destinations while traversing these pre-arranged portals. The difficulty was keeping destinations out of my head so that I wouldn't divert from the intended path. This was the first time I had played the flag game in real–life. Previously this activity was practiced in dreamland during sleep or meditation, never in real-time. It was going on three seconds as I walked through the second portal.

Brent followed my trail by stepping through the portal I'd left when I jumped out of his holding tank. Pistol poised in both hands aimed at the sky, he landed on the roof top where Martin and I had just been. Brent was immediately amused by the presence of the two portals. Being a competitive professional athlete in another life, Brent couldn't help but appreciate a good challenge. He lingered for a few seconds as he looked at the two choices. He was not entirely versed in reading fringes so he couldn't tell which one I had gone through. He quickly determined that he had a fifty percent chance of getting it right, and a one hundred percent chance of not knowing where or when either of the portals pointed to. Brent looked closely at the two portals and chose the portal on the left.

I held onto the black laundry bag instinctively, oblivious of bringing it with me from the roof top. I wasn't thinking entirely straight when I left Martin but now in a deep dark forest taking my second step towards the next portal three feet ahead of me, I realized I still had the bag. 'Right, right, center, left, right, just like we planned' I thought. The vision of my previous landing made me really wanted to just run down a beach and into the ocean, but I had to keep a clear head as I stepped through the portal so I wouldn't make the same mistake I did the first time I jumped. That was the whole reason for this elaborate exercise in time-line correction. 'Right, right, center, left, right, just like we planned'. Many lives depended on my success, our success, although the many lives were completely unaware of any potential danger. I stepped through the center portal and landed on a very tiny island that appeared to be in the middle of the Caribbean or some tropical sea, late at night with stars all around. The air was fresh, calm and warm. As I took my breath I became concerned that my thoughts of running into the ocean had brought me to this place. Sighting the next stage of the maze removed the concern.

There were two portal openings here positioned very close together as if someone who could see time portals may miss one of them. I thought of Martin and how literal he is. Precise and literal, he likely placed the portals like this for my amusement. I was losing my anxiety now as the oxygen was having a positive effect on my brain. I took the time to have two breaths of this fine sea-side air, and cleared my head mentally as I walked through the portal. 'Right, right, center, right, left, just like we planned'...This time I took the right one.

Brent was facing another two portals as he stood looking out over the Grand Canyon. He loved the view but decided he better change the rules of the game. Well there weren't any rules really the intention was obvious and he knew it, so he decided to employ some logical strategy of his own. Understanding that in this game, like in hockey, there was an exponential number of possible pathways that I could have taken. I being only one person with a head start advantage down a road with multiple forks would require my opponent to have multiple team mates to cover all of the possible angles. And even with multiple team mates, the head start made it impossible for his team to catch me. No team deployed now could cover all paths faster than I could traverse the single path I was already on.

He knew I had been in the Hotel in Buenos Aires and could go back there to attempt coming after me again, however he also knew that I was aware of his intentions at that point in time and would likely be prepared for a similar attempt. No, this would require a different strategy. Brent weighed the options before proceeding. He considered going back to the starting point and splitting off in both directions as two separate timelines. Then there would be two time traveling Brent's wandering down two separate paths that would need to eventually back-track and cover the other avenues. He could send himself to all possible portals, but it would be too difficult to map them all out or line up each instance of himself to follow along like good little soldiers each taking their own pathway. No, he knew that sending more than one of himself at any given time would result in an argument over who should go which way. There would likely even be a fist fight between them and he would never be able to consolidate any findings into one complete experience, no way to keep track of what everyone had seen. Damn he thought, time was pressing on and he needed to act now. Brent stepped through the left portal.

Sheila carefully inserted her subway token into the turnstile slot and walked through with a smile and a nod toward the TTC booth attendant at the Yonge Street Station. She made her way along with the crowds, everyone walking with a sense of purpose. Sheila thought it was as though they were salmon swimming up river to spawn. In this case however the collective group was traveling down. Down into the belly of the city where four very distinct arteries branched off, enabling these daily migratory animals to reach their destinations and return back to their domiciles later in the day to repeat the journey again tomorrow.

The only thing I had going for myself was the few seconds head start and the fact that I had traversed four portals now. Each reduced the odds of Brent successfully following me. We had planned the escape route and timing down to the second. 'Right, right, center, left, right, just like we planned'. Wait wasn't it 'Right, right, center, right, left?' I new Martin and Sheila would do their part and I was still on track and on time.

I landed and found myself standing in the deep end of a swimming pool, at the bottom, with at least six feet of water above me. The landing was interestingly different here. The reconfiguration process under water happened at the same speed as in normal air and with the same flicker effect however I heard no sound and the sensation was like waking up in a bowl of jelly. The water felt thick around me, gelatinous and heavy. The more I materialize the less viscous my surroundings felt. I could see two portals in front of me and instantly panicked about which one I was supposed to take. 'Right, right, center, left, right, just like we planned'. No this one was left. I'd lost count or got the order mixed up, which was it? I had completely landed now and was holding my breath. The clean salty sea air that smelled so good was now six feet under water in my lungs waiting to come out. It was causing me to float upward and I thought about Martin's words...'one deep breath between each portal.' Yeah sure pal, I'm gonna take a deep breath down here. I could afford to waste a few seconds, I postulated, but it didn't matter now because I knew I had lost track of the order. How the hell could I lose track of the order of five stupid maneuvers? I can remember the universal gravitational constant and the mass of the earth and moon, calculate the gravitational force that the full moon has on a 70 KG man standing on earth, but no, oh, no. I can't remember a five step freaking dance move? I began treading water in a reverse fashion to keep myself from floating up. I became aware of the laundry bag I was clinging to and thought of a little kid hanging on to his security blanket. I had to choose and I had to do it now. Was the last one center or left? Center or left? I swam through the portal on the left.

I knew I for certain I had gone off course when I landed next. I was supposed to now be in dreamland which would throw the dogs off the scent so to speak. Brent was aware that we trained in dreamland and we postulated that he would not at this point think to look for me there. This time however, I landed in the drying room of the condo unit that I had visited when I met my sister-in-law's Great Great Grand Daughter Zia. I was dripping wet so I thought this was a convenient place to land coming from the deep end of a swimming pool. I knew it was the exact condo Zia had shown me because she was leaving the bathroom at this very moment, and a past version of me was walking directly behind her. The déjà vu hit me hard and as I stumbled to the right I braced myself against the wall. The motion detector activated the drying agent, a pink cloud came over me from above and the suction of air began from below. I wondered now if I'd caused the jump to this location with my anxiety from being under water or having lost track of which order to take the portals. I couldn't see an escape route here. Where were the exit portals? With pink powder beginning to cover me I had to close my eyes.

The wet laundry bag still in my hand hung down and was covering most of the drain where the air would normally suck all the powder out. Most of the pink drying agent remained on me so I lifted the bag off of the drain and hit the button on the wall to manually repeat the drying process. This time I was left completely free of powder, my clothes were entirely dry and again my skin felt surprisingly smooth and soft. The déjà vu effect was now beginning to subside and I could see my escape route across the room. There were three glowing ovals against the opposite wall from where I stood inside the five by five foot cubicle. I placed the laundry bag in the center of the floor deliberately covering the drain before exiting the room. As I listened to my own voice reverberate from the other room, I remembered this discussion and thought about Devin. I lip-synched my own words 'Your Great-Great Aunt was a bit of a genius wouldn't you say?' There were only five portals in my intended route. Having gone off track, and now being unsure of where this sixth portal would take me, I made my decision and walked through the portal on the right.

Martin's jump from the roof top landed him in the third stall of the men's washroom of the Home Hotel in Buenos Aires. The room was empty as he left the stall and walked into the bar. November 4th 2010, 5:25 p.m. the night of the first kidnapping that changed the time line for the young tech engineers. Martin took a stool at the corner of the bar and surveyed the room as the bartender approached.

"Vhut ill it be?" Grunted the bartender.

"I'll have a beer." Martin stated politely with a smile. He was happy that he could drink while on duty.

The bartender stood in front of the tap drawing a pint and looking intensely at the table of young professionals in the corner. He checked the time on his watch before closing the draught tap and walking back to deliver the frosty mug of beer to Martin.

"Thanks. Oh, hey, your washroom is out of towels."

"Ah, danke." The bartender seemed agitated that something in the establishment was less than perfect on his watch and quickly reacted to fix it. Martin watched the bartender hurry over to the cupboard under the cash register and retrieve a paper towel roll. He looked at his watch again and glanced at the corner table before quickly darting out from behind the bar and in the direction of the men's room.

Brent had made his decision. He placed himself in his opponent's shoes and made the assumption that his opponent would want him to move quickly. His opponent would expect him to think outside the box and to move quickly would likely involve using reinforcements to tackle the numerous portals as quickly and efficiently as possible. They would expect him to come up with a strategy worthy of his German precision, an effective plan of attack. So rather than bring in reinforcements Brent decided to do the unexpected, he would take his time and traverse the entire maze himself, even if it took all week. This way he could be sure he covered all paths and would remember any signals or clues that he came across. He was not in any hurry. He was a time traveler— he had all the time in the world.

The front car of the train entered the platform, speeding past Sheila as she stood near the rear end of the platform. The train slowed as car after car passed by

Sheila until eventually the last car appeared out of the tunnel and the train came to a stop. The doors squealed open and Sheila stepped through the last door of the train along with a dozen or so other commuters who were now scrambling for seats. Sheila stood at the back of the train; there was standing room still but no available seats. It was like a game of adult musical chairs, Sheila thought, having witnessed a young couple in their twenties out maneuver an elderly woman for a spot on the triple bench seat. She felt embarrassed by the youngsters who had such little respect and lack of consideration for someone who needed to sit down. The doors closed and as the train began to accelerate the elderly woman lost her balance. A young man, who also looked to be in his twenties, stood and offered his spot to the woman who gratefully accepted and sat down. The woman scowled at the young couple who were too busy looking at each other and talking to notice.

The train had stopped at three stations before enough people cleared out to free up a seat for Sheila. She sat down in the second last seat on the train. To her left in the last seat was a man in his thirties and a young boy who was very excited to have a seat with a view out the back window of the train. The boy kneeled on his seat with his hands on the rear window watching the lights zip by overhead and shrink down to the size of a pinhead before disappearing as the tunnel curved to the left or right. Sheila closed her eyes and focused on the task she needed to carry out in Buenos Aires.

The bartender finished feeding the paper towel roll into the dispenser and closed the door. He was shocked to see in the mirror standing behind him was a young blonde woman who appeared to be drunk. Sheila placed her hand on the bartender's shoulder and braced herself as she stumbled forward falling to the floor. The bartender turned around and caught some of her weight as she fell and guided Sheila down onto the cool tile floor.

"Are you alright? Lady, are you alright?"

The bartender quickly wet some paper towel and dabbed Sheila's face and forehead with it. He noticed there was no smell of alcohol coming from the young woman who just fainted. He wondered why she was in the men's room, and it suddenly struck him that he may have just missed his chance to kidnap the first young professional. He looked at his watch. It was to take place just outside her hotel room right now. Maybe she was still at the table with the others. The bartender was getting up off the floor to hurry back to the bar for his little bottle of ether and the cloth. Sheila knew she needed to detain him for only five or ten more seconds at most. She grabbed his arm and began to cough. The bartender got up, pulled a paper cup from the dispenser mounted on the wall behind the sink and retrieved some water for Sheila. He seemed agitated as he looked at his watch. Sheila knew why and also knew that her job here was complete.

"Thank you so much. I don't know what came over me. I was completely disoriented and must have walked into the wrong washroom. I'm glad you were in here, thank you. I am O.K. now. Please if you must go, then go. I'm alright."

The bartender helped Sheila up from the floor, looked at his watch again and ran out the door. Sheila vanished.

Martin sprang into action when he heard two of the young professionals at the corner table announce they were about to leave. He walked over, arriving at the table just as two members of the group were getting up from their chairs and as Sheila was landing on the men's room floor.

"Excuse me. I'm sorry to interrupt but I thought I overheard one of you say you were developing a new digital image-projection technology?"

"Yes we were; why do you ask?" Anthony replied.

"Of course, apologies, I represent an investment group that is looking to expand our portfolio. I would love to set up a meeting with you to discuss a potential development contract."

"Can I ask, what is the main business of the investment group you represent?" Rita asked.

"We are in numerous ventures, but the majority of our three billion US dollars in capital is invested in the travel and leisure industry such as high-end resorts and time-share destinations. We are looking to expand through R&D. Please, I don't want to take up your time. I assume you are here for the conference?"

"Yes we are." Rita responded.

"O.K." Martin continued, "Then please stop by our booth and ask for this gentleman. He would love to discuss the development of your products. "

Martin handed them a business card which belonged to the Executive VP of Research and Development from the company that was to become the equity partner in their venture.

Brent's adventure through the portal maze was tedious but thorough. He was beginning to enjoy himself a little at the variety of locations that the maze architect had chosen. Why hadn't he included any dangerous locations Brent thought? He expected to land in a snake pit or right in front of a crocodile; maybe a shark tank or even an earthquake. But no danger presented itself at any of the locations until this one. Brent found himself underwater. He was standing in the deep end of a swimming pool, at the bottom, with at least six feet of water above him. There were two portals in close proximity and as he flickered into existence he noticed the portal on the left had a much more vibrant glow around the edges. Maybe it was the way the light hit it combined with the magnification of the water. He was sure this glow meant something. Maybe it was the first clue he thought to himself. Perhaps the more recent someone has created the portal the more vibrant the color around the edge. Or maybe the more recent someone had traversed the portal. After all, this elaborate maze was created for Victor to escape through while detaining me, Brent thought.

The water felt thick around him, gelatinous and heavy becoming less viscous as he materialized. Brent didn't hesitate; he swam quickly through the portal on the left with his pistol in his left hand. Brent landed in what appeared to be a shower stall at first glance. For a second he could see out through a dark glass door in front of him, but his presence seemed to immediately trigger the expulsion of a pink gas from the shower head above him. A muffled hissing sound came from below and Brent began to panic. He couldn't see a thing and began wiping at his eyes with his free hand. Not thinking he tensed his pistol grip accidentally causing the gun to discharge one round. The sound was deafening as the bullet lodged deep into the ceiling of the small space and sprayed marble tile chips across the width of the space. Brent attempted a step toward the glass door but he tripped on something that was under his feet causing him to fall hard to his left. His hands which normally would have been able to break his fall were covered in slippery pink drying agent. With the pistol in his left hand and being careful not to squeeze the trigger again, Brent found his attempt to brace himself against the left wall utterly useless. The pink material covering him removed all friction entirely so Brent's hand slid quickly along the wall. As he landed on the floor, the side of his head cracked solidly on the inner ledge of the chamber. Brent was instantly rendered unconscious.

Meditation and the
Snooze Button Effect

During our dreams, we visit a different plane of existence. Often times we reach a state of cosmic or "universal" consciousness at which time we reconnect with our higher-self. This higher self is the infinite energy that makes up the entire universe, and your connection to it is your spirit or soul. We connect with our higher self on a regular basis just to reconfirm that the path we are on in this life is in line with the intended path originally set out for us to travel. Like a child seeking approval from their parent for actions of uncertainty, we gain strength in this re-affirmation of our direction.

Time is not linear in our dreams because of this connection to our higher self energy source. Energy knows no time, and we humans have souls of pure energy that interact with our minds and bodies. So when we experience our true core, the spirit of our being, the soul, we are not bound by our accustomed frame of reference to time or space. This is what gives us the impression that a dream has spanned much more time than we know has elapsed. Have you ever hit snooze after your alarm clock went off, fell back to sleep and had a dream? Many things may have happened in that dream, many emotions and activities over what seemed like hours, and of course when your alarm activated again after only a five minute snooze cycle, you awoke feeling like you slept more like an hour. In fact, you likely only slept three or four minutes because it took at least a minute to get back to sleep and into REM. When you reawaken your brain, having a linear frame of reference snaps you back to the reality that it's been only five minutes. We accept this as reality because we are conditioned to live our lives according to arbitrarily chosen increments used to measure the duration between events. Your frame of reference around time and space is learned and conditioned and reaffirmed by schedules over and over each day as you grow and mature with human experience.

Within a single dream it is normal to experience ourselves in multiple instances existing in different times and even different life times. Our minds tend to mask this because the concept does not fit within our idea of normal. When we awake from a dream our current incarnation will remember the characters and events of the dream only from the current frame of reference; the life experiences of this life time. So the additional three instances of oneself present in one's dream may be remembered as friends or relatives rather than oneself.

The mind also erases most dreams from memory soon after we awake because so much of the content does not fit in with the every day norm of current life. Much of the activity that takes place in our dream doesn't make sense from our frame of reference during our awakened state. The best way to circumvent the mind's natural tendency to erase the interactions we have with our higher self in dreams is to experience these connections through meditation.

Meditation takes our spirit to the dream state while maintaining full conscious awareness. This is the key to intentionally engaging our mind's internal time travel application, and is the best control mechanism for training beginners. It allows us to experience short jumps to the ethereal plane where we can learn to interact consciously with our higher self and the spirits of others, while maintaining a connection to our current state remaining consciously aware of the passage of real-time in the present. In other words our spirit can leave our body to be active in a different place. We have a conscious experience in one location while the mind and body stay behind in another, and continue to experience the passage of time, albeit somewhat slowed down.

The physical act of time traveling during meditation is unique as it leaves the physical body in place here in the material plane while the spirit moves into cosmic conscious or ethereal plane. When we meditate and time travel within the ethereal plane the current time line does not stop for us. It appears to slow down considerably. When we return to the material plane during meditation we see that similarly to the "snooze button effect", some time has elapsed but it feels as though much more time should have passed. Our mind's frame of reference bends a little to accommodate the spirit's experience.

The act of time traveling for the more advanced traveler, one who has learned to engage their mind's internal time travel app from a complete awake state of consciousness, differs in that the physical body traverses space and time with the mind and spirit and is not limited to the ethereal plane. In this case the body is not left behind at the departure gate and the destination can be anywhere and anytime: past, present or future. If the traveler chooses the ethereal plane as the destination the experience will be identical to the traveler who arrives there through meditation. If the traveler chooses the material plane as the destination the experience will be dramatically different. The current timeline appears to come to a stand still at the traveler's departure point, only to resume upon their return. The time traveler in a material plane jump will always return to the exact point and time from which they departed, essentially picking up where they left off. To anyone else present, it appears nearly seamless in nature. As if almost nothing at all had occurred, nothing except a two second flicker to complete transparency and then a two second flicker back to full opacity.

Interactions while in the ethereal plane will have little to no direct impact on your present day life, however all interactions that a traveler has while in a physical time jump back to the past can potentially affect the outcome of present day situations and future interactions. The natural order or true progression of time can be altered by humans, but forces will always exist which will work to restore nature's balance. Some call this Karma, some call it Mother Nature's way, some call it the true time-line or time continuum.

The next time you hit the snooze button I challenge you not to think of the next five minutes seeming longer than five minutes. For those of you who have practiced meditation for more than a year, I would bet money that during your meditation you can accurately guess the number of minutes that have passed before you open your eyes. I know because I guess it right every time I meditate. I call it "harnessing the snooze button effect".

(Excerpt from Time Traveler's Handbook)

The Big Game Day

I woke up on Sunday morning feeling anxious but invigorated. Today was not only the day of the big World Series final, but also the day I was going to finalize the plan Maryanne, Martin and Sheila and I had put into play. Today, I would correct the alternate path of time I had created when I first experienced time travel. Today, I would restore life on earth back to the natural order of things. I was happy that Brent had not caught up to me yet but still I was extremely nervous that he might show up today at any time. What would I do if he just popped up out of nowhere to take me out? It would be easy enough for him to go back to BA and look at my travel documents, get my current address and poof, I'd be gone. I kept hearing the clip and the snap of the pistol being cocked when I was sitting on the floor of his holding tank. Had he completed the maze, or had he just given up?

It was not unlike most Sunday mornings around our house. Coffee and poached eggs for breakfast, feed Oliver and put him outside for a few minutes to do his business. We cleaned up the breakfast dishes and tidied up the house somewhat to make it presentable to our guests. Devin insisted that I don't over clean. We didn't want to give the guests the impression that our house was a model home or in my opinion more like a decor museum.

At noon we went out to run errands and shop. We picked up beer and snacks and all the ingredients to make chili. We stopped at a few other stores that weren't on our list. The impromptu 'stop-by' was always somewhat challenging for me. Devin would say 'Let's just pop into Home Sense for a minute, I want to see if there is anything interesting for the spare bedroom'. In a case like this we usually would end up going to two or three locations and buying jewelry to give to a relative next Christmas; or a shelving unit for the garage. Not something for the spare bedroom. Either way it was usually an exercise in patience that contributed to my character building every time.

I shop like a hunter, a predator who is looking for a very specific and predetermined species. I even wrote down on paper what I was going hunting for, and as such I cannot hunt anything other than the intended game. How can I go fishing when my mind is set on shooting a rabbit? It's defined right here on my list. Devin's mind doesn't work that way. Her mind is more like the person dreaming or a time traveler for whom the past present and future co-exist—Multi-dimensional you might say. For example she recalls what I wore to a social get-together a year ago, the last time we saw a particular friend. 'Don't wear that.' She'll say, 'You wore that the last time we saw Andy and Michelle.'

I, on the other hand, have a more linear, single-dimensional way of thinking. I can't remember what I ate for dinner last Friday. I can remember music that I've played on piano since I was a twelve, but some things just don't stay in there. Or maybe they stay in and just don't come back out? Perhaps I can't recall every experience I've had.

We returned home with a chest of drawers and a couple desk top organizers for my music studio along with a lovely pair of earrings for Devin's friend Kim's birthday which was still nine months away. The chest of drawers took me some time to get down the stairs to my studio but once in place it looked as though it belonged there. It was a great new addition that completed the space and made me think 'How did I function in here without it.' We took a few minutes to organize all the stuff that was cluttering up my desk top and stored most of it in the new unit. The rest of the clutter was now organized in the two desk top organizers. Man, she is good. I just wanted to get stuff to make chili and lo and behold, a brand new piece was added to my music studio décor.

"Devin, I know I get cranky when you take us on a detour and buy stuff like this, but wow, thank you, it's awesome to have some semblance of order down here."

"Yes you do get cranky, and you are very welcome. I just hope that your creative juices will flow even better now that you have a nicely organized space."

"And remind me again why are you not doing this as a business? You have the eye and the passion. What are you missing?"

"Let's not go there. I mean I love it and all but I don't know that I could deal with the people."

It was three O'clock and I was quite aware that I needed to get moving if I would have the pot of chili ready by four O'clock. Man, where did the time go? Then Brent came drifting back into my head. How had he faired in the maze? Did he see anything that could be a clue to my whereabouts? Did he bring along some help or did he have something else in mind? I was fine here and now so I assumed all was still right in the world and the plan was still in the works. I went to work on prepping and pulling together the food for later this afternoon.

Devin's friend Kim and her husband Mike were the first to arrive at four o'clock sharp. I had known them for several years and had become close friends with Mike over the past few months especially since we had moved to their neighborhood.

Paul and Suzanne arrived soon after Kim and Mike followed by Devin's brother, Kevin. The kitchen was lively while I opened beers for the guys and Devin poured white wine for the ladies. Oliver was excited to be entertaining guests and knew he would be pampered for the duration of their visit. He gravitated towards Kevin, the last to join us, in order to welcome him to the pack.

"I had a dream that you guys got another dog." Kevin offered while he was thoroughly scratching Oliver behind the ears.

"Really?" Devin followed Kevin's statement, "I was thinking that we should get a little brother for Oliver."

"Let's think that one through a little later." I objected.

"Too late" Devin continued, "I already thought it through, we'll call him Simon."

"You really should get another dog." Kevin added.

"Simon is a great name." I agreed thinking of the little dog we lost weeks ago.

"Simon." Suzanne added, "There's a name you don't hear very often."

We talked for a few minutes more about great dog names and travel destinations while the rest of our friends arrived. We ate our chili around the kitchen island and eventually the men retreated to the family room to watch the start of the game. The ladies stayed in the kitchen chatting about movies and celebrities. We settled into the game but I had a difficult time sitting still and focusing on the present. My mind kept going back to the plan and the current time of day. I kept myself busy by getting beers for the guys and keeping the lady's wine glasses topped up. I would join in on the conversation in the kitchen with the three women sitting at the island talking about the upcoming landscape project or latest trend in fashion. The guys were engrossed in baseball and knew most of the players by name. The only player I knew by name caught me off guard. I heard the name of the pitcher for the Kansa City Royals, Steve Bolins and it nearly knocked me over. I hadn't stayed in touch with Steve since my old high school days. He and I played on the same volleyball team for five years. He and I played baseball together for three years. Then it hit me. Steve was the pitcher that struck Brent out at the high school game I time-jumped back to. Of course, Brent's career was thrown off so someone needed to fill the gap. Steve

Bolins, as it was, turned out to be the person who filled that gap.

Mind Travelers - Chapter 5

Game On! Part 4

Sheila returned from Buenos Aires and noticed some subtle changes within the subway car, undoubtedly caused by the timeline correction. The boy who was playfully watching the lights fly by overhead and diminish in size as they grew further and further away from him was with his mother now, not his father. The young belligerent couple that had rushed to take the elderly lady's seat now stood next to the elderly lady. The lady was no longer scowling at the two of them in disgust and was seated where the young couple had originally occupied.

Sheila's head began to ache in concert with several other people aboard the train. The woman with the young boy at the back suddenly noticed that she now had a nose bleed. She pulled some tissue out of her purse and took control of the dripping blood. The boy was so amused with the light show in the tunnel that he didn't notice a thing.

Sheila's job was complete. She had set up several time jump portals with Martin as part of the maze and detained the bartender long enough for Martin to make certain that the proper business networking connection would occur. Brent would be looking through the various portals in the maze for Victor. Victor would be getting ready to make the final move now after the kidnappings had been prevented. But something felt out of place. Sheila couldn't put her finger on it but she trusted her instincts which told her that there was more at play than she was aware of.

Sheila, having returned to the fast moving subway train car now closed her eyes and began to meditate. She would go to her father despite having been told to stay away until this was all resolved. A few moments later Sheila was standing at the edge of the fog looking in on her father. There was someone standing with him and she could sense immediate danger in the mood of the scene. Harold's anxiety and fear quickly reached her like a radiating heat that one feels when opening an oven door and Sheila, now sensing Harold's fear, instinctively wanted to react quickly. Sheila felt the urge to run into the clearing straight towards her father. She resisted, staying where she was but keeping close watch on the two. After a few moments the man walked to the edge of the fog then disappeared.

Sheila ran to her father who was not in the least surprised to see her.

"Are you OK?" Sheila asked.

"It was Brent. He's still in the maze but must have gone to sleep. He wasn't here 'in body' only 'in spirit'." Harold offered, "He was looking for Victor. He said he knows I mentored Victor and that if I didn't tell him where to find Victor I would never come out of this coma. Sheila. Go. Follow him now and keep him detained. It won't be long now."

"OK Dad, just like the game right?"

"That's right. Just like the game. Be careful."

Sheila ran to where Brent had disappeared into the fog. She quickly found the portal and took a couple seconds to read its fringe pattern but Sheila didn't jump through it. She could read the detail of the fringe and knew exactly where and when Brent had come from. She was familiar with the place because she had set up one of the portals at this location herself. No she didn't jump instead she went back to the train where she was currently meditating.

Sheila opened her left eye to take a glimpse of her watch. She knew instinctively that only two minutes had transpired, but like most people who meditate Sheila felt the need to confirm her ability to harness and confirm the snooze button effect. It was a way to reconnect to the present here and now. Like the dream one has between the snooze cycles on an alarm clock, Sheila felt she had been gone for much, much longer. Sheila focused her time jump on the spa inside the condo unit Victor had told them about. The one that Martin and her had visited earlier today while building the maze.

Sheila arrived at the condo spa via one of the three existing portals positioned across from the drying chamber, the center one. Having created this one herself, she knew how to revisit the same portal even though she was arriving from a different departure location. There was no sign of Brent anywhere. Sheila cautiously looked around the bedroom and living room for Brent but he was nowhere to be found. She walked back into the spa and stood squarely facing the three portals with her back to the drying chamber. The chamber was not currently visible and because it was not in an active state, the door to the chamber appeared the same as the tile walls throughout the spa. She looked closely at the three portals to get a read on which one Victor had gone through and to see if Brent had traversed either of them. It was instantly obvious to Sheila that Brent had not left this room through any of these portals.

Sheila's walk through the condo had activated a silent alarm which was received by Zia the attending condo showroom tour guide. Zia in turn alerted security to come and deal with the intruder, a female approximate age 22, blonde, 5ft 6in tall. She could see her on the security cameras which covered the entire interior of the unit, with the exception of the drying chamber.

Sheila knew that the entry portal to the room would be in plain site of the three exits, but she was only involved in creating one of the exits. Having no knowledge of the entry portal in the interior of the drying chamber, she turned around and looked at the tile wall. She heard a noise coming from behind or inside the wall, a groaning like someone with an extreme headache.

Brent had come to and was now remembering what circumstances had brought him to this place. He rubbed his eyes with his hands and thought that he was currently coated with olive oil. Brent opened his eyes slightly but all was completely dark. He remembered the pink gas or powder that was sprayed on him and felt relief that it wasn't a gas chamber of some sort devised to kill him. He now felt the cloth that had become tangled around his feet and reached around to pull the cloth out from under him. As Brent stood up the pink powder began to spray again. Brent closed his eyes expecting to be smothered again, but there was a hissing sound below his feet that accompanied the spraying noise from above.

Now that the chamber was active, the outside tile door had become transparent. A shocked Sheila looking directly at the chamber could now see Brent standing not three feet in front of her covered in a pink substance with his eyes closed and his cheeks puffed out as though he were holding his breathe. She instantly let out a yelp that she was certain Brent heard.

Brent standing with his eyes closed and holding his breath didn't hear the little yelp that Sheila made not three feet in front of him. The loud sound of the spraying had stopped but the even louder hissing sound of the drain remained and had drowned out Sheila's voice. Even louder still was the pounding in Brent's head from the gunshot which went off right next to his ear followed by the smack he took on the side of his head when he hit the floor. He became aware that there was some light in the chamber now.

Sheila, still in shock at the sight of Brent, watched as the pink agent was sucked down from Brent's head and shoulders and eventually right down to his shoes. She heard the condo door open and a deep voice yelling.

"Security, come out with your hands up. You are trespassing and will be punished to the full extent of the law." Sheila looked towards the bedroom and back at Brent.

Brent didn't dare open his eyes all the way as a dozen

questions flooded his mind. How long had he been knocked, out he wondered; where are the exit portals out from this place; what is this pink substance that was all over him; why had the hissing now stopped. Brent cautiously opened his eyes. Who was this blonde girl in front of him? What is this cloth bag he was standing on? Brent looked down. He recognized the laundry bag that covered the top half of Victor the last time he saw him. Blood dripped from Brent's chin onto his hand as he looked down at the laundry bag. He quickly looked up and saw Sheila's reaction. Sheila let out a scream, and began to turn to run. Brent had quickly put all the pieces together. This woman must be working with Victor. The bag was the clue that proved Victor had been here, and the reaction that the girl had when she saw him could only mean one thing. He had to pursue her now and quickly. He scrambled for the door and nearly tripped on the short step.

Brent watched as Sheila turned and started towards the center portal. He fumbled with the drying chamber door being overly careful not to squeeze the trigger of the pistol again. As the chamber door opened Brent took a quick shot at Sheila's legs. It was a feeble attempt being that the gun was in his left hand. The bullet hit the wall several feet off the mark a half second before Sheila vanished through the center portal. Brent stepped out of the chamber crossing the room as quickly as he could move, his head still throbbing, blood running down from his temple and dripping off of his ear and chin. Brent transferred the pistol from his left hand to his right as he followed Sheila through the center portal less than three seconds behind her.

Only a few seconds later, two heavily padded security guards stepped into the spa, infrared glasses on and taser guns set to stun, raised and ready.

One security guard yelled, "Put down the weapon and come out with your hands up."

"Where is he? Look the drying chamber." The

second guard asked.

The two guards could see that the drying chamber door was visible. They both knew this meant someone had activated it within the last thirty seconds. The first guard approached the glass door with caution and upon squaring off to the door, could see the chamber was empty. The second guard pointed out the series of eight or ten drops of blood on the floor that spanned the width of the spa from the drying chamber to the opposite wall. The infrared glasses showed that the blood was still warm but neither guard was able to see the portals that were so carefully placed as part of the maze for Brent. The first guard opened the chamber door and stepped inside to retrieve a cloth bag of some sort that lay on the floor. The two guards stood silent looking at the bag and the drops of blood, dumbfounded.

Sheila landed back at the exact same spot that she had left from, sitting on the second to last seat on the last car of a subway train traveling through the subway tunnel at sixty miles per hour. Brent had arrived one and a half seconds later via the same portal as Sheila. The problem Brent faced now was that Sheila, having landed on the moving train, had traveled over one hundred feet during the one and a half seconds. Sheila's portal however, the one that Brent had just arrived through, had remained in a fixed position relative to the earth while the moving train and its contents continued on their path.

Imagine the surprise that the young boy must have felt when he saw a man appear out of thin air a hundred feet behind the train, hovering five feet above the tracks for a moment, and then fall to the ground. By the time the shock of this surprise allowed the boy to regain his faculties enough to tell his mother, the man had disappeared around the bend in the tunnel.

I was watching Steve Bolins pitching for the Kansas City Royals and having a hard time keeping to myself the fact that I was on the receiving end of that pitch only a handful of years earlier. Well OK, two handfuls of years earlier. It seemed like only yesterday that we shared time and space on the field and on the hard court. He was a much better baseball player than I ever would be, even back in high school. I chose to be a back catcher because I was quick and nimble, not because I could run or throw well. Watching Steve play now brought loads of memories flooding back.

It was getting close to the time I needed to complete the final task of our master plan. To course-correct the true time continuum and get things back where they belonged. I was to complete my part of the plan at 6:30 p.m. which would give Martin and Sheila enough time to complete their respective parts and prepare themselves for the shock this final adjustment would cause for most of us. We didn't know how the last piece would affect our lives or our relationships, but based on what Harold had told us, we felt that the three of us would somehow remain a strong team and good friends even after this last time line change. We had Harold's words of reassurance to comfort us. He had said we would become each other's best friends and allies one day. I wondered if this was that day.

The time was 6:25; I looked around and offered to top up the lady's wine and the guy's beers. Devin and Kim were drinking Malbec and Suzanne was drinking Chardonnay. I took my leave, retiring to the powder room in what seemed like slow motion to take care of the business at hand. The slow motion effect was likely my imagination adding emotion to the act of walking. Like the hero who is on his mission to save the world, hair blowing in the wind, hand poised and ready to draw his six shooter. Several stereotype hero images came to me and I had to chuckle when I, the hero in this movie went into the powder room, closed the door and sat down on the lid of the toilet.

I closed my eyes and took three slow, deep breaths. I could hear the game progressing in the other room. Steve had just struck someone out and the man on first base had stolen second. Two out, man on second the announcer trumpeted. I began to repeat my mantra and felt my heart rate quickly diminish and time slowed down along with my breathing. In my mind's eye I could see the familiar scene that comes as the physical transition from mass to energy begins. It appears to be a mountain landscape with the peaks of the mountains just above my line of sight. There appears over the mountains a brilliant sunrise that begins as a deep orange and rises in intensity to a golden yellow and then pure white light that grows and completely engulfs me. My spirit had connected to the cosmic energy, the stuff dreams are made of. I was in the fog of the time traveler's training ground. I was in Dreamland yet still completely aware of my physical surroundings in my house.

Steve had just pitched a strike. I focused on my mantra while I thought about the meditation that began the entire journey. Would I still be able to time travel after this? Would things go back to how they were before I screwed up? Would Devin remember all the weekend getaways? Would she remember the trips we took to Italy in the past, to New York in the future? Would she remember any of it?

I could hear the commentators, "There's the windup and the pitch, ball one. One ball, one strike and a man on second."

I walked through the fog to a clearing where I came upon a familiar scene. I had witnessed this before. Harold and Martin and a number of others running and jumping through portals. It was the scene where it had all began. I stayed along the fringe of the fog so I wouldn't give away my presence to my previous self who had also just materialized on scene. He was in the fringe of the fog too, just behind Harold and to his right. Steve threw another ball. "Ball two, one strike, a man on second."

I continued to circle around behind the location that my previous self was standing. I could sense my own presence without the déjà vu effect. Dreamland didn't involve atoms so there was no duplication of matter, only energy existing alongside itself. Similar portions of the same higher self, one of whom had never time traveled, one of whom had. I slowly walked up behind myself and waited for the right moment to act. Sheila came through one of the portals and saw my previous self but they didn't recognize each other. She ran over to Martin and whispered something in his ear. Martin smiled and followed the next opponent through the energy hoop that she had just come through.

I could sense my previous self was beginning to feel the urge coming on; it was nearly time for me to take my first jump, the one that landed me on the pitcher's mound. The commentator from the living room proclaimed "The wind up and the pitch, strike two! Two balls, two strikes with a man on second."

It was time. I put my hand on my previous self's shoulder and said "Victor, listen carefully." My previous self turned around to face me. There was a look of surprise and disbelief on his face. "I know that you want to join the game but you must not. If you do, the course of history will change and the future will be altered forever. You can learn the game from this man over here. His name is Harold and he is here to teach you the game; to mentor you. Go introduce yourself. Trust in him but don't enter through one of these portals without his guidance."

Like a deer in the headlights, my previous self stared at me and didn't say a word. He blinked a couple times and turned back towards the game.
I watched my previous self walk over to Harold and introduce himself. Harold patted him on the shoulder and said "Hello Victor, I've been expecting you. Welcome to the game."

I walked away from the clearing and focused my mind on my powder room back home. The fog engulfed me then disappeared, giving way to a brilliant light directly in front of me. The light shrunk down to a small orb which rose up and out of my line of sight. I returned my awareness to the present location which had engulfed my entire house. It was as though I was hovering above my home looking down and seeing everything within it, my guests, the TV and myself sitting in the powder room, Oliver and the ladies at the kitchen island. I took a couple deep breaths and was now squarely focused within the powder room. I opened my eyes slowly. Two and a half minutes had gone by since I first sat down. I lightly clenched my fists a few times to get the blood circulating in my arms and I wiggled my feet to induce circulation in my lower legs.

I got up slowly and was about to exit the powder room but felt light headed.
"And there's the pitch, Ball three. It's a full count with a man on second."
I braced myself against the sink and noticed the commentator's voice had changed, my head began to ache and my nose started to bleed. I grabbed some tissue and held it to my nose with my head back. "The pressure is on for Schuhmacher now with a man on second and a full count." My nosebleed wasn't bad; I could tell it had stopped. I started out to the family room and was trying to make sense of what I had just heard "Schuhmacher?"

I was a little shocked by the scene. In the kitchen Devin and Kim now had chardonnay in their glasses while Suzanne had red wine. In the family room, there sitting on the couch was, amongst my other guests, my old friend Steve Bolins, and low and behold. larger than life. sitting on Steve's lap was my long lost dog Simon. I looked around to confirm Oliver was still with us and to my relief there he was sprawled out in front of the fireplace. Most everything else was the same with the exception of some minor details. Everyone's clothes were different and there were a few décor accessories and photos I had never seen before here in the family room.

"Victor, watch this, Brent is going to hit a homer. I

can smell it." Steve spoke to me as though he'd been here since 4 o'clock.

"I wouldn't bet against it." I replied as normally as I could

The commentator's voice spoke through our banter, "There's the wind up and the pitch..." There was a crack of the bat followed by a half second of silence. "It's a solid baseline hit down third. Schuhmacher gets an RBI as Jones crosses the plate, Brent holds up at second."

"Hey Devin, has Victor ever told you we played against Brent in high school? Or about the time he let him hit a grand slam to beat us in the finals?"

"Hey man, I just called 'em, you pitched 'em." I retorted.

"Yeah, yeah he's told me that a million times," Devin piped up, "only I get the sense, Steve, you wish you would have struck him out?"

"That I do, Devin, that I do."

"Sweetheart, I suddenly have a massive headache. I'm going to take an Advil and lay down for a minute." My head was pounding and my nose was leaking blood again.

"Are you O.K.? You don't look so good. Victor is your nose bleeding?" Devin passed me her napkin from the island counter top.

"Yeah, sorry folks I just need to lie down and close my eyes for a bit."

Two security guards were looking at blood droplets left on the floor of the spa by Brent. One guard had a black cloth laundry bag in his right hand. The blood, the bullet hole in the wall and the laundry bag faded completely, disappearing from existence over the course of the next three seconds. The two men looked at each other in amazement and then suddenly, they forgot what it was that they had come into the condo unit for. They had forgotten what they were looking at that had just amazed them seconds before. When they asked Zia why they were alerted, she said she didn't remember even calling them.

The young boy watched the tunnel lights overhead zipping quickly past him from the rear window of the train. The man who just materialized out of thin air five feet above the tracks fell to the ground and shrunk into the distance disappearing as the train moved quickly down the tunnel and around the bend out of sight.

Brent stood up, blood dripping down one side of his face onto the steel rail, his head pounding. He thought to himself that he had been beaten. His opponent was worthy and had outmaneuvered him. Brent pondered his current position and felt deep down that he was destined for a much higher purpose. This was not the intended life for him, of that he felt certain and a slight smile came over his face just before his body vanished into thin air.

Messing with Timelines
Part 5 - Role Reversal

Harold had a scowl on his face as the nurse wheeled him to the front door of the hospital. Maryanne smiled at Harold and extended her hand to help him up get up and into the car.

"I'm not crippled you know. I can make it under my own steam."

Maryanne smiled at the nurse who rolled her eyes back in Maryanne's direction, then said goodbye to Harold.

"I know Harold, I know. Come on let's get you home."

"How are the kids doing?"

"They're both fine as far as I know. They've been a little distant the last few days."

"Well I don't blame them with all the recent changes."

"Well yes, but they don't remember how things were. The changes aren't consciously registered in their minds"

"No, they likely just sense a different vibration than before. Something they can't put their finger on."

"I know it needed to be done Harold but with Victor gone there is an empty place to fill."

"An empty place indeed, but Victor will be back in a couple years and in the mean time Devin is coming along nicely. She will be ready to join the team in a few more days."

"Please make sure you keep a close eye on her? She has a vivid imagination and we don't want her wandering off the way Victor did his first time."

"Good point, of course Victor wasn't under my

mentorship at that point. He's a pretty special case you know. I've never met anyone else that has reached Dreamland on their own."

"You mean other than me?"

"That's what I meant, other than you. I've never met anyone who has reached cosmic consciousness and interacted with me; through dreams yes, but not through meditation. I will take special care with Devin and I know she will bring Victor along with her eventually. "

I awoke in the middle of the night on Wednesday. Oliver was leaning against my right leg, twitching as he was likely dreaming of something, probably chasing squirrels or maybe another dog. It was 3:35 a.m. and for some reason I began thinking about the game this past Sunday. I had gone to bed and left the guests with Devin. I remembered excusing myself, my head was hurting at the time and I had a nose bleed. I couldn't remember much now about the game.

My skin was hot and dry from the sun I had exposed myself to on a recent vacation to Buenos Aires. My arms were peeling and itchy so I got up to use the washroom and moisturize again. When I returned it was 3:50 a.m. and I noticed that Devin was sweating. She didn't seem agitated in any way. She wasn't tossing or turning, just sweating. I lifted the comforter up and could see by the dull moon light filtering through the bedroom curtains that the top sheet was wet and sticking to her neck and chest.

Devin woke startled and in a sweat that confused her. "What are you doing? Why are you over top of me?" She asked.

"Why are you sweating and out of breath?"

"I don't know. I was dreaming."

"That's weird, that you would have a physical reaction like that to a dream."

"I dreamt I was on a team playing in a game of some sort. We were playing against another team, capture the flag I think. But it was weird we were chasing each other through these holes that lead to god knows where, everywhere and back again. The object was to get the flag from the other team and bring it home. It was so real and I think it isn't the first time either."

"What do you mean it isn't the first time?"

"I think I've had the same dream a few times now. Only at first I was a spectator and this guy, the coach invited me to play along. I think I played last night too and maybe the night before."

"So you are having a recurring dream that leaves you out of breath and sweaty? You would think it would at least be a sex dream, not a game of tag."

"Not Tag! Capture the flag." Devin corrected me.

"Capture the flag then, either way you shouldn't be sweating so much."

"I know. A dream has never made me sweat like this before."

"Here have some water. Your head isn't hot. You don't have a fever. In your dream you said you were jumping into holes?"

"Not 'into' as much as 'through'. The holes weren't in the ground they were hovering above the ground. Like someone picked the hole up by one side and hung it on a clothes line."

"Weird. And why would you jump through these hanging holes?"

"It was a game. We chased each of the other team members till one of us got a hold of their flag then we would try to bring it back to our base before they could steal it back. You know Capture the Flag, you probably played it when you were a kid?"

"Never by jumping into holes. You look like you've cooled down a bit. Try and get some sleep."

"OK. Thanks for the water. Goodnight."

"Goodnight."

Devin had the same dream every night for the next two weeks. Each morning at about 3:45 a.m. she woke up with a serious sweat on and a strong memory of the dream; the game, the players and the coach. I suggested getting psychiatric help or dream therapy. She wasn't biting.

A Different Weekend Getaway
- Pitter Patter let's Find Kruder

We had been back from Buenos Aires four weeks now. The tan, the memories and most of the joy had faded along with two thirds of the weight I had gained from my excessive consumption of wine and red meat on the trip thank goodness. It felt good being back at work but it seemed there was something now missing in my life. I couldn't figure out what that something was. It just felt like there was a void of some sort. I chalked it up to post vacation blues and decided I would talk with Devin about planning our next trip. I was thinking Greece or maybe Turkey would be interesting and different. I needed something to look forward to and planning a travel destination would at least fill that void.

Something kept bringing my mind back to the baseball game the day after we returned from Argentina. I thought about the people that were there and how they were integrated into my life. Paul and Suzanne, Kim, Mike and Kevin, everyone seemed to have a solid place in my life with the exception of Steve. Steve Bolins was there sitting on the couch with Simon when I came out of the powder room with a nose bleed. How did I get the nose bleed and the headache? He and I went back many years, back to high school for that matter, but I couldn't remember much about his current situation. What was he doing lately? Where did he work? Was he married? Had he been married? How did he get to our house? I didn't remember him arriving, only being there. It seemed right but now in hind-sight his presence didn't feel right at all. I couldn't remember anything about Steve that happened since high school.

I arrived home to find Devin at the kitchen island researching Turkey on her iPad. As coincidental as that seemed, I didn't feel compelled to mention the fact that I was thinking of the same destination today. Instead I asked.

"Devin, when was the last time I saw Steve?"

"Steve Bolins?"

"Yeah Steve Bolins and I mean before we got back from Argentina, when was the last time I hung out with him?"

"I don't know. Didn't you get together with him last summer to go to a Jay's game?"

"I might have, I can't remember though. It's like I have no memory of the guy since high school."

Devin looked at me with a puzzled expression. "You've hung out dozens of times since then for sure. Listen I was thinking of Turkey for our next trip but I want to run something by you first."

"Yeah, what's that?" I asked.

"I've stumbled on something quite unique that I think you will like. It may take you some time to get used to but when you open your mind to it I think you will be intrigued."

"OK" I said, "Let me have it, what's this about."

"Sweetheart you trust me right?" Devin chirped.

"Yes, to a certain degree."

"Trust me enough to take my hand and close your eyes for ten seconds?"

Now I was intrigued, what could possibly happen in ten seconds?

"I don't know. What are you going to do?" I asked.

"Close your eyes."

Devin took my hand as I closed my eyes. There was a flash of brilliant white light and then an entire outdoor meadow scene flickered into existence all around us as if it were being built from scratch, piece by piece, inside of a still 360 degree photograph. Even with my eyes closed I could see it building clearly. Each flicker added more detail to the scene and each flicker came quicker than the last. Finally the flicker sped to a frequency that was no longer detectable and I opened my eyes up wide. We were standing on a hill top with nothing but green fields as far as the eye could see. A gentle breeze caused the tall grass to sway in a way that made me think of a green lake full of fish, playfully swimming just below the surface, making the grass move this way and that haphazardly in every direction.

"What the hell just happened?" I gasped, rubbing my eyes in disbelief.

"We just time traveled." Devin bleated out with a cheery smile.

"Time travel; impossible!" I said trying to convince myself that the scene before me was an illusion of some sort. "We can't time travel. You can't time travel. It hasn't been invented yet."

Devin spun around once with her arms outstretched.

"Oh yes it has. Besides, when time travel is invented is irrelevant. It's been invented and developed and I know how to do it. That's all that matters. Now guess where we are?"

I looked around for landmarks or any sort of clue as to our location.

"We appear to be in a very large field of tall grass?" I said, stating the obvious.

"Of course we're in a large field of tall grass silly, but do you know where this field is?"

Off in the distance something caught my eye. It looked like a heard of cattle that were moving across the horizon but were moving too fast to be cattle. Plus I didn't see any men on horseback keeping them in line.

"That looks like a heard of buffalo." I said pointing to the moving pack. "Are we in Montana or the Great Plains where the buffalo once roamed?"

"It would appear so wouldn't it? Feel the breeze and the warmth of the sun? Come with me." We walked approximately three feet straight ahead where Devin put her hand out and a door suddenly appeared as if out of thin air. We walked through the door and on to a patio which had a small bistro set and two lounge chairs. The meadow was visible behind me and to both sides. In front of me however was another door leading into a building. Walking onto the patio, a peculiar insect flew in front of me and hovered uncomfortably close to my mouth. Only for a split second but it was large enough to catch my curiosity and the fact that it made no sound at all piqued my interest. It flew away so quickly I didn't have a chance to get a good look at what it was. We crossed this patio which had miraculously appeared at the wave of Devin's hand, and were now entering into the most amazing looking apartment I had ever seen.

"Wow. How did you know there was a patio there? And how did this apartment get here? What the hell is this place?" I turned around and took another look at the bison off in the distance and the Great Plains just off the deck. I was amazed and very confused. First the time travel thing now this; had she actually done it, I thought? "So where or when exactly are we?"

"This is a design lab where we experiment with décor and home entertainment concepts. The model suite we are in is being developed for the largest luxury hotel chain in the world."

"Model suite; is it for a hotel or condominium?" I asked.

"Both." Devin replied. "The hotel industry is very

different in 2120. Developers build and sell units like this suite as a condominium but also install a management company at each property to enable the building to operate as a hotel. So there is a mix of owners and renters in most of their properties. Some owners rent out their units when they are away for extended periods. Some are time-share units. Everything is consumer focused and driven by customer demand."

We walked through the unit and out onto a large balcony which my eyes were telling me was overlooking Time Square in New York City. The city was buzzing with people and traffic.

"How is this possible? We were on the Great Plains a minute ago."

"Actually Victor we never left Toronto. The Great Plains and this scene of New York are virtual realities, videos of the future."

"So this scene of New York is video?"

"Taken within the last twelve months, and see the advertisements playing on the digital screens around Time Square? They are all customizable to user profile data of the habitants of this unit. Notice right now all the ads seem to be geared towards a middle aged man?"

"You're right; laser shave, Johnny Walker Purple, nice car ad there and I see Molson's is still in business. Not a cosmetic or feminine hygiene ad anywhere in site."

"Come on, let's eat." Devin turned around and I followed her back inside.

"Sounds good, what's for dinner?" I asked as we entered the kitchen.

"Oh, actually most people these days don't consume solid food."

"What? No buffalo steaks?"

"Food is in the form of a drink. It's much less taxing on the human body and far more efficient way to deliver everything the body requires."

"Wait a second, you said 2120. That's the year? We're in 2120?

"That's right! Amazing isn't it?"

"Well yes, but not so great if you are a carnivore for starters and also not so great if you want to go out for a walk. You might end up on the Great Plains with no clue as to where your front door is. Upside is you could take down a buffalo and have a cook-out."

"Technically no, the bison in the Great Plains video are computer generated, CGI. The physical space out there, the virtual viewing room as we call it is only two meters deep by seven meters wide and five meters tall. It's not much bigger than an average walk-in closet these days. The balcony has a virtual viewing space roughly the same size. Now the nutrition in this drink for example, is far more than you would ever receive in an ordinary meal in our day. You may have seen an insect like robot fly in front of you for a split second on our way in?"

"Robot...more like a bumble bee."

"No, that was a flying robot designed to catch your breath while you are exhaling. It grabs a sample of your breath and sends the composition analysis to a central computer for the purpose of identifying your nutrient deficiencies. Then it synthesizes the perfect concoction for you to consume as a beverage."

"Listen to you! When did you get this scientific jargon down? It's making me excited."

We stood in the kitchen next to an island of approximately three meters by two meters. It had a beautiful speckled marble top and a number of futuristic and unidentifiable metal contraptions protruding up from the surface. Being the cook in the family I was interested in learning as much as I could about the culinary advancements of the next 100 plus years, but Devin had no patience for this type of knowledge transfer. She was typing a few characters into the marble top's built-in interface and before I could ask what she was doing a trap door opened and two tall dark blue colored beverages elevated up out of the opening.

"Here…"She said passing one of the drinks to me and holding the other up for me to clink my glass against it. "…dinner is served."

I looked at Devin as if she was kidding, but sadly she was not. I tasted the dark blue liquid and was surprised at its velvet consistency and rich flavor.

"I took the liberty of ordering you a tame one. I wouldn't want you getting out of control while we are out of our time zone." Devin said with a bit of a smirk.

"So first of all, this tastes really good, but more importantly, how long have you been time traveling?"

"Well it's funny because you know the dreams I've been having? The ones with the game and I wake up sweating?"

"Right, the last few weeks."

"Well I've discovered that the whole game is a training ground for time travelers. I have a coach and team mates to practice with. We were meeting up in our dreams somehow, and the game was a way of learning to control time travel through out of body experience. Our mind and spirits at play while the body remained in bed. Now we've graduated to a whole new level of time traveling, one where our bodies come along with us."

"Out of body experience… right…right…How do you know it wasn't a dream?" The blue beverage was beginning to make my scalp and the pit of my stomach tingle.

"Because the same people were in my dream for three weeks, and we were doing the same thing every night."

"So you've been dreaming the same thing for three weeks?"

"No really. When I was in the game I was jumping through portals to all sorts of locations and time periods, but it was a series of controlled training exercises. Because my physical body stayed in the physical plain, time kept moving forward so it felt like a dream when I woke up. The sweating was my body's response to my mind and spirit's experience. My body didn't want to be separate. And now I can initiate the time jump myself and take my body with me. And the best part…when I return no time has passed."

"So you're telling me that you've been time traveling for quite a while now?"

"Well, yes and no. Technically I have been time traveling for three and a half weeks, three weeks in training and four days on my own."

I was enjoying my liquid dinner so much at this point that I forgot to portray indignation to Devin's traveling around without me. My head was beginning to buzz and the tingle in my stomach was now in my chest.

"So you some how just stumbled upon this hi-tech lab in the last couple days?"

"No not really. I've been here almost five months altogether."

"Five months? How the hell?"

"I realized that when I get back to my real-time from a jump, no time has passed. So I figured if time stands still while I'm gone, I can spend as much time as I want in the future and it has no effect on my present. I've come here two or three times a day over the past four days and usually stay for a week or two, maybe three each time. While I'm here I work most of the time and sleep in the master bedroom."

As Devin explained the double life she suddenly had created for herself I truly had an epiphany, or perhaps it was the blue dinner drink that was taking a complete hold of my psyche. Regardless, I realized that the reason she had become very close with me the past few days was all the time she spent away. She missed me. I also realized that the model suite we were in must have been developed by a company that Devin was a partner in. I assume a very big and powerful company if it is supplying the largest luxury hotel chain in the world. Likely it is a research and development division owned by said luxury hotel chain.

The interface on the counter, the insignia on the doors even the mosaic inlay on the patio and bistro furniture. All displayed the regal letters **KB** proudly.

I should have been feeling many emotions at this point not the least of which would have been jealousy or betrayal. I should be jealous and feel betrayed that the love of my life, my better half could spend months away from me without feeling a sense of guilt for non-disclosure. But what I felt was as far from betrayal as it gets. I felt closer to Devin than I had in a long time. The blue dinner had opened my mind to a broader reality than I had been able to conceive anytime before. This was truly a mind expanding experience. I was also very happy that Devin had become immersed in her true passion, interior and exterior design.

"So the work that you do here; all of this hi-tech

stuff, do you work with other people?"

"My partner Holger. Holger Kruder. He is the "K" in "**KB**" and I'm the "B". Together we are "Kruder Barkin". Come I'll introduce you." Devin turned and began walking towards the patio door.

Devin sang as we walked through the back patio doors. "Pitter patter let's find Kruder."

Everything Happens for a Reason

The Tibetan Book, of the Dead also known as 'The Great Liberation upon Hearing in the Intermediate State', is believed to have been written by Padma Sambhava in the 8th century A.D. The book is meant to be a guide for the deceased and is read out loud to the dead during the time between death and the next rebirth which can be up to 49 days. This is done so the deceased can gain awareness in order to reach nirvana and be liberated from the cycle of rebirth.

The book teaches that upon death, the body loses its natural awareness so it creates its own reality similar to what it would experience in a dream. This dream unfolds in a series of stages which contain a variety of extremely peaceful visions and a variety of extremely wrathful ones. The dream emulates heaven and hell and the end result is dictated by the reaction of the deceased to the dream itself. If the soul reacts with fear or negativity, jealousy or anger to any of the numerous deities it encounters in the dream, it is drawn back towards rebirth and becomes reincarnated; sent back to live another life. By maintaining the awareness that these deities are deliberately trying to evoke a negative response and reacting with joy, will have a positive outcome, nirvana. The only way to liberation is to respond with the joy of a pure heart. The soul during the 49 days following death will either be liberated to remain in the clear light forever or their karma for the next incarnation will be determined and rebirth will soon follow.

We know that the souls of the dead are all around us every minute, just vibrating at a frequency beyond our perception. We marvel at those who have the capability to communicate with the souls who have moved on. We marvel because they can do something we can not. Do we marvel at a dog's ability to hear frequencies outside our range? Of course not, yet we struggle to believe in the abilities we possess within ourselves. We neglect to marvel at our own capabilities. We marvel at an artist or a musician who expresses something that resonates deeply within us. We marvel at their "talent" and wish we could express in the same fashion. We can express in the same fashion, or a similar fashion that is unique to us. We just first need to free the energy associated with the desire.

We are frequently amazed by the imaginations of young people even though we still have the same amazing imaginations within us. We may have let our imagination lie dormant for some time; we may have allowed ourselves to be conditioned to hide our imagination while we conform to the norm. How many times have you been told "You can do anything you set your mind to." maybe three or four times in your life? Be careful what you set your mind to because you may shock yourself when you achieve it. That statement is a sad testament to society because most of us have likely been told what we can not do on a daily basis for our entire life.

Everything happens for a reason. The reason may not always be a good reason, nor will it always align with what you desire but it will happen for a reason. Any time traveler understands that good and evil are merely our own human perceptions that reflect in emotions of fear or joy. What some perceive to be good, others perceive to be evil. Do you perceive the force before you as having a selfish agenda or selfless agenda? If it is a selfless agenda, can it be trusted? Where does the evil truly reside, externally or internally?

Everything happens for a reason. It's what balances the universe, our existence, our planet and our lives. Like the wax within a lava lamp we gain heat energy from the bulb and rise as a blob to the top and hang out with the other blobs and then we cool down and lose our energy, drift back down only to regain energy from the lamp in the base and cycle up and down again. Life is the balance and all things that happen therein. Oh sure, we can maneuver and manipulate somewhat, steer our own destiny, grab life by the horns as it were, but in the grand scheme of life, everything happens for a reason. Whether we believe we caused an effect or perceive ourselves as the effected, all things are meant to happen and they happen for a reason.

Everything happens for a reason. The true timeline is what is meant to be, and any and all deviations from this true timeline, which cross an infinite number of possible alternate realities, will eventually be returned to its natural order. Our lives are not meant to be devoted to discovering the reason for the events that occur, our lives are meant to be devoted to learning the lessons that reside within each of our daily life experiences.

The human mind has the capability to develop abilities far beyond the current scope of human understanding. This has always been the case since the dawn of man. The universal energy or cosmic consciousness that connects us all does not segregate or differentiate between the living and the dead. It connects our souls to the past and to the future as a system of energy cycling in and out of various states. Sometimes the soul energy is connected to a mind and body like a molecule of H_2O in a frozen state. When the solid H_2O receives more energy it vibrates faster causing it to melt and transpose into a liquid then vibrating faster still it becomes a gas and eventually breaks into its base components. Our soul is pure energy that separates from our mind and body when vibrating at a higher frequency. Similar to the pure Oxygen atom floating around on its own until eventually joining up again with two Hydrogen atoms to reform into water, the soul takes some time on its own to determine which Mind/Body to combine with during its next incarnation.

Everything happens for a reason. What is your reason? The human journey on this planet has been a constant search for the meaning of life, the reason for our existence. The Time Traveler's Handbook was written to assist you in discovering your reason. It was written to teach you and all who read it that you can do anything you set your mind to. Time travelers for centuries have helped guide souls along their path to reaching enlightenment, or return to the physical plain through rebirth, or teach others to time travel, or band together to help insure the true timeline is kept in tact.

Everything happens for a reason. Welcome to the journey that will help you discover your reason.

- Introduction to The Time Traveler's Handbook

The Absent Handshake

Devin led me out the back door and off the patio onto the Great Plains once again. We made a right hand turn almost immediately as though there was a wall only feet from the end of the patio. I stuck out my left arm as we walked and sure enough I felt a wall there. The Great Plains image that was so realistically presented on the wall began to ripple as if my hand was cutting through a vertical sheet of water. Devin put her hand up in front of her face and a door appeared which we walked through. Once inside the door, we continued down a dark narrow corridor to an exit at the far end. We went through the exit door at the end of the corridor and found ourselves in a massive office overlooking central park in New York City. A young man got up from his seat and carefully placed a book on the very large desk,.

"Devin good to see you! What brings you in on a Saturday?"

"Holger, I'd like to introduce you to."

"Victor I presume?" Holger stood up behind the desk.

"Victor this is my partner Holger, Holger I'd like you to meet my husband Victor."

I reached out as one does, gesturing to shake someone's hand. I assumed he would come around and shake my hand, oddly he did not. Instead he awkwardly placed his hands in his pockets and remained behind the desk.

"Ah, Victor it is truly a pleasure to meet you. Devin has told me all about you. At last I can put a face to the name. How was your trip? Have you seen the lab yet?"

"Yes thank you the trip was fine, rather quick in fact. The lab is interesting, very intriguing. Did you invent the visual surround display?" I asked pointing to Time Square?"

Holger let out a hearty laugh. There was something very familiar about Holger but I couldn't quite pin point it. I felt like we had met before.

"Oh heaven's no, the display has been sixty years in the making, I am not even forty years old myself. Most of the technology here is a culmination of many research and development projects over many, many years. We merely have borrowed bits and pieces from several such projects to combine the best of the best into the most remarkable and marketable products." Holger's words seemed to pour off his tongue like a politician who has rehearsed his address at the ribbon cutting ceremony or a salesman giving his elevator speech. I was certain this was not the first time he had spoken these words. I became instantly suspicious.

"Holger, with all due respect, your age is irrelevant. You could be a teenager and still have invented and developed this technology provided you can travel through time. You can time travel can you not?" I asked as I looked at the book on the desk titled 'The Time Traveler's Handbook'. I noticed the name of the Author – Steve Bolins.

"Ah you see the book on my desk. Yes of course I can time travel. I wrote the book on it as you can see here." Holger pointed to the book and I could plainly see that Holger Kruder was credited as the author. I had to look twice because only a couple seconds earlier the author's name was Steve Bolins. My head suddenly began to ache as I pondered this. "Victor, I believe you are a friend of my Grandfather? Steve Bolins." Holger stated, conveniently changing the subject.

"Steve Bolin's yes of course I knew him well." I don't know why I used the past tense in describing Steve. I think it was out of habit because I couldn't remember anything about him since high school aside from his recent visit to watch the game at our house a few weeks ago. "He was your Grandfather?" I thought that he had written a book of some kind but I was losing the memory of what book it was.

"Steve was my grandfather. I barely knew him myself. We lived in different countries while he was alive. You say 'you knew him well', has he already passed on in your current time?"

"Oh, I meant I was much closer to him in high school than I have been later on in life. I knew him well once, but I don't know him at all now."

"Ah, I see. Even though he came to your house to watch a sporting match only three weeks ago, you say you don't know him at all now? I find that curious. Why would you invite someone to your home who you don't know at all?"

Listening to Holger speak I was overtaken by the strangest feeling. The words didn't mean anything to me. The fact that he knew Steve had been at our house three weeks ago didn't faze me at all. It didn't even make me curious why he knew. I was drawn for some reason to the book on the desk. Seeing The Time Traveler's Handbook on the desk, struck a chord with me as I tried to remember the author's name and suddenly Holger's words blurred into oblivion and memories began to flood my head. Memories flashed that I didn't know I had inside of me. Memories of a hospital bed in the fog. Memories of a man named Harold who had been some sort of mentor or coach. Memories of a young couple named Martin and Sheila who I trained and worked with on some kind of important job. Emotions accompanied these memories and I felt my life had depended upon my relationship with these strangers. Anxiety began to well up inside me. The memories didn't give any answers they just raised more questions. My head began to hurt and blood started to run from my left nostril.

"Victor, your nose! Are you feeling OK? Come with me, let's get you cleaned up."

"Oh, man, I am so sorry. I don't know what's going on." I said dabbing my fingers in the blood that had run down to my lips.

Devin escorted me to the washroom where we got my nose bleed under control with a damp paper towel.

"Why is your nose bleeding?" Devin was visibly upset that I had caused a scene in front of her partner.

"I have no idea. My head started pounding all of a sudden and then this." I was somewhat baffled at the memories and mixed emotions that I had just experienced.

"This has been happening too often Victor. We have to get you to a doctor and get this checked out."

"Is there a place I can lie down for a few minutes?"

"Yes of course, come with me." Devin brought me to a small office that was furnished with a beautiful mahogany desk with plush leather chairs and a matching couch along one wall. "Here, lie down and keep this on your nose. I'll come get you in a half hour."

"Thanks. Sorry about this. Something happened in there when Holger was talking."

"What do you mean something happened."

"While he was talking I got the weirdest feelings and a bunch of odd memories came to me. It was like I was dreaming even though I was wide awake. Then a flood of anxiety came over me right before you snapped me out of it by saying my name."

"Well just relax and I'll be back to get you soon. Try not to bleed on anything." Devin closed the door as she backed out of the room.

I lay there on the oversized leather couch feeling a little embarrassed for what just happened. I couldn't help thinking that there was something familiar yet weird about Mr. Holger Kruder. He seemed nice enough but why wouldn't he come out from behind the desk to shake my hand. Perhaps in this time people don't shake hands anymore. Maybe it's not socially appropriate in this day and age. Perhaps it is a hygiene issue. I mulled this around in my mind for a few more seconds and realized my head was no longer pounding. I felt a little dizzy so I closed my eyes and allowed myself to relax for a minute. Just as I was on the verge of sleep, about to fall into the abyss I had a vision of being in a fog, walking and listening to sounds. I heard shuffling and scuffle sounds as though a number of people were playing basketball on an asphalt surface. I stepped through the fog and came upon an interesting scene.

There were people running and disappearing as if they were jumping through a series of invisible holes in the air. Others were materializing from the same invisible holes. Running in short spurts with a sense of urgency to make it to the next hole as quickly as they could, but for what reason? I could tell it was a game but I couldn't understand why I was seeing this and why it appeared to be so real. Then I saw two familiar faces, Sheila and Martin. I don't know how I knew them, I had never met them before to my knowledge, but I knew their names. Sheila stopped and looked at me. Our eyes met and we instantly felt a connection. Martin did the same after a few moments and joined Sheila who was standing in the middle of the playing area about fifty meters from me. I realized at this point that Devin was now standing right beside me.

"Come with me, there's someone you should meet." Devin guided me over to a man standing on the sideline who appeared to be the coach. "Harold, I would like to introduce you to…"

"Victor…we've been expecting you. It's great to finally meet you." Harold enthusiastically held out his hand to shake mine.

As odd as it felt to be in this mystical place, I felt relieved that people here were still open to handshakes. As I reached out to take his right hand I could see in his other hand he was holding a copy of The Time Traveler's Handbook. The author's name was not fully exposed but I could tell from what I was able to see that it was certainly not Holger Kruder. When I took Harold's hand and shook it, I felt a warm glow come over me that was the most peaceful feeling I had felt in my entire life. The encounter was less than five seconds but in that time I felt a surge of positive energy course through the physical connection I had made with Harold into my hand and it filled my entire being. At the same time I saw visions of a past that I knew to be real but were not part of my conscious memory. In one vision Steve Bolins and I were working together on a big project. I think it was a restaurant or a hotel or both, and there were other familiar faces in the vision. A man setting up the bar, the same man that tended bar in Argentina, the same man that kidnapped me, the man Sheila distracted while the young entrepreneurs were directed to the meeting that would define their future. A memory of Martin laying a maze of portals out intended for Brent. Brent? Who was Brent? Where did all this memory come from? Certainly I couldn't have lived these experiences? I just met Sheila and Martin. We hadn't even been formally introduced and yet I was remembering things I had done with them.

"Would you like to join us Victor?" Harold asked as he let go of my hand. His words hit my ears but I was stunned. It took me a moment to get my wits about me and digest the question. "Are you ready to join the game Victor?"

"Yes, yes of course. I'd like to follow Martin and Sheila if that's alright?"

"You know their names? Victor, I'm impressed." Devin was complimentary of my insight.

"Of course you will follow Sheila and Martin. You three including Devin you four, will make a great team."

Recurring Dreams and Telepathy

Have you ever had a recurring dream? You know the type that is the same each time and has the same people and places and emotions attached to it? Ever wonder what that dream means? Well stop wondering. Dreams don't mean anything. They are mini out of body experiences that occur when our mind and spirit connect to our higher self. The spirit, as part of the universal cosmic energy that connects us to all other life, requires frequent interaction with its "higher-self" on a regular basis the same way humans need contact with other humans. The mind, being closely attached to the spirit, comes along for the ride and then attempts to decode what it experienced. The decoding process is generally based upon the frame of reference of an earth-bound mind in a conscious state which holds fast and strong to a set of beliefs instilled by the society it conforms to. This, simply put, means that most humans are not open-minded enough to realize the dream as an actual out of body experience, but instead look to interpret the hidden meaning within the dream because society has taught us that dreams are some sort of reflection of our mind; like a movie reel of our sub-conscious being played back to us in order for us to process recent life experiences.

The recurring dream then must be a reflection that is stuck in our psyche? It must mean that we haven't grown from an experience or moved past a certain hurdle right? Wrong! The recurring dream is the reconnection of the spirit to its originating energy source, the same energy source that your spirit connects and everyone else on the planet connects to when we dream, the same energy source that all living things are connected to. The recurring dream is the mind's interpretation of the familiarity of this connection. It's the mind becoming accustomed to the connection to our "higher-self".

We have all experienced a high pitch ringing in our ears. Have you ever been told that it means 'someone is talking or thinking about you'? It's true. Have you ever been told that ringing in the left ear means someone is thinking or speaking about you in a positive light and the right ear means they are thinking negative thoughts or speaking negative words about you? Also true. What you probably haven't heard is that the very moment you think of the person who is transmitting this high frequency your way, is the same moment the ringing will stop and the transmitter will become the receiver and have a ringing in their ears. If you are thinking positively or negatively about the person the ringing will be in their left or right ear respectively.

We do this every day sub-consciously; well most of us do it without knowing it. Some people have consciously labored to develop this ability into a complete mental telepathy capability whereby whole conversations can take place. Ringing in the ears is like a Morse code message being transmitted across a microscopic thin slice of the universal energy or cosmic consciousness to the recipient. It was a very small connection that was discovered and developed into what today has become a channel of communication enabling us to transmit or receive full concepts in a few seconds, concepts that include details enough to fill dozens of pages of text.

Recurring dreams were the key to developing the telepathic communications channel. When a select group of individuals were open minded enough and had the imagination to attempt to become lucid in and meet in their respective dreams they discovered that not only was it possible, but that they could communicate without talking. The communication started as a simple ringing in the ears and with a little practice and fine tuning of the technique, the throttle on the bandwidth was opened up and the ringing became thoughts, emotions, words, images and eventually complete concepts. Over time the technique was developed to a certain extent to be practiced in a fully conscious state. The conscious mind however dramatically impedes this ability, essentially throwing static across the channel so it is common for telepathics to communicate during meditation or from their dream state.

Further to the telepathy aspect of the original experiments, the ability for individuals to meet and interact while within a lucid dream opened up a whole new dimension which became the training grounds for time travel.

- Excerpt from The Time Traveler's Handbook

Out of Time

Still in my semi-conscious state, my body lying on the leather couch in one of Holger Kruder's other offices, my mind and spirit flashed out from the group discussion in the fog and back to reality. I had come from dreamland where I had seen Devin and Harold. Harold had the book in his hand. The same book...the handbook. Was this a dream or was I having an out of body experience? Maybe this was a premonition of some future event, or a past one. But why did Harold have the same book that was on Kruder's desk? Why was the author different? Was it a coincidence or did it have some real meaning? It made sense that two time travelers would possess a book on time travel. The same way two physics students would have a book on physics, or Artists would have sketch books. But I could sense that there was something more to this. The visions I had when I shook Harold's hand, the kidnapper and Brent Schuhmacher, the warm feeling from Harold's energy, the connection I felt when I saw Martin and Sheila. Dream or not, it all had to mean something. I felt I had the ability to go back to the fog at will, so I made an attempt.

I slipped back into my semi-conscious meditative state, re-emerged amongst the fog and walked into the clearing of the playing field. It felt as if I hadn't left. I joined Devin, Martin and Sheila on the asphalt where they were lined up waiting to start the game. I didn't need an introduction. Neither did Sheila or Martin. There was a connection between us that was understood without having to speak, a telepathic communication of concepts along with memories and visions of things in the past. Within a matter of seconds I had downloaded so much information that I didn't need training, I had been here before. I could see the portals now around the playing area fringes shimmering in the dull light that were invisible only minutes before. I knew exactly what we were about to do. We weren't here to play a game. We were setting out to change the future back to the true timeline.

"Pitter patter, let's find Kruder!" Sheila whispered as she led us through the nearest portal. Devin followed next, then Martin and my self.

As I approached the portal I could see that the fringe contained three distinct patterns which I immediately associated to the people that traversed ahead of me. I don't know how I was able to read this, but it came to me easily like the solution to a simple math question, as if I had just calculated seven times three. The experience of entering the portal awakened something in me and I remembered completely that I had been a time traveler before. Was it in a previous life or just an alternate timeline?

I passed through the portal and I thought I would land in the presence of others who went before me but instead I found myself in a room with a desk, two plush chairs and a leather couch. There was a non-time-traveler version of my self laying on the couch, eyes closed with a bloody paper towel held to his nose. The version of myself on the couch opened his eyes and, upon seeing me standing next to the couch, immediately sat up.

"What in the hell?" Asked the seated me.

"No, Victor, you're not hallucinating." I said calmly, "I'm you, just a slightly different version? I'm from an alternate timeline."

"So the fog, the game it's all real?"

"Listen carefully. The man you just met, your wife's partner, Kruder? Well he isn't a good person. He pirated your wife's ideas and a lot of other people's and is capitalizing on them in an alternate timeline. He taught Devin to time travel so that he could put her to work developing his stolen products while he sells them to a number of multi-national conglomerates for his own benefit. He's done this with several brilliant minds. Now that you are here he knows he's in danger of losing everything so he's gone back in time to alter your past in order to control your future. You had a nose bleed and a splitting headache right? Don't answer. Trust me when I say that you have about thirty seconds before one of two things happens."

"What two things?" Seated me said holding the bloody paper towel to his nose with one hand and the side of his head with the other.

"Well the good outcome would be if Holger is distracted and does not succeed in erasing you from the past."

"And the bad outcome?"

"The bad outcome would be if Holger is not distracted and succeeds in erasing you the past."

"Erase? Erase. What do we do?"

"My friends are distracting Holger in a few different places and times right now, seven to be exact, so that you don't get erased. Now, as an insurance policy, just in case my friends do not succeed you should come with me to a safe place. Stand up and walk this way. We've got about five seconds left."

Seated me stood up and took my arm. We walked toward the portal I had created when I arrived. My other self couldn't see this gateway but I could read the fringe and knew it was created by me, and only I had passed through it. I needed to make the transition "Now close your eyes, this maybe a little too bright for you."

Having recently absorbed from Sheila and Martin an enormous amount of knowledge about time travel and the effects of multi-stepping, I was a bit concerned about the task at hand. What I was about to do was not something I had any knowledge of. Had Sheila and Martin deliberately withheld the information or was it something that had never been done by either of them? The multi-stepping I had done in the past was when I had time traveled to one spot and then again from that spot via "Past Time" or meditation, "twice removed so to speak" as Harold once put it. But this time I wasn't just taking my wife as a passenger to some other time, and then taking myself to another time. This time I was also bringing my previous self as a passenger who was also on a different time, and had meditated into a second jump. And I was the one from the second jump now ready to take my previous self along with. This was essentially me three times removed with my self as a passenger. 'Bunsen' Ray Bernier, my high school physics teacher's voice came through my mind at this very moment "If you think too much about that time travel stuff, it will drive you crazy."

As I moved through the portal along with my other self, I gave in to the thought that something special was about to happen, something unique and powerful. The scene faded to bright gold then up the spectrum to white. My entire life flashed before my eyes in less than a second. I saw it like a movie in fast forward but with every single detail and emotion that accompanied each and every experience at every moment in my lifetime. Nothing was left out, a lifetime of experience and emotion, not missing one moment of my life from birth. The embarrassing memory of my first fist fight, piano lessons, exhilaration of playing concerts, the first time I dunked a basketball, my first date, every date, every breakfast lunch and dinner, every discussion and every moment of every day up to the point when Devin took me into the future. All of this flooded through in next to no time at all. I felt numb as my brain relived the entire forty years that had gone before me.

When we were completely through the portal I could see my future and my past all in one 360 degree panoramic environment. It was like a large photograph that didn't have any boundary or borders no beginning or end. This scene was everything I had already experienced and everything that was still to happen in my future. My entire forty years in this lifetime laid out to my left and what appeared to be another sixty years laid out to my right. I knew I was going to live to one hundred, no mistake, I could see the date and circumstance of my death. Funny I don't die of old age even at one hundred.

The scene appeared to be shrinking or shrink wrapping around me. Perhaps my awareness was expanding but now I realized my other self was gone. The other me brought here for safe keeping was no longer with present, or at least he was not visible even though I felt his energy all around me. The visual scene of my current lifetime had shrunk down into a sphere which was now only a small part of my field of vision. There appeared to be many spheres all around me, floating up and down. It was like I was inside a giant lava lamp with hundreds of spheres, spheres hovering at different distances and of various sizes. There was only one small shrinking sphere that corresponded to my current life and the rest looked as though they belonged to other people. My current life suddenly felt insignificant amongst all these other lives.

I could feel now that these other spheres, these lives did not belong to other people. These were also mine. I was acutely aware now that these were other lifetimes which I had already lived or were yet to be experienced in future incarnations of my soul. I saw in an instant an eternity of incarnations floating around me so quickly, yet I could feel the emotional experiences of each one as I glimpsed them. I was at this very moment pure energy traveling at the speed of light. I maintained conscious awareness and could see there was no future and no past, everything just existed here and now. I was caught in the moment, truly and completely out of time.

The scene was like looking at the universe revolving around me as though I existed at the center. Then I saw it, the reason for my existence. In amongst the hundreds maybe thousands of lifetimes I was witnessing in this moment of time travel I was suddenly aware of one sphere floating in front of me. It belonged to Holger Kruder and it was an incarnation of me. This was my soul to be born more than two hundred years into my future. There was no question this sphere in front of me was Holger Kruder. Not a nice man but a man none the

300

less that is linked to me, my energy, a man who may be instrumental in forming a very negative future. And this other sphere just off to one side? This is Harold, the next incarnation of my soul only sixty years hence. Harold my coach, my mentor my father figure who will hold my soul in his body during my next go around. That kind of makes him my son in a way. I knew there was a good reason for the way Harold resonated with me. Now I knew why Kruder didn't shake my hand. He knew I would feel his energy and be able make the connection that our souls are one.

The life I was living had become at this very moment clearly defined in it's future direction. My life's reason was revealed as having a specific purpose. That purpose was for me to introduce time travel to others in the physical world and to maintain the true timeline going forward, at least for the next couple hundred years. Everything happens for a reason, and my reason became clear when Harold and Holger were revealed as my future incarnations. This gave me my reason for existence.

It was obvious now that my distant future incarnation, Kruder, if left to his own devices was going to violate the true timeline. Clearly my reason in this lifetime was to attempt to maintain the true path from deviation until Kruder's lifetime and beyond. In order to do that, I needed to engage him and beat him at his own game. You've heard the saying 'Keep your friends close but keep your enemies closer?' well it was clear that my job now was to keep my enemy, Kruder, as close as I could. It did seem strange to think of my future incarnation as my enemy, but have you also heard the saying 'You are your own worst enemy.' Knowing that Kruder is me put a whole new and somewhat literal meaning to that saying. What did happen to Kruder just now? What had my team mates done to distract him from destroying that version of me that had lay on the couch, bloody nose and pounding headache not thirty seconds ago? What happened to that version of me that I brought into this time jump? Where did he go? Did he and I just melt together? What would Devin do when she went back to the lab? Would the lab still be there? All of these questions seemed to ground me back into my present time. I could feel a change in state coming on, a transformation of energy.

My surroundings looked similar to a photo of the cosmos through an electron telescope. I felt like I was floating in space with visibility light years into the future and past, and the constellations, galaxies and solar systems floating around me. The scene began quickly to expand away from me and as it did suddenly everything intensified in brightness up to a blazing gold light that turned bright white for a split second then faded down.

When the white light subsided I found myself back home with Devin at the very moment in time that we had left to visit the décor lab. Oliver and Simon were on the couch in where we had left them in their usual positions, Oliver on the seat and Simon spread-eagle on one of the back cushions, both looking up at us expectantly in anticipation of some command or another. It had been four weeks since we returned from Buenos Aries and I pondered that one of my guests for the Sunday afternoon game I had hosted, Steve Bolins had been a bit of an anomaly in my mind. I knew him well in high school. And up until today, this very minute as a matter of fact, I couldn't remember a thing about him since high school. According to Holger Kruder, Steve had written a book about time travel. I knew Steve well enough in high school to know he wouldn't have written a book, and certainly not one about time travel. I was in some of Steve's classes and Physics was not his strong suit. What happened to Steve and why was there no memory of him in my brain until now? For some reason the memory of Steve being in a hiking accident during college was becoming a solid concept in my mind complete with images of Steve on a stretcher and in the hospital. During a fall from a thirty foot ledge, Steve had broken his pitching arm against a tree half the way down, and broke his left leg upon impact at the bottom of the fall. I had been on the trail with him when it happened and I remember now that on a particularly narrow ledge Steve tripped on some loose rocks then quickly slipped off the edge. I had been the one to get him out alive and back to safety via air ambulance. Why had I lost that memory? Saving a friend's life and riding with him in a helicopter to the roof top of a hospital is not something one would normally forget? This accident ended Steve's baseball career and two years later I helped Steve move to Toronto to take over his uncle's restaurant. Steve became a successful restaurateur in Toronto where he lives with his wife and two teenagers. The memory was now firmly fixed in my mind and I no longer questioned the gap from high school to present. I had no reason to.

"Hey baby I'm going shopping with Suzanne in a few minutes. Do you need anything?" Devin shouted down the stairs to me.

"No I'm good. What are you shopping for?" I asked as I walked up the stairs from my studio.

"For three hours, maybe four. We're going to a décor shop. I hear they have some really cool installations demonstrating some new hi-tech decor ideas. Did you want to come?"

"Oh no, I think I'll hang out with the dogs. Actually, I have an idea for a book which I am going to start drafting out."

"A book? You're gonna write a book? What's your book going to be about?"

"Oh, I don't know. It's hard to describe. I just feel like writing an adventure story."

"Will I be in it?" Devin asked in her cute and playful way.

"Maybe, do you want to be in it?" I bounced back to her.

"If I'm cute and playful." She answered, again in her cute and playful way.

"And smart and hot?" I added.

"Sure, smart and hot works."

"You'll be in my book of course. Go on get out of here. Have fun shopping, spend a lot, and I want to hear all about the new hi-tech stuff when you get back."

Devin put on her coat and went out through to the garage. As I walked downstairs to my studio I heard the garage door open. Devin climbed into her car, closed the car door and started her engine. I sat down at my desk, booted up my computer and launched Microsoft Word. I knew what I needed to write. I knew I had to write this particular book and that over time several authors would assume credit for the work. This book was going to motivate my future incarnation Harold to become a protector of the true time-line. It would also motivate Holger many years later to become a technology pirate fulfilling the purpose of Harold's life's work thereby enabling my mind travel training. I immediately felt empowered with a sense that from this desk I could change the outcome of my entire world and several of my future incarnations along with it. I began typing.

The Time Traveler's Handbook
By: Victor Stephens

Chapter 1: Introduction –
Everything Happens For a Reason

The Tibetan Book of the Dead, also known as "The Great Liberation upon Hearing in the Intermediate State" is believed to have been written by Padma Sambhava in the 8th century A.D. The book is meant to be a guide for the deceased and is read out loud to the dead during the time between death and the next rebirth which can be up to 49 days. This is done so the deceased can gain awareness in order to reach nirvana and be liberated from the cycle of rebirth.

Mind Travelers – synopsis

Warning, spoiler Alert! The following contains vital story-line and plot elements which may spoil the enjoyment of reading this book.

Victor Stephens played back-catcher on the high school baseball team along with his close friend Steve Bolins who was the pitcher. After high school Victor remained in Wisconsin while Steve attended Michigan State University on a baseball scholarship, and so they lost touch during their college years. Steve's path to becoming a professional baseball player was quickly diverted when he broke his pitching arm and left leg in a hiking mishap. With no hope of achieving stardom as a pro ball player, Steve went into the hospitality industry and became a successful owner-operator of two restaurants in downtown Toronto.

Victor, having stumbled on his ability to time travel, ventures back twenty years inadvertently causing an alternate reality. Upon his return from the past Victor discovers how he has affected the present as several positive and negative changes reveal themselves. Victor realizes he must go back and correct his mistake to restore the natural order of things. One such change is the corruption of a would-be professional baseball player Brent Schuhmacher who has instead become a time traveling technology pirate in this new alternate reality. To right his wrong, Victor must first fully train in the art of time travel and work with a team to orchestrate the correction of a twenty year time-line gone awry.

During his four weeks of training Victor learns much about life and death, traveling extensively on his own as well as with his wife Devin to many locations past and future. Victor becomes an expert mind traveler and together with time travel friends Sheila and Martin the team of three, go about exacting the necessary steps to getting the world back on track to the time-line that was meant to be. Once the task of restoring the true-time line is complete Victor no longer possesses any memory of his ability to time travel. In this reality it is not Victor but Devin his wife who is being mentored by Harold along with Sheila and Martin to learn the art of traversing space and time.

Devin is an excellent interior designer and superior decorator employed as a National Account Sales Manager in a prominent corporation. Satisfied in her job but having a new found ability to jump ahead in time decides to leave her sales career and go into business for herself. Literally able to see into the future Devin discovers that a number of new technological advancements in interior decorating, design and Home Entertainment align closely to her own interests and current ideas.

Devin partners with a man from the future that controls the largest luxury décor, home entertainment and technology company in the world. Focused on developing leading edge experiential applications for the elite hospitality market, Devin does not realize that it is her partner who has chosen her.

When the team discover that Holger is the mastermind behind the technology pirates from the future Harold, Devin and her team mates set out to shut him down once and for all. In the process Victor discovers that he shares something in common with Holger and Harold. This realization gives Victor a renewed focus and direction in his life as he discovers his true reason for being.

Inspiration

Here are some of the publications that inspired the writing of this book.

Douglas C. Giancoli: **Physics**: Principles with Applications, Prentice Hall 1980

Barbara Anne Brennan: **Hands of Light**: A Guide to Healing Through the Human Energy Field, Bantam; REV Edition 1988

Carlos Castaneda; **Teachings of Don Juan**; A Yaqui Way of Knowledge, Washington Square Press; 30th Anniversary edition 1985

Carlos Castaneda; **A Separate Reality**; Further Conversations with don Juan, Washington Square Press; 1991

Stephen Leberge PHD; **Exploring the World of Lucid Dreaming**; Ballantine Books 1991

Robert A. Monroe; **Journeys Out of the Body**; Three Rivers Press; 1992

Shirley MacLaine, **Out on a Limb**, Bantam Books, 1986

Mind Travelers

ISBN 978-1-304-69971-8

9 781304 699718

Contact Jacques Vincent Leroux
vince.leroux@mindtravelers.ca
Visit: www.mindtravelers.ca

Acknowledgments

Thanks to my Father, Jacques Bernard Leroux, for introducing me to Transcendental Meditation when I was twelve years of age. This was an important moment in my life because it opened the door for me to develop a much higher awareness of my internal and external worlds than would have otherwise been possible. I am glad I stepped through this door and stayed with it. Also thanks Dad for being such a good story teller. Your life stories have taught me well and helped me learn how to tell a story.

Thanks to my Mother, Mary Strobl, who inspired me by telling me I could achieve anything I set my mind to. One day I hope that will include time travel, but for now, I will stick to meditation. Thanks Mom for being the first to proof-read my initial print draft and for the first round of edits. Thanks most of all for the early encouragement which, to this day, gives me the confidence to try my hand at new creative adventures such as penning a novel or a trilogy.

Thanks to Sandy, the second person to read my initial print draft. Thanks Sandy for the edits and for the enthusiastic evaluation of the story. Yes I would love to make a movie of this so please feel free to recommend the book to any film or television producers you may happen to meet. I hope you enjoy the second and third novels as much as you id the first.

Thanks to Adam Wilson, the third person to proof read my novel. I thought the third draft was ready to publish but fortunately, I had you Adam, to take the final run through and help me tighten it up. Thanks for the final touches, catching so many little yet obvious areas for improvement and giving the novel a literary quality that only a master of the English language such as yourself could offer. I am honored that you enjoyed the story given the number of pencil mark-ups you graciously made along the way.